FATES FULFILLED

Copyright © Jules Barnard 2021

This book is a work of fiction. The names, characters, places, and incidents are either products of the author's imagination or have been used fictitiously and are not to be construed as real. Any resemblance to persons, living or dead, actual events, locales, or organizations is entirely coincidental.

All rights are reserved. Except for use in any review, the reproduction or utilization of this work in whole or in part in any form is forbidden without the prior written permission of the copyright owner of this book.

This book is licensed for your personal enjoyment only. This book may not be re-sold or given away to other people. If you would like to share this book with another person, please purchase an additional copy for each recipient. Thank you for respecting the hard work of this author.

FATES FULFILLED

J. BARNARD

JBARNARDAUTHOR.COM

N
Old Kingdom
Sunland
Dark Kingdom
New Kingdom
River
TiRNaN

CHAPTER

ONE

"A FEMALE CHILD OF DARK FAE BLOOD WILL SAVE THE LAND FROZEN IN WINTER—OR LEAVE THEM IN A RUIN OF THEIR OWN MAKING." ~ UNKNOWN ELDER, DARK KINGDOM

Lex shoved her sociology notebook into her backpack and glanced at her brooding uncle sitting on the bed. "What's wrong with you today?"

Jasper blinked and looked away. "Nothing. I just don't understand why I can't go with you."

"I told you, you're not signed up for the class." She grabbed her wallet and dropped it into her backpack. Jasper —or Jas, as she called him—was only a few years older than Lex, but after the accident that had taken her mother's life when she was thirteen, Jasper became her guardian. And he took his guardianship literally, believing himself her bodyguard too. "My professor noticed you last time, and he's not going to let you get away with it."

Lex had social anxieties, and she often depended on Jas

to help her navigate society. But sometimes, his overprotectiveness was a pain in the ass.

Jas's frown deepened. "It's not too late for me to register for your courses. It would be like last year."

The corner of her mouth pulled back. "I've got issues, but even I knew that was overkill. Not to mention, you hated the classes and bitched the entire time."

She could tell by the look on his face that she was right. Even so, he shook his head stubbornly. "I have a bad feeling about today."

She sighed and looked around one last time for anything she'd missed. "I'll only be gone a couple of hours, and I haven't had a panic attack in six months. Everything will be fine."

His lips flattened into a tense, straight line. "Come immediately home afterward." The look in his eye said he was a hairsbreadth from following her.

Jas was totally obsessing.

"Why don't you go upstairs?" she suggested. "Maybe Alice is around?"

His pale green eyes flashed. He had the biggest crush on Lex's dorm neighbor, though he would never admit it.

"Perhaps I shall." He hoisted his long limbs off her bed —the only place to sit in her dorm room—and stretched his arms above his head.

Lex let out a sigh of relief.

Jas didn't grow up in any one place, and his accent sounded like a combination of British and German. Add the hot accent to a handsome façade, and her uncle was catnip to college coeds. But for some reason, he refused to date. That didn't mean he was immune. Shy Alice with the soft brown eyes was one of Jas's weaknesses. And Lex's best bet at distracting him.

Lex had never met Jas's family, but she'd heard tales of their competitive nature and cold winters. Lots about the cold winters. One of these days she'd visit her extended family. Just as soon as she got her anxiety under control.

"I'll catch you back here in a couple of hours." She leaned up—way up—and pecked him on the cheek. Lex was tall for a woman, but she felt short compared to Jasper.

He moved toward the door, then froze, his hand on the knob. "It is cold, Lex," he said softly, but with an intensity that made the hairs on the back of her neck stand on end. He looked over his shoulder. "Do you not feel the chill?"

What in the what? "Um...sure. I've got on my sweat-shirt." It wasn't *that* cold in Northern California, where she attended Dawson University—not like Germany or the myriad other locations he'd lived—but she'd agree to anything to get her uncle moving on, and a conversation about the weather wasn't going to speed things up.

He squeezed the back of his neck. "Call me as soon as you return. Are you certain I can't wait outside your classroom?"

For the love of God, what was wrong with him? "Please don't. You'll only make me look like an even bigger social pariah than I already am."

"They don't know you." His expression softened. "You must not let their ignorance upset you."

Her uncle was kind, but with her six-foot-two height, no men found Lex attractive, and the women on her campus stared at her as though she were a freak.

"It doesn't bother me," she said, silently adding *mostly* to that statement.

He hesitated, then gave her a nod and opened the door. Lex pulled her backpack around to make sure it was zipped, but she sensed Jas's attention on her. She held her breath.

After a moment, he stepped out and closed the door behind him.

This was insane. Jas couldn't follow her anymore. At her age, it was getting weird.

Lex wanted to be stronger. Strong enough to live without the constant emotional support of her uncle. But thoughts of that would have to wait. Because her darn sociology paper was due, and nothing would stop her from turning it in on time after she'd stayed up half the night to complete it.

She hurried for the door.

Seconds later, she was speed-walking down the industrial carpeted hallway of the off-campus housing where she lived, her hoodie over her head and her eyes downcast. Her anxiety lessened when she didn't make eye contact. Most people stepped aside or walked around her.

But not today.

Caught up in thoughts of Jas and her paper, Lex didn't notice the tall man wearing all black and standing in the center of the hallway, until he was a few feet in front of her.

Lex stopped abruptly before she ran into him, thankfully.

But the moment she looked up, her breath caught and an ice-cold shiver ran down her spine.

GARRIN BRANIMIR, Prince of Dark Kingdom, strode down the dingy hallway where the Fae kept their half-human, half-Fae Halven, and paused near a dark-haired female on his right. The woman grinned as she passed.

She was attractive. For a human. Or Halven, given the building.

Hundreds of years ago, Fae from other kingdoms in the Faery realm of Tirnan built Dawson University to monitor their half-blood offspring, known as Halven. Particularly those Halven who developed magical powers. As far as anyone knew, no Halven born of Dark Fae blood existed due to the Land of Ice that blocked Dark Kingdom from any other living being, including in the Earth realm. But Garrin suspected the one he searched for could be hidden here.

The prophecy stated a female with Dark blood would save his people. Garrin had run out of options in Dark Kingdom. No one possessed the power needed to create safe passage to other lands. The Earth realm was his last hope for finding *the one*.

He fanned his hand in front of the female's face before she passed. He'd been testing all females in the building for weeks. So far, none had deflected his magic.

The brunette blinked, then stumbled. Then her lips turned blue, and she began to choke, her dark eyes watering as ice formed across her face. Sounds of suffocation came from her throat.

She was indeed Halven. He wasn't as good at sensing magic levels as those with the ability, but he could tell she was more than human now that he was close. Only she wasn't the one for whom he searched. She was simply a half-blood, like all the rest.

Garrin sighed and waved forward the two soldiers behind him. "Heal her and blur her memory."

This girl might not be *the one*, but Garrin would search for the female who was until his dying breath, which should give him a millennium, give or take.

"Your Highness," Amund said, a portal creator and one such Fae with the ability to sense energy levels. "The earthbound Fae soldiers have discovered our presence."

Garrin let out a long-suffering sigh. He'd spent the last hundred years attempting to cross the barrier separating his kingdom from the others of Tirnan. It had been nigh impossible to make it across the Land of Ice weakened, only to be attacked by deadly Fae soldiers from other lands. Until an uprising left said lands vulnerable. He'd finally breached the borders of the other kingdoms and made it to the Earth realm, and he wasn't about to turn back now. "The Fae living on Earth are a nuisance. How am I to find the girl with them nipping at my heels?"

Amund stared off in the distance. "We have two minutes before they discover us."

His men had returned the brunette to the dwelling from whence she came, and Garrin looked down the hallway one last time. "Very well. We will return another—"

Someone exited a door halfway down. A female. Tall.

Garrin didn't get a good look at her face because she'd pulled a hood over her head that dipped below her eyes, but he held up his hand in a staying motion. There was something about this one... He was drawn to her.

"I sense no power," Amund said.

Fae were taller than humans, and many Halven took on the trait. "I will test her anyway." The closer she got, his urge to be near her grew.

"Your Highness, please hurry." Amund glanced back. "We have a minute at most."

The female kept her head down as she moved closer. She didn't appear to see Garrin standing there.

Odd, that. At over seven feet, Garrin wasn't easily missed in the Earth realm. The girl was so preoccupied, in fact, that she nearly ran into him.

She stopped abruptly a couple of feet away, and her chin tilted up. Her face flushed, and she averted her gaze.

But not before Garrin caught sight of her beautiful golden eyes, the mysterious energy behind them hitting him like a bolt of lightning.

There was no time. Garrin needed to test her quickly and be gone. He pursed his lips and exhaled, giving her more of his powers than he'd given other females they'd encountered.

She blinked, and ice crystallized around her nose and lips...and melted as quickly as it had formed.

Her gaze collided with his, her expression one of surprise.

Garrin's entire body lit up with desire so powerful it took his breath away.

He stepped back, astonished at his reaction to the woman, and at what he'd discovered. For so long he'd fought death and starvation and battled enemies to reach *the one*. No Dark Fae were thought to live in the Earth realm, but Garrin suspected she was hiding here, and now he'd found her in the form of a Halven.

Elation coursed through him. After all this time, he'd succeeded where no other Fae had for hundreds of years.

He would save his people from isolation. He would make his father proud...and he would have the female.

A smile slowly pulled at the corners of his mouth. "Take her."

TWO

Lex woke with a pounding headache. But like all her aches and pains, this one disappeared within minutes. She was a fast healer, and yes, that was odd, but that wasn't why she was hyperventilating.

The man.

He was the most terrifying person she'd ever seen, standing inside the dorm. Short black hair, dark stubble that accented full lips, and a chiseled jawline. But it was his eyes that truly alarmed her.

The color should have made them beautiful—pale blue and clear as a summer sky. But it was the cold intent behind them that struck her numb.

And that was the last thing she remembered.

The room she was in now was pitch-dark, with the exception of a lit firepit, and the air held a crisp bite with the scent of dirt and decaying leaves.

Her vision acclimated to the dark and she saw three shadows standing off to the side.

Lex crawled backward. "Where am I?" Her voice

bounced off the walls that felt as though they were closing in on her.

Long legs clad in all black approached, and a man hunched in front of her. *The man.* "That is all you wish to know?"

Her mouth parted and her heart rapped against her chest. His eyes were bright even in this dim light, but she couldn't hold them for long, fear making her peripheral vision darken and narrow.

"Very well," he said when she didn't answer. "I suppose you would call this a cave. My apologies for the lodging. We were in a hurry, and this is somewhere we'll not be tracked."

Lex breathed in slowly, attempting to stave off the panic flooding her. "I have to get back. To-to Jasper."

"Impossible," he said, no hesitation, no softening of his tone.

Lex turned from the man and clawed her way up the cave wall until she was standing. She patted the surface, searching for an exit. "Please," she gasped. "I can't stay here."

Forget her paper and keeping her word to Jasper. She was trapped inside a cramped, dark space with strangers. The panic attack she'd staved off for months was gaining steam, bubbling up, and siphoning her breath.

The man stood next to her now, studying the side of her face. "What is wrong with you, Halven? Why do you breathe so heavily? I assure you, there is plenty of air in here, even for one such as you."

Her palms grew cold and clammy, and her vision winked. "I..."

Darkness enveloped her.

WHEN LEX NEXT WOKE, she was on her back, and the man from before was leaning over her. "You are a curious female."

Her heart raced, the shaking returning to her limbs. "Have to get back. Find Jasper."

"Who is this Jasper person?" He glanced to the side and tipped up his chin. "She is doing it again. Calm her, Zirel. She is not well."

Another man, just as tall as the first, moved closer and hovered over her. His hair was lighter—red? He rested a large palm on her head.

Lex flinched at the touch, but no pain accompanied it. Instead, the panic that had tightened her chest and made it impossible to breathe eased.

"That is better," the man with the strange eyes said to Zirel. "Her color is back." His gaze swept her features. "My guard Amund says he senses your energy level now that we've taken you from the building where you lived."

Energy level? "Who are you? What do you want with me?" Her chest might have stopped pounding, but her brain was going haywire, this way and that and nowhere at all. She couldn't be away from Jas for long or the anxiety would cripple her. It always did.

"My apologies," the man said, and delivered a charming grin that might have disarmed a normal person. But Lex wasn't normal. "I am Garrin Branimir, Fae prince of Dark Kingdom. And you are?"

Lex's jaw unhinged. "Fae prince?"

She'd been kidnapped by a madman.

"Please let me go," she begged.

This time, Garrin's eyes softened. "We cannot."

She was having a bad dream she couldn't wake from. That had to be it.

Lex sat up and scooted back. She used the cave wall for leverage to straighten her legs and stand, but the men blocked the exit.

When her head stopped spinning, she darted around them in the direction where pitch-darkness turned gray and what she hoped led out of the cave.

And was immediately ensnared by the prince's arm, her body pressed to his broad, warm chest.

More heat than normal radiated off him as he tipped his head toward her ear, his mouth inches away. "You cannot leave, Halven. And it would be better if you accepted it."

She attempted to hit him where it hurt, but his body was solid and unyielding, and he dodged her. Every time she tried, he shifted just enough that she slammed her fist into his muscular thigh instead of his nuts. *Dammit!*

He chuckled, his deep voice filling the space around her. "You can't hurt me, Halven."

She let out a harsh sigh. "Why do you keep calling me that?"

He eased his hold and turned her to face him without letting her go. "Because it is what you are. Created by the mating of one of my kind and a human."

For a moment, Lex couldn't speak. Couldn't get her mind to wrap around his words. "Your kind? You called yourself a Fae prince."

He grinned, and her eyes widened. He might be a devil, but he was a handsome devil. "Now you are catching on. We are from Tirnan, the Fae realm, as is one of your sires... Curious, that. I wonder who in my kingdom created you? What did you say your name was?"

She hadn't. And what was with this guy? He'd

kidnapped her, but he didn't know her name? "I'm Lex. Make note of it, because you've got the wrong girl."

"Lex." He said it as though the word stuck to his tongue like peanut butter. "That is an odd name. But Halven are an odd breed. I give you permission to call me Garrin."

Breed? Like some dog? "What is a Fae?" she snapped. His companion must have done something to her when he touched her head, because she was braver with these men than any other strangers in her life.

"Ah," he said, and glanced at the other two men. "If you don't know you are Halven, you wouldn't know our history." Garrin gestured to himself. "I and my people descended from the mating of angels and a few honored humans. We live in a realm known as Tirnan."

"Oh my God." He was certifiable. And big. And how was she going to get past him? Lex glanced around desperately.

He cocked his head. "No, the *grandchildren* of God. Please pay attention." He looked at the others leerily. "We've been told Halven are lesser beings, but I didn't take your kind for having low intelligence."

Zirel, with the magical touch that slowed her heart rate, shrugged his broad shoulders, his cropped red hair brighter now that he stood in the faint light of the fire. "Perhaps the Halven brain is..." He made a small space between his thumb and forefinger.

Were they calling her dimwitted? "I'm not slow, you arrogant asses."

The one Garrin had called Amund laughed low, and Garrin shot him a deadly look.

"Take me home *now*," she said.

Garrin motioned for Zirel to block the entrance. "You cannot go home. Others search for you as we speak. Dark Kingdom is fortunate to have found you first. As far as we know, the prophecy has spread wide in Tirnan, and others wish to use you against us."

These men didn't seem like lunatics, not that she knew what lunatics looked like. They were well dressed, if strangely, and they were healthy-looking, if extremely tall... Lex gripped her hands together. "What are you going to do with me?" she managed to get out.

"Take you to my home," Garrin said.

"To, to..." Visions of what men did to hapless females choked her.

Garrin's brow furrowed as though he were confused at her response. "To introduce you to my people. And to find your magic."

So they weren't going to... *Wait*— "What magic?"

"You are a powerful Halven, Lex. I do not understand how it could be either, but the prophecy is real."

Her eyes widened. "I'm the weakest person I know. You've got the wrong girl!"

Garrin's wide, full lips compressed. "I am never wrong. Dark Kingdom lies a great distance through the Land of Ice. We must leave this cave and prepare for the journey."

"You're not listening to me. And what do you mean *Land of Ice*...as in snow? You're not taking me to-to the snow, are you?" Lex's mind whirled, her words coming out choppy.

"There is a great deal of snow in the Land of Ice," he said absently as he grabbed a pack and shoved garments of some kind inside. They looked puffy, like coats people wore for heavy winter.

Lex sank to the ground. She couldn't get past these men, but she wouldn't go willingly. Suddenly, the cave didn't seem so bad after all. "I won't leave."

Garrin stopped what he was doing and frowned. "You

will eat something, and then our journey begins. It will be long and grueling. Unless you have perfected your abilities? I assumed not, but..." He looked hopeful.

She threw up her hands. "What abilities? Of course I can't help you. Have you listened to anything I've said? I'm not the person you're searching for."

He let out a soft sigh. "You are her; you will see. However, without your magic, we must make the journey the hard way."

Lex grabbed the sides of her head. It wasn't pounding in pain and her heart wasn't racing, but her mind spun like a tornado. "Why are you doing this to me?"

Garrin paced away, his back to her, and said, "To save my people."

THREE

Lex stared at the food in her hand. "Tacos?"

Garrin sniffed the taco he'd just unwrapped. "I was surprised as well. It's rather flavorful, this human food." He took a large bite, eating half in one fell swoop. "We are conspicuous in your land, but the establishment allowed us to drive our vehicle to a window to procure the meal. But do not worry. Soon we will be in Tirnan, where the food is excellent." He grinned and tossed the last bite into his mouth.

The picture he painted of three seven-foot men pulling up to a drive-through would be funny if she weren't being kidnapped.

Lex's stomach roiled and the food in her hand grew cold. Was she Halven?

Now that she wasn't having a panic attack, she studied the three guys doing what men do best the world over and eating their weight in food. They were attractive—beautiful, even—with straight features and athletic, tall bodies. Not to mention confident. All adjectives that didn't apply to

Lex. She *was* tall, but that was the only thing she had in common with them.

She set her taco down and rubbed her forehead. If she could only think straight. "How far is this Land of Ice?" Maybe if she went and showed Garrin she wasn't magical, he'd let her go?

He hesitated as though deciding what to tell her. Which wasn't reassuring. "We will travel to Tirnan, the Fae realm —a relatively simple journey to navigate via portal. Traversing the Land of Ice and reaching our kingdom...that is more of a challenge."

A cold sweat broke out on Lex's forehead. "Because of all the ice and snow?"

Garrin frowned. "You are not eating."

"My stomach..." Lex pressed her arm to her belly. "I can't eat."

"Help her," she heard Garrin say.

Zirel reached over a Frisbee-sized palm and flattened it on her stomach.

Lex squirmed away, but not fast enough. Heat infused her abdomen, and the coiled muscles and sinew eased.

She glared at Zirel. "Warn me before you do that. It's super creepy."

He shot her a grin, and Lex blinked. Good Lord, even the assistant was hot.

Compared to these men, Lex was homely as hell. If there was any truth to her being part Fae, she hadn't gotten the good-looking genes.

"We will be on strict rations while traveling." Garrin nodded at her food. "You must eat now. Our kind can survive long stretches without nourishment, but not yours."

It had to have been hours since Garrin and his men

kidnapped her from her dorm, given where they were. Dawson was located on a river delta, miles from mountains and caves. No one was going to find her here. No one was going to rescue her before they took her away for good.

"You don't understand," Lex said, her mouth tacky and dry. "I have...problems. If you think my panic attack earlier was bad, just wait until you put me near snow."

Garrin set his food down. "What is this panic attack you speak of?"

"Fear—irrational fear. I can't control it. The one time I saw snow, my heart raced so fast I passed out. Other times, I feel like I'm having a heart attack with all the signs and symptoms."

Garrin looked to Zirel, who nodded.

"We will heal you," Garrin said.

Lex shook her head. "My body, maybe, but not my mind. I won't pass out if Zirel does his"—she waved vaguely at the redhead, because what in the hell *had* he done?—"but inside, my mind will be a wreck. Please." She reached over and touched Garrin's shoulder. And immediately retracted it as though she'd been burned. A spark of heat radiated up her arm, and she rubbed it. "Please, don't do this."

Garrin's eyes were bluer than she'd ever seen them, nearly illuminated in the dim light set by the fire. "It is my duty. I must."

"Doesn't what I want matter?" Lex had never mattered to anyone except her mother, and now Jas, but it was worth a shot.

"No," he said.

She wrapped her arms around her knees and rocked back and forth. Garrin didn't realize it yet, but he was on a fool's mission. Because she wouldn't survive the Land of Ice long enough to help him.

~

LEX WAS A STRANGE FEMALE, fearful of the unknown when the known could be so much more deadly.

Garrin and Zirel had barely escaped the Land of Ice with their immortal lives. Hope had sprung when Amund, with his portal-creating powers, joined them after they reached New Kingdom, but not for long. Garrin had believed Lex would have command of her abilities, given her age. Only it seemed not.

Without Lex's powers, there was no way to remove the magic-blocking barriers that prevented his people from safely coming and going. No way to create a megaportal to other realms and lands. Amund didn't possess such magic. No one did.

Portal makers were capable of taking short jumps within a kingdom with a couple of people on board, not flights across tens of thousands of miles. Travel across the Land of Ice took months and was cold and dangerous.

And that worried Garrin. If Fae perished in the Land of Ice, how would a Halven with no abilities survive?

Amund swiveled his head to the side. "They are here," he said sharply.

"Who?" Lex paused from nibbling the food Garrin had finally convinced her to eat.

Garrin sighed harshly. The Fae soldiers on Earth shouldn't have found them for days. And now Garrin, his men, and Lex must leave before they'd properly prepared, and before the girl had sufficiently eaten. If the cold and snow she so feared didn't kill her, lack of nutrition would. But he had no choice. "Create the portal."

Amund raised his hand to the cave wall, moving it in a circular motion just above the surface. But before he could finish, four soldiers stormed inside.

"Lex!" one of the men shouted.

"Jasper?" Lex stood and moved toward the male—a Fae like Garrin, though Lex couldn't know that. She hadn't known Garrin and his men were Fae when she first encountered them.

"Stay back," the man Lex called Jasper said. He was dressed in black, along with the rest of the Fae soldiers, who were quickly brandishing swords, including a black-haired female with eyes like Garrin's.

Shimmers of light from Amund's portal bounced off the walls of the cave.

"*Now*, Amund." Garrin unsheathed his sword. "Take the girl."

"No!" Lex shouted, and scurried away from Amund.

Garrin moved between her and the soldiers, and he and Zirel fought back the men, clashes of metal on metal rending the cool night air.

Eyeing an opening, Garrin charged with his sword, forcing Jasper toward the entrance before the soldier could make his way to Lex.

The Fae sidestepped a powerful blow and slashed back, aiming for Garrin's head.

Garrin ignored a light nudge on his back as he blocked blow after blow from the soldiers. He swung his blade, missing Jasper's sword arm but slicing the man's side.

Garrin straightened while the other man stumbled, and a pounding on his back caught his attention. He looked over his shoulder.

The small Halven was beating him with her fists.

Did she think to harm him? "Stand back, female. You'll only hurt yourself."

"Don't kill Jas! Let me go! I don't belong here."

"Belong or not—you are mine now."

An animal cry sounded from the Fae who sought Lex. He stormed forward, his pale skin red with fury.

Garrin shoved Lex aside and deflected a blow that nearly clipped her.

Rage had Garrin's chest pulling taut. The man Lex so favored had nearly injured her.

Garrin could use his magic, but it might frighten Lex, and he didn't need it to best the others. He made several strikes with his sword in quick succession and forced Jasper to retreat.

Garrin feinted a move, and when Jasper went to block it, Garrin kicked the Fae in the chest, sending him flying out of the cave.

"No!" Lex launched herself onto Garrin's back, and he sighed.

"Female, what did I say about hurting yourself?" She was trying to strangle him, but it felt more like a neck rub. "Very well. This serves my purpose."

Garrin held on to Lex with one arm behind him and ran to where Amund stood, his face strained as he held open the portal. Garrin jumped inside and tucked his sword close to his body, away from the woman on his back.

Colorful magic inside the portal momentarily blinded Garrin, but he sensed the pull of the landing. At the last moment, he spun and protected Lex from the fall, swiftly rolling them out of the way before Zirel and Amund crashed down.

"We must hurry," Amund said, panting. No magic

came without effort, and Amund had portaled them to the cave and now to Tirnan. "There was a portal creator with the soldiers. A woman they call Camille. I met her when I supported New Kingdom's queen, Theodora Rainer."

"Rainer? The human lover?" Garrin climbed to his feet and pulled Lex up with him.

After they found Amund in New Kingdom, he'd told them stories of Theodora Joelle Rainer, the New Kingdom princess who'd married a human and borne his child. It was her full-grown Halven offspring who'd saved Tirnan from a disease made to kill every immortal Fae. Only Dark Kingdom had remained untouchable. Not even disease penetrated the magical barrier that set his people apart from the rest of Tirnan.

Garrin felt a blow to his stomach and looked at the woman in front of him. "That one I felt, little Halven." He cocked his head to the side. "You are stronger in Tirnan." He glanced at Amund. "Is this normal?"

Amund was the most knowledgeable out of the three of them when it came to Halven, having fought beside the New Kingdom queen's Halven child. But on this matter, Amund merely shrugged.

Excellent. Even Amund didn't understand Garrin's Halven.

Lex's light brown eyes flared with anger. "You jerk! Where is Jas? What did you do to him?"

"Your Fae friend? I assume he is braving the mountains where I left him. Or he and his men are on their way here..." Garrin looked at Amund.

"On it." Amund waved his hand in the air, drawing on his magic, though his hand shook.

Amund would be able to create the portal, but it would

take longer. His power was waning, and they hadn't much time.

Garrin ushered Lex closer to his men. "The soldiers from New Kingdom will arrive within seconds. As will your friends who wished to cut out our hearts. We must go."

"*Your* heart," Lex said. "They wish to cut out *your* heart, not mine. I'm not going anywhere with you." Lex glared at the shimmer of the beginnings of another portal. "And not in there. What *was* that?" She looked around suspiciously. "How did it take us here?"

Garrin sighed. "Will you always be this difficult?"

"Yes! You kidnapped me and took me through *thin air* to this place!" She gestured forcefully at the sky. "There are three moons. Three! And the stars are red. I'll probably die of radioactive contamination."

Garrin looked around and spotted what he sought. "We are in Tirnan, the Fae realm. Your homeland. Or, at least, the homeland of one of your sires. As long as we aren't confronted by other Fae, you'll be safe." He quickly paced to the closest Allon tree and started plucking leaves. Zirel scavenged for fruit and more leaves a few feet away. "Fae in Tirnan despise Halven, so stay close."

"H-how will they know I'm Halven?" she said, inching nearer.

He stashed the leaves into the bag they'd brought, filled with warm clothes for Lex and he and his men. "I'll explain later." He fisted more leaves. "This isn't what I planned, but it will have to do. We haven't time."

A rumbling came in the distance, and Garrin looked past Lex.

She gripped his arm. "What is that?"

He signaled to Amund, who was bent at the waist, his tanned skin pale, and ushered Lex toward the new portal.

"It is the sound of deadly New Kingdom soldiers alerted of our arrival by a Presence Charm." He threw the bag of provisions to Zirel. "Useful magic, Presence Charms." He pulled out his sword. "Except when you're doing the invading. We leave. Now."

Lex looked around. "I don't see anyone."

And she wouldn't. Not until the soldiers were upon them.

New Kingdom Fae possessed elemental powers—the ability to control fire, water molecules, and other natural elements. They were likely hidden among the fog that grew closer.

"It does not matter that a Halven sits on the New Kingdom throne. Most believe her rule temporary. Either way, they will kill first and talk later if they discover you."

"Just me? Why won't they kill you?"

"They'll try to kill me, but I'm harder to get rid of. Now go!" Garrin shoved her stubborn body closer to the portal and ran in the opposite direction and toward the deadly fog.

There was no avoiding using his power now. He raised his free hand, and flames jutted at the dense gray mist.

Screams cracked the night sky, and the figures of Fae soldiers aflame emerged from the dissipating fog.

But Fae healed fast, and a little burn for an otherwise healthy Fae was nothing.

Garrin stabbed the soldiers closest to him, slashing and maiming others, and only pausing to glance back and ensure Lex was in the portal.

But what he saw made fear lance his chest.

Lex fought Zirel's attempts to usher her into the portal, and Amund had collapsed to one knee, his hand raised, attempting to keep hold of his magic.

Garrin stabbed his way through the frontline of soldiers, blocked a lightning bolt and several boulders aimed at his head, and threw one massive fire torch at his enemies before running for Lex.

She grabbed his arm as he neared. "Take me back!"

"I've already told you." He picked her up, one arm under her knees and the other behind her back. "I can't," he said, and jumped into the portal.

FOUR

Amund's portal deposited them at the perimeter of New Kingdom and the Land of Ice, where towering, snow-covered mountains spanned as far as the eye could see.

Lex jerked out of Garrin's arms and glared. "Damn you!" Her gaze was hot as the fire Garrin could throw with his hands. Until she looked beyond him.

Her eyes rounded, and her body tensed. "Nooo!" she screamed.

And continued to scream.

Garrin stared at the female, confused at her lack of control. His chest tightened as her cries turned hoarse, choking sounds coming from her throat.

Lex's eyes glassed over, and Garrin signaled to Zirel, but Zirel was already running to him.

Zirel touched Lex's forehead, and she fell limp in Garrin's arms.

"Her fear is a problem," Zirel said.

Garrin was as frustrated as his men, and fearful for the fragile female. "The only way to Dark Kingdom is through the Land of Ice." He gently set Lex on the ground and searched for signs of New Kingdom soldiers who may have followed them.

The portal creator huddled not far away, his complexion gray, his chest rising and falling in exhaustion. "Amund?"

The burly Fae rubbed his face. "I need but a moment."

In a moment, New Kingdom guards would track them. "Can you get us deep enough inside the Land of Ice?"

Amund nodded. "One more portal. That is all I have in me until I rest."

Amund was in terrible shape. Should he be attacked in his condition, he would succumb to his injuries, unable to heal. But they were out of options. "It is enough."

With Amund's help, they soon passed into the great white abyss.

Inside the Land of Ice, mountains jutted toward the sky, craggy, in shades of gray, blue, and white, the peaks stretching farther than even Fae, with superior sensory perception, could see. There was no anchor in this land, and disorientation was a death sentence.

Exhausted, they huddled together and blocked the cold wind from Lex's small form.

Zirel stared at the girl, who looked peaceful in sleep. "She will wake soon."

"Yes," Garrin said.

Zirel peered around. The wind blew so hard that it was difficult to stand, let alone walk. "She is terrified of this place—not that I fault her."

"Nor I," Garrin said, "but it will make the trip more difficult."

Amund lay on his side, unmoving, his eyes closed. "If

she was truly the prophesied one, she would be able to take us to Dark Kingdom."

Garrin steeled his gaze. "It is unfortunate the girl shows no sign of her powers, but there is something about her... I am certain she is the one the elders spoke of. Our circumstances may have changed, but not our purpose. We will not fail our people. We will bring the girl with us."

He grabbed the canvas bag that held their supplies and pulled out a heavy coat made of Fae material resistant to cold. He eased Lex's arms through the sleeves and secured the front, tucking her head and long hair inside the hood. Next, he covered her hands with gloves.

His brow furrowed. She would remain warm for a time. But it wasn't the cold that concerned Garrin. It was the strange fear of snow she carried with her.

He looked at Zirel. "You must keep the girl asleep while we travel."

Zirel gave a quick nod. "Yes, Your Highness."

Lex was lying on frozen ground so cold it seeped straight to her bones. "Thirsty," she said, and tried to open her eyes. When she finally managed it, she struggled to focus. "Cold."

Rustling came from above, and a warm blanket covered her.

She rubbed her eyes, finally getting them to adjust, and looked down. At some point, someone had put her in a coat and gloves—not that it made a difference when lying in snow. Another coat now rested on top of her.

"Better?" Garrin leaned over in nothing but a sweater,

while the other two Fae crouched nearby in coats like the one that covered her.

Garrin had given her his outerwear. In the middle of this awful, arctic place.

She closed her eyes against the images that flashed across her mind. The ones she'd had before she passed out. Given the temperature beneath her back and the clothing the men wore, she was still living her worst nightmare.

"It isn't too late to return me." Her teeth chattered, and it was difficult to swallow. All she wanted was to return to her uncle.

Was Jas really Fae like them? These men sounded like Jasper, with their English accent that held tinges of Germanic influence, but it was hard to imagine it being true. "I won't tell anyone you took me. I promise."

"Shh." Garrin's strong arm slipped beneath her back and lifted her upright. He placed a bowl to her mouth, and she flinched. "The bowl is made of ice, but you must drink the water. You are dehydrated."

Lex sipped and experienced the sensation of freezing from the inside. She winced and turned her head. The coat Garrin had laid over her was losing the heat from his body. She shifted and pulled it closer. "I'm so cold."

Garrin murmured something off to the side, then his face was in front of her again. "The coat contains our magic and protects against the worst of the cold, but not all. You retain heat better when I carry you, but we must rest for the night and give you more food. You're not eating enough."

Her body shook, her tongue thick. "I told you I wasn't strong enough. Not for this. Not for anything. We have to go back."

A haze of regret crossed Garrin's cool gaze. "We've traveled for several weeks, and—"

Her eyes widened. "Several *weeks*?"

"—there is no turning back if you are to survive. We must get you to Dark Kingdom as soon as possible." He reached to the side, then held out something brown. "Eat more leaves."

She made a face, her memory hazy but clearing the longer she stayed awake. "You've been feeding me those. They taste awful." She looked past Garrin at the frozen landscape. The cool wind cut through her flesh, and her throat bobbed. "How has so much time passed without me knowing?"

"Zirel is a healer, but he can also blur memory to some degree. We felt it best for you not to remember much of this land."

If only she could forget the entire experience. "When will we be past the snow?"

Garrin's expression stiffened, and Zirel and Amund glanced at each other. "Not for a while," Garrin said.

She'd never forgive Garrin for taking her to this place. She might not have had much back home, but at least she'd been safe. "Jas said he sensed the cold." She looked at Garrin. "*You* are the cold." Her tears chilled and froze in their descent before she could wipe them away. "Should have listened to him. Should have listened..."

Amund leaned closer, crowding her along with Garrin. "What is she talking about?"

"Lex," Garrin said, his tone low and commanding. "You will not be harmed. This is my land, and I will protect you."

"Protect me? But the snow..." She shook her head, visions of an avalanche making her heart race. "This is torture."

Garrin's strong throat bobbed. He glanced off, and when his gaze returned to hers, it was hard and unyielding.

"You must eat and drink more, but you cannot allow your-self to panic. It drains you of energy." He took off his glove and set a shockingly warm and gentle hand on her cheek. "Be calm, Lex. You are safe. The snow cannot hurt you."

She wanted to lash out at his arrogance. Instead, she looked into Garrin's bright eyes and saw an emotion that mirrored her own. "I'm scared."

Zirel moved closer, but Garrin raised his hand in a staying motion. "She must get used to this land." He sat beside her, and that was when Lex fully saw her surroundings.

The snow and ice and mountains—she couldn't stay here. It would smother her. It would stomp her out like an ant on a roadway. She moaned, and her head throbbed.

Garrin pulled her to his side, his arm wrapped tightly around her. He placed his gloveless hand on her forehead, where he stroked her hair back beneath her hood.

"It's too cold. The snow," she said, but her breathing slowed at his touch, and she no longer felt the sharp blade of panic she had a moment ago. The vision of the avalanche was still in her mental periphery, but blurred and harder to grasp.

"If you remain calm, Zirel won't need to make you unconscious—"

She turned sharply and stared at him. "Is that what you've been doing to me?" She hadn't believed him when he said they'd been here for weeks. It seemed impossible, but if he'd been knocking her out and messing with her memories?

Lex tried to move away, but Garrin held her close.

"The land frightens you, making you incoherent," Garrin said. "Our actions were necessary."

She squeezed her eyes closed. "None of this is necessary. Why didn't you return me when you could?" Lex felt lightheaded, her chest moving up and down too rapidly.

"Control your breathing, and I will build a dwelling to keep you warm tonight."

Her palms clenched and the wind on the mountaintop whipped the fur lining of her hood. "You aren't listening to me. I wouldn't need a dwelling if you hadn't taken me!" This time she scooted away, and he allowed her.

Garrin stood and looked off. "If I could save my people any other way…"

Lex's eyes burned with tears she held inside. They'd only freeze on her face anyway. "And *I'm* your best option?"

He glanced back. "Unfortunately."

Lex huffed out a breath. This jerk… "I'm going to fail, and then what? I die, and you find option B? I suppose one human life isn't a big deal in the scheme of things."

"It is far more complicated than that." Garrin's face was less expressive than his eyes. But right now, those eyes grew haunted.

He moved a couple feet away and looked out at the white horizon. "Dark Fae have traversed this unforgiving land for millennia. It was only during the last few hundred years that travel through the Land of Ice became nearly impossible. Our magic falters when it never did before. We've lost many lives attempting to escape our prison." He looked back. "The prophesied one is the only way out. *You* are the only way for my people to leave Dark Kingdom. And to leave we must go through the Land of Ice."

Lex pressed her fingers to her forehead. "You're talking in riddles, and my head feels like someone is stabbing it with a knife. For the hundredth time, I don't have powers. I can't send us through space like Amund or heal like Zirel. And I can't help you cross this awful place."

"But you will."

Lex growled in anger. Garrin was stubborn, and now they'd die because of it.

His mouth twitched. "You are feeling better if you are making angry animal sounds. You must no longer fear me."

She wasn't hyperventilating, no. Not since he'd distracted her with his warm hand stroking her forehead. And as seriously pissed off as she was at his taking her from the only security she'd ever known, he was right; she didn't fear him anymore.

How could she fear a man who risked death by giving her his only coat? Seriously, why wasn't he freezing? Zirel and Amund had on their coats, and even they bounced on their heels to keep warm in the frigid wind. "I'm too annoyed to fear you."

"I will keep that in mind the next time you panic," Garrin said, his mouth turned up.

She shot him a death glare.

Choking sounds came from the other men.

Garrin's brow quirked. "You know, Lex, I'm not used to insolence from females."

Her teeth chattered harder. She huddled inside the hood and pulled his coat closer to her face. "Jas says I'm more headstrong than people realize. I must be getting used to you."

"I would like for you to grow used to me." Longing simmered in his eyes, then he said, "If I could have avoided all this..." His jaw clenched, and he seemed to grapple for words. "It is of no matter. I hadn't anticipated your powers would not be formed. We expected you to be in possession of your magical ability, given your year of study. How old *are* you?"

So she wasn't what he expected? Shocker. That was what she'd been telling him all along. "Twenty."

"Twenty?" Garrin's chin jutted back.

"It is odd," Amund said, his brow furrowed.

She looked at Zirel, who was also staring at her strangely. This was getting annoying. "What is odd?"

"You are past the age in which Halven come into their powers." Garrin picked up a handful of snow in his gloved hand, and Lex watched it melt faster than it should. Especially in below-freezing temperatures without a coat. He glanced at his men. "Once we are in Dark Kingdom, we will speak with the elders and inquire as to why her ability lies dormant."

Her jaw dropped. "You kidnapped me…and you're not even sure what I can do?"

Garrin bristled and wiped the moisture from the snow onto his pants. "The prophecy didn't specify when you'd come into your magic, or even what it would be—only that a child of Dark blood would become my people's savior. No one from Dark Kingdom has stepped forward to claim such an ability in the hundreds of years of our isolation. The only conclusion was that the prophesied one lived elsewhere."

Lex let out a pained sigh. "That sounds like an extremely vague prophecy."

"Perhaps, but our elders are never wrong. Come." He stretched out his hand to her. "It grows dark and cold. I will show you something, if you allow it."

Lex reached for Garrin's gloved hand, and a shock wave of sensation ran up her frozen limb through the layers of clothing that protected her.

She slammed her eyes shut. The charge she felt whenever they touched was getting annoying.

He tipped his head in the direction of an area that was

relatively flat on the mountain. Lex peeked at it and took in a dizzying view of the rest of the area.

She closed her eyes and breathed in and out slowly.

When she opened her eyes again, Garrin was watching her patiently as though waiting for her to calm. "You've witnessed Zirel's ability to heal and Amund's ability to create portals for travel. Are you not curious about my abilities?"

He was trying to distract her—and it helped. She couldn't deny she was curious, though she wasn't about to tell him that. "No, but you'll probably show me anyway."

He chuckled and held up his gloved hand. He turned it over as though studying it. "Fae handle temperature variations better than humans, but even my men cannot withstand the Land of Ice for long without proper protection. I will show you one of my abilities that will keep us warm overnight, but if you feel frightened, you must calm yourself like you did a moment ago."

Lex gripped the edges of the coat that dwarfed her body and huddled inside the fabric. She was turning into an icicle even with Garrin's outerwear layered above her own. "I have no idea what you plan to do, so I can't promise you anything."

His mouth turned up. He didn't look at her like the campus curiosity she was back home. He didn't avert his eyes when he spoke to her, and he seemed pleased at her stubbornness. "You experienced some of my magic in your dormitory. Do you remember?"

A shiver added to her existing chills and coursed through her. "I remember the cold. And then it was gone and we were inside the cave."

"You are part Dark Fae, Lex, and what I gave you was a taste of my powers. Your innate ability to deflect my magic indicated you are my kind and not another Fae from another part of Tirnan. You are whom I say you are, no matter how you spent your life before I found you."

The wind blew harder around Garrin, whipping his wavy, dark hair across his forehead.

And then he raised his hands, and the snow around them rose too.

FIVE

Garrin raised his hands and drew on his power. The snow around them rose and compacted, slowly forming a dome around them. He was careful not to move too quickly, but even so, Lex gasped.

"Do not be afraid. I have complete control. I can throw the snow across the horizon or compact it, as I am doing now."

Lex swiveled her head back and forth at the walls forming around her. She huddled inside her coat and blinked several times, shivering harder than normal.

"Breathe, Lex, as you did earlier," Garrin said as he worked. "The dome will protect us from the elements, not harm us."

Garrin turned toward one side of the dome and brought his hands together as though in prayer. He slowly separated them, and the ice and snow trenched and formed a tunnel that led to the outside, allowing air circulation while keeping heat in. Finally, Garrin blew on the interior walls, warming the compacted snow until it melted. Then he blew again and cooled the melting snow, turning it into an icy, hard shell.

"My prince," Zirel said, and Garrin looked over his shoulder.

Lex shook near an interior dome wall, her eyes glassed over.

Garrin rushed to her. "Can you hear me?"

No answer.

He tore off his gloves and grasped the sides of her face with his palms. "Look at me, Lex."

Her teeth chattered violently.

"*Lexandra*," he said, "look at me now."

Lex's gaze collided with Garrin's. "Wha...? How do you know my name? No one knows my name. Except for Jas."

He rubbed her temples gently. She was so fragile. For the first time, he truly feared she wouldn't reach his kingdom alive.

The notion was unsettling. This woman did not deserve to die. And the thought of it made him wish to shelter her. "You told me they call you Lex," he said in a calm tone.

She swallowed. "I never told you my full name."

"Your given name is traditional in our land, with Lex as the diminutive. Lexandra means defender of people," he said, smoothing his thumbs over her forehead. "And you were born to defend and protect."

Her shaking grew less violent the longer she listened to him.

Garrin slowly lowered his palms, but he remained within arm's reach.

"Aside from the fact that just looking at the walls of this igloo brings on a panic attack," she said, "how did you make it?"

"It is my gift—one we call ice and fire in Dark Kingdom. And when you are ready, your gift will help many too."

She closed her eyes. "This person you're searching for—they can't be the only one able to help."

He glanced down and let out a resigned breath. "If the myths are to be believed, there is no other."

She looked at Garrin, her gaze hard. "The myths are wrong."

No matter what happened, there was no doubt in Garrin's mind that Lex was special. He felt it when he touched her. If only he understood her ability and how to manifest it. "The prophecies have never been wrong. You forget who sired Fae. Angels do not lie."

"The *angels* made the prophecy?"

He nodded. "According to the elders."

Lex didn't show signs of panic, but she retreated into herself for the rest of the evening, and Garrin didn't know what to make of it. She fought so hard to convince him she wasn't special, but Garrin sensed that she was with every part of his being.

He remained close to Lex, awake long after his men had fallen asleep. Each time she began to shake, he reached over and calmed her with a touch. He managed to get her to eat a few Allon leaves and drink the water he'd melted from the snow, and finally, she slept more peacefully.

"She is correct," Amund said, rolling to his side to face Garrin.

Garrin stared at the ceiling, his hands beneath his head. "I thought you were asleep."

"We don't know for certain that she is *the one*."

Garrin rubbed his beard. It had grown while they scouted for Lex in the Earth realm, and he hadn't bothered to cut it. It was good protection against the cold. "The only way to hide her among humans was to keep her with our kind at the university. We checked hundreds of females, and she is the only one who withstood my powers."

"But she hasn't any magic."

"That we know of," Garrin said, and looked across the dome. "You said yourself that you sensed her to be Halven."

"I was wrong," Amund said.

"Wrong?"

"I no longer believe she is Halven."

Garrin lifted on one elbow. "Explain."

Amund looked at the sleeping woman. "Once we entered the Fae realm, her energy level bloomed—and it has continued to grow."

"What are you saying?" Garrin asked.

"Lex is not Halven. She is full Fae."

CHAPTER
SIX

Lex woke slowly from a dream of her mother, where Lex was happy and unafraid...peering into the eyes of three incredibly tall men looking down at her with worry.

She sat up abruptly and scooted back. "What's wrong?"

"You aren't what I believed you to be," Garrin said.

Lex rubbed her eyes. These guys had a terrifying way of waking a girl. "You're just now figuring that out?" Good Lord, maybe now they'd return her.

"Lex," Garrin said, and crouched. "You aren't Halven, because you are Fae—full Fae. Amund says your energy level has been changing since we entered Tirnan."

Lex attempted to make sense of his words. There was no way she was like them. First and foremost, she wasn't strong, and she certainly wasn't beautiful like these men. Not to mention the absence of anything resembling a magical power.

"Search your memory," Garrin said. "You must recall something."

She thought back for a moment, then shook her head.

"Everything before my mother's death is either murky or nonexistent. I figured it was from the trauma."

Lex remembered Jas vividly, but her mother was only clear in her dreams, or more specifically, her nightmares. This morning's dream was entirely unusual in that she and her mother were together and happy.

"I remember my mother dying in an avalanche. But Jas says I wasn't there. I must have made up images of what I think her death was like. I don't know."

She covered her face. No matter how hard she'd tried, she couldn't get the images of her mother buried in snow out of her head.

Gentle hands tugged at Lex's wrists until she looked up.

"If someone didn't want you to remember," Garrin said, "you wouldn't recall the past. Not clearly."

"You think someone did this to me?"

Garrin glanced at Amund knowingly. "We believe so."

Something had brought these men into her life. According to Garrin, they'd been traveling for weeks in this freezing wasteland with little food. Granted, she felt like crap, but shouldn't she be dead? And then there was Jas. He'd fought them as though he were Fae, and not her young uncle all the college coeds wanted to date.

Frustration simmered beneath her skin. How could Jas have lied to her all these years? Or had he? He never told her he was human. It's what she'd assumed.

"Maybe I'm not full Fae. Maybe I'm extra Halven." That sounded entirely dumb even to her ears, but she needed to hold on to something normal, and being half human was better than full Fae.

Garrin stood and paced the large igloo. "If you were noble Fae, that would make you 'extra Halven,' as you call it. But it would only explain a Halven with higher energy levels. Not someone presenting as Fae."

"I don't feel Fae."

He raised his brow. "How would you know?"

"Shouldn't I feel something?"

His shoulders sank noticeably. "You should possess a power. But the magic that hid your energy level when we found you must be suppressing your abilities as well." He rubbed his beard and looked down as though contemplating.

After a moment, he looked around. "We've stayed too long. The sun has risen. We must leave."

Lex got to her feet. "What sun? Everything is white and gray."

"Be that as it may," Garrin said, "it is warmer during the day than at night. We cannot stay inside a snow dome forever. We will run out of food unless we keep moving."

Food? He called those leaves food? And even if it was warmer during the day, it wasn't comfortable. She was covered from head to toe in more layers than she'd worn in her life, and the cold ate right through them. "I'll walk. Maybe the exercise will help me stay warm."

Lex clapped her hands together and stomped her feet to get feeling back in them. She had a pounding headache and felt like she could sleep for a day or two, but being carried was humiliating.

Garrin and the other men looked at each other.

"This is not a good idea," Zirel said. "The terrain is steep."

"What if you panic?" Garrin asked her. "You've grown used to the dome. But once we step outside...?"

He had a point. "I might freak out, but I can control it better now." She hoped.

Garrin looked at her as though he didn't believe her, and she glared back.

"I'm tired of being knocked out by Zirel," she said. "I can do this."

Lex made it about a mile and was darn proud of how well she'd managed to ignore the snow sinking under her feet. She still felt anxious, but she continued her deep-breathing exercises and kept her gaze low and not on the monstrous white mountains.

Until she slid on a narrow section, her feet flying over the edge.

Her arms flailed, hands grasping at nothing but snow that slipped through her gloved fingers. She screamed.

Garrin caught her hand before she rolled off the mountain.

A loud roaring filled her ears, and she gasped for breath.

Knees trenched in the snow and still holding her, Garrin hauled her up until she lay half on top of him.

His chest rose and fell beneath her cheek. "Are you okay?"

She couldn't answer. In the span of a heartbeat, she'd nearly plummeted to her death.

"Say something, Lex."

Black fog filled the corners of her vision.

Garrin sat up, bringing her with him. He gripped her shoulders. "Lexandra, listen to me. I told you, I will not allow harm to come to you."

No matter how powerful Garrin was, he couldn't save her from herself. What if he missed her next time? And once they figured out she was of no use to them, what then?

She shook off Garrin's hands and bent over until her vision cleared. Then she stood slowly and trudged forward, stumbling, and catching herself.

She'd die in this place. They thought her Fae and powerful, and she was only a scared nobody.

Perhaps this was her destiny. To perish the way her mother had.

Tears pricked her eyes.

Hours later, when her legs would go no farther, she collapsed to her knees.

Without missing a beat, Garrin swept her up and into his arms.

Lex was too tired to protest. She tucked her head into Garrin's warm chest, covering what was exposed of her face from the cold. Being in his arms felt incredibly good, and it had nothing to do with the warmth of his body.

The heavy weight of sleep pulled her under.

~

WHEN LEX WOKE, she was lying inside another damn igloo. She'd only managed to walk one day—and not even a full day—before nearly getting herself killed. It had been so exhausting that she didn't remember Garrin setting her down.

She turned her head and studied the man beside her.

Garrin lay on his side with his eyes closed. His arms were crossed, hands tucked inside his armpits as though to protect from the cold, but he didn't perpetually shiver the way she did. His breathing was even and slow. And he was so close that she felt the warmth from his breath on her face.

He smelled of pine needles, and she smiled. The sweet, earthy scent of his breath was probably due to all those leaves they'd been eating.

Her gaze traveled down his facial features. His forehead

was broad and smooth, the lines of his nose straight. All three Fae had serious facial hair after this many weeks traveling, but up close, Garrin's wide mouth and rose-hued lips looked soft and pillowy next to his beard.

Do Fae kiss?

She squeezed her eyes closed. What was wrong with her?

Garrin was warm, and she had the urge to scoot closer and curl within the shelter of his body—the man who'd *kidnapped* her. The cold had either frozen her brain cells or she had Stockholm syndrome. Either way, she wasn't herself.

He was super arrogant, and somehow that was both infuriating and humorous at the same time. When she didn't give in to his demands, he smiled. What sort of masochist smiled when someone wouldn't do what they wanted?

Apparently, women in his land didn't talk back to him. No wonder he was so spoiled.

She ignored her better judgment, scooted closer to Garrin, and breathed in his scent, because she'd become *that person*. The kind of woman who was so desperate she smelled guys while they slept. She'd lost her mind. Or maybe, whether she wanted to or not, she was growing attached to the arrogant, masochistic prince.

He smelled good. Really good. Whatever happened to body odor, and why was she the only one with it after all these weeks?

Lex rolled her eyes in frustration and looked across the igloo. Zirel and Amund's shadowed figures sprawled near the opening, one of them snoring lightly. The only other sounds were the wind whistling outside and the snow crunching beneath her when she moved.

These Fae were growing on her, but this place she could do without.

She let out a deep breath and blinked back tears. She didn't know how much longer she could do this. Her arms and legs were constantly weighted down by exhaustion and cold, and she needed to travel again tomorrow? And the next day? How many more days? According to Garrin, they weren't even halfway.

She turned to cuddle back into his body. And his cool eyes were leveled on her.

"Get some sleep," he said, his gaze warm and slightly hooded.

She swallowed and kept a straight face. "You're very controlling, you know that?"

His mouth twitched. He reached over, tucked her against him, and closed his eyes.

It should feel awkward to be in his arms, but Garrin wasn't a stranger anymore, and the only awkward thing was the feelings she was beginning to have for him.

The heat from his body broke the chill, and the comfort she experienced instantly lulled her.

She was dozing before she knew it.

Lex rose the next day and felt a jolt of energy she hadn't yesterday. She'd been eating more, and maybe that was the explanation. No matter what, she was determined to keep up with the guys today.

She stretched her arms above her head, and her back cracked like an eighty-year-old's. A whiff of something less than pleasant crossed her nose.

She lifted her arm and sniffed her armpit. "Oh, that's bad."

Garrin looked up from packing their rations into the pack he carried. "What's bad?"

"Aren't you guys dying without a shower?"

"We're used to our own smell," Zirel said before ducking out of the igloo to join Amund outside.

"That's because you don't smell," she called out, annoyed.

It had been several weeks, and her hair felt like butter had been smoothed down it. She needed a bath.

Garrin stopped what he was doing and stared. "You

wish to bathe? We are on a frozen mountaintop," he pointed out unnecessarily.

She shifted her feet, her breath visible in the frigid air. "I know, but the need to bathe is battling with the cold in terms of discomfort. How is it that Fae don't have body odor?"

He lifted his eyebrow. "You do not smell."

What was he talking about? She could smell herself!

She shook her head and went to leave the igloo. "Never mind." It wasn't like she expected him to do anything. They had their hands full trying to stay warm and sleeping in a Fae-made igloo without food or running water. Of course there was no way to take a bath.

Garrin caught her arm before she passed. "Wait a moment." She looked up, and his gaze appeared hesitant. "I can offer you a shower, but I can't guarantee you'll be warm."

She blinked in surprise. "How cold are we talking? Because if I get any colder, I might pass out."

"I can warm the water—"

She held up her hand. "You can give me a shower *and* warm water?"

"It will not be a long shower. A minute and then you must put on your clothes. And it will delay us."

The idea of getting naked in a freezing igloo did not appeal—until he'd mentioned warm water.

Thus far, Garrin had only given her cold water to drink. "If it's only a minute and I dress quickly, I'm up for trying it. But you really expect me to undress?"

"Is there another way to shower?"

Good point.

What if this was her last luxury in life?

It turned out taking even a cold shower ranked high

when things like food and proper shelter weren't an option. "Okay, what do I need to do?"

Without a word, Garrin created an ice partition between him and Lex inside the igloo. It was about six inches deep and six feet high, and if she stood on her tiptoes, she could see his face.

"Undress," he said, and a shiver ran down her spine.

That word spoken from his lips was distracting.

Was she really doing this? Getting naked in front of Garrin? True, he couldn't see her through the foggy partition, and Zirel and Amund were out somewhere taking their morning constitutional, but... "No peeking."

He made a sound in the back of his throat. "I assure you, I am capable of controlling myself."

Lex frowned. Did he have to make it sound so easy?

"Fine." She stripped off her clothes rapid-fire, tossed them over the partition—and thought she might turn into an ice cube on the spot.

Her teeth chattered and her body shivered uncontrollably, the snow beneath her feet burning, it was so cold. "This was a bad idea. I can't do it. Too cold," she said, but before she got out the last word, a rain of warm water drizzled on her head.

"Aah." She reached up and rubbed the heated water into her hair and down her body, trying to soak up the warmth. "More!"

More warm water poured down her, and when she looked up, she saw that it was coming from the ceiling. Garrin was melting the igloo on top of her head.

Lex ran her hands through her damp hair and squeezed out whatever she could to clean it, and then he handed her what looked like a snowball. "You said you wouldn't peek!"

"I'm not looking. That is to wash yourself."

She stared at the snowball. "What, like an ice loofa?" She tossed it from hand to hand—the thing was cold, and her bare hands weren't happy.

"I do not know what a loofa is. The shaved ice will melt quickly under the water, but it can be used to clean before it melts."

She rubbed the ice under her arms and down her body, shaking and shivering at the warmth from above and the cold in her hands. "Okay, I'm done." Even with the warm water dripping on her, the snow under her feet was freezing and now slushy.

The water coming from above her head stopped. Just in time, too, because she could see the hazy blue-gray sky. Garrin handed her a small rag. "Dry off with this first."

She did as he said, and he handed her clothes piece by piece so they didn't sit in the snow while she dressed.

Lex hurried around the partition and hopped on her bare feet. "Cold, cold. Shoes."

But instead of handing over her shoes, Garrin picked her up.

"What are you doing?"

"Keeping you warm," he said, and sank onto the blanket they'd slept on, with Lex in his lap.

The blanket was made of the same material their coats were and stayed dry on top of the snow.

He opened his coat and wrapped it around her, which put her flush with his superheated chest.

She felt the ridges of his muscles through the thick knit tunic he wore and cuddled into him, tucking up her bared feet.

"You'll need to put on your boots," he said.

"Can't," she said without moving. "Too cold, and you're warm."

He rubbed his hands in her hair, his fingers sifting through it and massaging her scalp.

"What are you doing?" she said, because his hands were like heating pads. She closed her eyes, and an uncontrolled hum of pleasure came from the back of her throat.

"Drying your hair."

And somehow that seemed totally normal, a guy drying her hair with his bare hands.

He must have decided her hair was dry enough, because he stopped after a minute or two, and Lex frowned.

She reluctantly reached for her socks and the thick boots they'd given her after she'd stopped panicking in the Land of Ice, careful not to dislodge herself from the Garrin cocoon. Once her boots were on, she gripped the edges of his coat and pulled them together until she couldn't see out.

"We should leave, Lex." She shook her head, and he sighed. "Much as I am enjoying holding you, we must leave and make up the time we lost."

Did he really enjoy holding her? As much as she enjoyed being held by him?

"What would happen if we didn't go?" Staying warm and cuddling with Garrin seemed more important for survival at the moment.

She felt his chin rest on the top of her head. "We are running out of food."

Until he said that.

CHAPTER

EIGHT

Day after day they traveled, and Garrin was fairly confident they were going in the right direction. One never knew in the Land of Ice. But after centuries of trudging through the terrain, and with Amund's sense of power levels centering them somewhere between Dark Kingdom and New Kingdom, he was certain they were on the right track.

Only every day that passed, Lex weakened, particularly this last week with the cold snap that had hit them.

This morning, she collapsed shortly after they'd started the long, arduous walk, and Garrin ran to her.

"Can't," she said, her lips barely moving. "Don't feel well."

"Shh." He cradled her in his arms. "Conserve your energy," he said, then shouted for Zirel.

Zirel and Amund hurried over, their cheeks gaunt, lips cracked, with dark circles marring the skin beneath their eyes. Garrin suspected he looked no better.

If he and his men were this bad off from malnutrition, cold, and lack of proper sleep, he could only imagine how

52

Lex's health fared. She might present with a Fae's energy level, but her body wasn't sustaining like a Fae's.

After spending the last three weeks walking on her own and slowly losing energy, her lips were beyond blue; they were gray. Every night he lay awake worrying about her. He'd lost much of his magic due to exhaustion and could barely keep himself, let alone her, warm throughout the night.

He pulled off her gloves, and she whimpered. Her fingertips were charred-looking. Garrin's stomach turned, and he clutched her closer.

"She is dying," Zirel said.

"No." Garrin's jaw firmed. He wouldn't allow it. He looked at Amund hopefully. "Your powers?"

Amund couldn't take them any great distance, or they would have done so after they'd entered Tirnan, and now he was just as weakened as Garrin. But perhaps if they jumped through a few short portals, they could get close enough that Lex would be able to survive the last leg of the journey.

Amund's cheeks were burnished from the bitter wind battering them daily. None of them healed like normal in the Land of Ice. "Drained after the last few jumps."

With their food stores depleted, none of them had the resources to gain back magic.

Garrin looked at Lex, scanning her features desperately. "She cannot die."

Zirel and Amund sank down, surrounding Lex and trapping in whatever heat they had left.

Amund lifted his head and closed his eyes, breathing in and out. "We are near the Great Ravine," he finally said.

The Great Ravine marked the halfway point between Dark Kingdom and the other kingdoms of Tirnan. They were farther behind than Garrin had thought. Not only that, but the Great Ravine was said to be the origin of the magic that prevented Dark Fae from leaving their land. Many had fallen to their demise in its jagged depths.

Some Fae had built bridges to cross the ravine—only to fall into oblivion when the edifice collapsed. Others were drained of all powers and could go no farther, forced to return. While still others made it past the ravine, only to become disoriented and incapable of finding their way back. No matter how strong, no Fae survived several months without food in freezing temperatures. There was a limit to their endurance, and the Land of Ice, with its magic-blocking barrier and thousands of miles of terrain, tested all limits. And won.

Until Garrin, it was believed no others had crossed the Land of Ice and survived. But Garrin and Zirel had found Amund in New Kingdom...

"You made it to New Kingdom, as did Zirel and I," Garrin said. "We can get her to Dark Kingdom. We must."

Amund nodded. "Twice."

"Twice?" Garrin asked.

"Once to escape," Amund said, "and once when the Great War commenced."

Portal creators were rare, but a few had been born of noble Fae blood over the last few thousand years. Due to his unique magic, Amund was the only Dark Fae, aside from Garrin, who had any hope of escaping his kingdom. It was said he'd returned once to fight in a rebellion within their land. Until Garrin discovered Amund in New Kingdom months ago, he'd believed the story myth.

"How many more portal creators are hidden in Tirnan and Earth?" Garrin asked.

Amund shrugged. "I don't know for certain. I've only seen the one female."

"The black-haired woman at the Earth cave."

Amund nodded. "I survived by portaling myself and no others. It took dozens of attempts. I also brought food to last me months, not a handful of Allon leaves stuffed inside my clothes."

Garrin held Lex closer, trying to keep her warm. Everything that could go wrong had gone wrong. They'd left civilization in a hurry without proper preparation, and Lex didn't have her powers. And now her health failed. He swallowed thickly, his desperation to save her a palpable thing.

He leaned over, his face close to her nose. She breathed. Barely. But she no longer appeared conscious.

He formed an ice cup and managed to get a few droplets of water down her throat, but that was all.

Amund looked off. "I can do maybe one jump to the edge of the ravine. If His Highness wishes it."

In other words, one more portal could kill him. But he'd do it. For his prince.

"It won't be enough," Garrin said. "Even without the physical signs, you sense her energy draining as well as I. She is dying. We've traveled halfway. Go back or continue on; either way, she won't survive."

"We had to take the chance," Zirel said softly.

It was why Garrin and Zirel had never given up, even after losing their friends in past attempts to cross the frozen land. It didn't quell the burden he carried.

He looked across the area, snarling. "What if the angels meant for us to remain in Dark Kingdom? What if my father was wrong?" At the rate they were going, *none* of them would survive the trip back. "What have I done?"

Garrin wasn't the prince his people needed. He'd failed them.

He rested his hand above Lex's chest, willing energy into her body.

Amund made a light noise, and Garrin looked up. "What is it?"

He was staring across the landscape. "A great deal of land lies between here and help, but perhaps..."

Garrin exhaled. "Say it." He had to face whatever lay ahead.

"Perhaps once we pass the ravine," Amund said, "she will strengthen."

Garrin frowned. "How?"

"She is Fae, and not as strong as you, but even Zirel and I feel the weight of the magic that blocks our powers and energy here. If we cross the ravine, Lex might strengthen and live long enough for the rest of the journey."

Garrin shook his head sharply. "It will take *days* to cross the ravine. She doesn't have that long."

"We crossed the ravine by walking to the narrowest section on our way to the other kingdoms," Zirel noted.

Amund nodded. "That is not so far. I sense it. I can portal us there."

Garrin looked up, exasperated. "We jumped and climbed from that narrow section to make it across. It was a risk, and our strength was not depleted as it is now."

"There is no other way, my prince," Zirel said.

Garrin cradled Lex's head and didn't speak for a long moment. "I take all the risk," he finally said. "She is the priority. If something should happen to me, get her to the king."

Zirel bowed his head.

"Very well," Amund said.

Amund raised his hands. It took longer than normal for the air to waver and the portal to form, but when it did, Amund turned to them, his skin gray from the energy loss. "Hurry. I cannot hold it."

Garrin stood with Lex in his arms, entered the portal, and collapsed to his knees on the other side, his strength more depleted than he'd thought.

Zirel and Amund tumbled through the portal after him, collapsing just as Garrin had.

Garrin took a moment to catch his breath, his arms shaking. Lex had lost so much weight that she was light in his arms. But with his strength drained, he was weaker than he cared to admit.

Fighting exhaustion, Garrin climbed to his feet.

Zirel rose next, but Amund didn't move.

The healer leaned over Amund, then looked up. "He lives. Barely." Zirel had lost the ability to heal weeks ago and could not help their companion.

He pointed to the edge of the ravine farther down. "This section. The vee shape shortens the distance. But if we jump..."

They could die. Lex could die. But if they did nothing, they were sure to perish. "You go first," Garrin said. "I will bring Lex. Should I falter, you grab her."

Garrin was asking his men to put Lex ahead of their prince. But Lex was no mere Fae. He didn't know her magic, didn't know how she might help his kingdom, but he felt in his soul that she was special. And if he survived, he would prove it.

"Amund will follow after me and Lex." Garrin doubted Amund could do much after creating the portal, but he had to believe Amund could make the leap.

He had to believe they all could.

NINE

Garrin created an ice ledge with what little power he had left and shortened the distance across the ravine. He hadn't enough energy to make a bridge. Not that he'd attempt it. Too many bridges had failed under eerie circumstances at the Great Ravine.

Which meant that so could his ledge.

He ran a heavy hand down his face and looked at Lex at his feet, huddled in his coat he'd covered her with.

"Go," he said to Zirel. "Make the leap."

There was no time to second-guess their actions. This was their only option, and even if it worked, Garrin wasn't sure how he'd get Lex to his kingdom before she...

He wouldn't think of it. He'd come to care for her, and he refused to imagine anything worse happening.

Zirel took several steps back, then, with a running start, he jumped, using the ice ledge as his leaping-off point.

Garrin held his breath as his friend flew across the ravine no human or Fae eye could see to the bottom of.

The healer hit the ledge of the opposite side and clung

to the cliff, half of his body dangling off the edge. After a moment, Zirel slowly pulled himself up and over.

He stood and raised his hand, signaling for Garrin to proceed.

Garrin looked at Amund, who lay on his back.

The soldier waved a hand in a shooing motion. "I'll be right behind you."

Amund didn't appear in any condition to cross the ravine. Given the urgency with which they needed to reach Dark Kingdom, Amund's ability was extremely useful to steer them in the right direction, but the longer they waited, the worse Lex's condition got.

Garrin and Zirel had had slightly warmer weather and vastly improved provisions on their way across the Land of Ice. The return trip was the worst he'd encountered. Even so, Garrin owed it to his men to return them home safely with or without him.

He secured his coat around Lex, knotting the sleeves across her waist to tighten the extra layer, and brushed off frost that had formed around her nose and eyes.

He swallowed and held back an emotion he'd never experienced. It very much felt like the panic he'd seen in Lex. Only he wasn't worried for himself; he was worried for her.

There was no room for error. Garrin picked Lex up with numb arms. Like Zirel, he paced several steps back, took in deep breaths, and ran as fast as he could toward the ravine. At the last second, he leapt off the icy ledge he'd created, clutching Lex to his chest.

Garrin had a split second to realize he wouldn't make it across.

He twisted and hurtled Lex toward the other side of the ravine.

In the span of a heartbeat, Garrin saw Zirel fling his body forward and grasp the hood of the coat secured to Lex —before she slid out of his grip.

"No!" Garrin shouted as he fell, arms windmilling through frigid air.

But there was nothing to grab on to. He was in the center of the ravine, falling head over heels, and he couldn't see Lex anymore.

And then he glimpsed her. Her small body hit an outcropping above him and flopped like a rag doll.

He reached for his magic, willing it to respond.

Snow flurries whipped around his face, but that was all he could conjure.

Nothing solid.

Nothing to cushion Lex's fall. His energy and magic were drained.

It was over, he thought as he plummeted, his body aching with the knowledge he was responsible. Why had he never considered he'd fail her?

Garrin roared, the sound bouncing off the cavernous walls. His eyelids iced over from moisture, his hair freezing along with his limbs.

And then he was falling no more. His rapid descent slowed to a stop until he was suspended inside the seemingly bottomless ravine.

He looked up and saw Lex suspended as well. "Lex!"

She didn't move.

Garrin swung his limbs, attempting to reach the side of the ravine, but he went nowhere.

A light caught his eye. He stopped flailing and searched for the source. Because it wasn't coming from him. He'd barely the strength to breathe, let alone summon fire.

The yellow glow grew and...heated?

And then it became blinding, heating the walls of the ravine until a mist formed and the walls dripped with condensation.

One wall in particular.

The wall of the ravine across from Lex dissipated as though melting in on itself, forming an alcove with the bright light emerging from inside.

Garrin reached for the knife he kept in his boot and pulled it out.

But it wasn't a beast or even an army coming for them in the mysterious ravine.

It was a woman.

The woman who emerged wore simple village clothes from his kingdom. She looked pale as she wiped at her eyes and searched beyond the alcove.

When she saw Lex suspended in air, she let out a pained cry and ran to the edge, her arms outstretched.

Lex's body floated to the woman. She cradled Lex in her arms on the cave floor, rocking and running her hands down Lex's face.

Before Garrin could figure out what was happening, the woman's head swung in his direction.

He started to fall again, descending to the infinite bottom. Yet all he could think was Lex was in the arms of a stranger, her body near death. "Lexandra!"

Garrin halted midair as though he were on a string, the abruptness knocking the air from his lungs.

He slowly floated up, level with the alcove where Lex and the woman were.

"Who are you?" the woman asked. "And how do you know my daughter?"

Daughter?

TEN

"I am Garrin Branimir," he said. "Prince of Dark Kingdom."

The woman blinked several times as though surprised, and then her nostrils flared in anger. "Why have you brought my daughter here?"

Garrin looked down and jerked at the vertigo that rushed through him. "Can we discuss this on land?"

"No," the woman said.

Now Garrin saw the resemblance. Only Lex dared to defy him, and it seemed this woman did too.

"I am taking Lex to my kingdom," he said. No need to tell the woman he'd taken Lex against her will. "She is very ill from our journey and needs help. Are you truly her mother?" It was a strange twist of fate to be saved by Lex's mother inside the Great Ravine.

"Are you truly the son of Casone?" Bitterness filled the woman's tone, and it didn't bode well that she knew his father by name.

But Fae didn't lie, not even to save themselves. "Yes."

Garrin's father wanted what was best for his people,

but he could be ruthless in his means. Lex's mother might have been on the receiving end of his father's wrath, considering from where she emerged.

"Please release me and let me help your daughter."

After what felt like a century suspended over the ravine, Garrin slowly floated to the alcove ledge, where he finally touched ground.

He bent over, hands on his knees as he caught his breath. He was still power-starved, and just plain starved, after weeks of giving Lex his rations.

He slowly straightened. "Thank you. We must get Lex to my people, where she can be healed." He hesitated, glancing around. "How did you come to be here?"

The woman sighed harshly, still holding Lex. "Your father, of course."

Garrin closed his eyes. It was just as he'd feared. "I am sorry."

"As am I. 'Twas around the time of your birth... What human year did you say it was?"

He hadn't, but he rattled off the year the humans went by, and the woman's eyes enlarged.

"No," she said. "It can't be... Time runs differently in our realm, which is why I had the spell slow Lex's age and make her forget..." She shook her head, looking crestfallen.

Garrin took a chance and moved closer. "What did you say your name was?"

The woman blinked and looked up. "I am Isle Meinrad, but we don't have time for greetings. We must return to the human realm, where Lex will be safe."

"We cannot," Garrin said, his brow furrowed. "Do you not see that she is dying?"

Isle's face winced in pain. She scanned Lex's body, then glared at Garrin. "What have you done to my child?"

Garrin could fault no one but himself. "I will do everything in my power to get her help. But our only hope is to move forward, beyond the ravine." His men were somewhere above, but Garrin was so far down that he couldn't see them. "I don't suppose you know of a way out?"

"When your father banished me, he froze my powers in addition to my body." She gently eased Lex onto the floor and stood. Cautiously, she approached the edge of the alcove. "As soon as I sensed Lex, I was able to draw on her powers to regain mine."

Garrin shook his head. What was she saying? "Lex has no discernible powers. Our hope is that she strengthens as soon as we get her beyond the ravine, where most lose abilities due to the magic here."

"Most do," Isle said distractedly as she moved from the edge. "But not my daughter. Her powers are different. They were locked away, waiting until the time we were reunited and the spell was broken."

"Spell?" Garrin glanced at Lex, noting her coloring had not improved. "We must go. I fear Lex will not survive long."

Isle moved to her daughter. "Do you not know Lex's ability? She's been in hiding, but I assumed you had discovered it if you found her."

"She is the prophesied one," he said.

"A prophecy, is it?" Isle sank to her knees and cradled Lex's face. "The elders have been busy while I was away if they sent you on a treasure hunt. Your father murdered or isolated the only Fae who knew about Lex. It's why I went to such lengths to hide her. But she is old enough now. And I am here to protect her."

Isle's narrow throat bobbed and her eyes glistened.

"The others have been trapped for so long...well before you and I were born."

"Who has been trapped?"

She looked up. "Dark Fae. Your father has kept us imprisoned for centuries."

Garrin attempted to slow his pounding heart. Isle's words made no sense, but she wouldn't say something she didn't believe. "You're mistaken. My father has been as much a prisoner of this land as the rest of us. Few have managed to escape. Most who have escaped lost their lives to the hatred of Old and New Kingdom soldiers. And no one has managed to release our people en masse."

She huffed out a sigh. "We don't have time to argue this. You are the king's son. I assume you have power over water?"

Among other things, Garrin thought. "When I am hale. Which I am not."

She looked him up and down, taking in his eyes, which he knew were sunken. His beard had grown at least an inch longer too. "Your mind is sound; thus, you are healthy enough. The ravine is too deep for me to lift us to the top. Use your abilities and stair us."

When strong, Garrin could create stairs of ice to climb the ravine. But not now. Now he couldn't put together a flurry. "I assure you, I've tried. I would do anything to save your daughter."

Isle seemed taken aback at that. She moved closer, her gaze intent. "Anything to save my daughter?" She laughed humorlessly. "Oh, what twisted irony." She peered at him skeptically. "Have you any notion why your father entombed me?"

No, he hadn't, and when he didn't say anything, she answered for him. "I possessed knowledge your father wished to hide. What he didn't know is that I'd hidden something from him. *Lex.* I've spent two hundred years waiting to be reunited with her. I will not see harm come to her—not by you, should you change your mind about saving her, and not by your father."

Two hundred years? Lex had been hidden that long? It was beyond belief.

He shook his head. "What you said about my father can't possibly be true, but we haven't the time to debate it. What do you propose we do to get out of here?"

"We use Lex's power the way her gift was intended."

Garrin pressed his fingers to his temple, the pounding of his head blocking out the rush of the wind. He'd gone too long without a coat, and Lex's mother spoke nonsense. "What power?"

Isle's eyes narrowed. "I don't trust you, Dark Prince. I will tell you, because we are in a most unfortunate situation, but do not cross me or you will regret it."

He let out a measured breath. "As I said, I only wish for your daughter's safety."

"Which you've put in peril!"

The moment required patience, and he had little left. He closed his eyes and said something he never did. "Please."

She stared for a long moment, then looked worriedly at Lex as though weighing her daughter's safety against her mistrust for Garrin. "My daughter has the ability to manipulate and magnify powers. *All* powers." She looked at him intently. "Do you understand what I am saying, Dark Prince?"

Lex was *the one*. He'd always believed it, and Isle's words proved it. "I've never heard of such magic."

"That is because no other Fae possesses it."

"One needs power in order to magnify it," he said. "And

I have none at the moment, as is the case with my men. How would Lex be able to conjure it?"

"Your power is there. It is merely held back by the exhaustion of your Fae form. My daughter might not be able to control her magic in her current state, but I can."

Lex's mother was quite possibly mad. But he'd been plunging to his death moments ago, and now he wasn't. He was open to discussion. "How can Lex do this if she is unconscious?"

"The same way her power allowed me to melt the ice tomb your father created. I have the power of telekinesis and a minor ability with fire when I exert myself. As soon as I sensed my daughter, I reached for her magic and activated my own, breaking my imprisonment."

Isle motioned for Garrin to come closer. "You do not know Lex the way I do. I can call to her power because I am her mother. If you want to reach her magic, you will need to touch her. It will be easier that way."

Not know Lex? She was stubborn. Beautiful. And under the worst of circumstances, humorous without meaning to be. If they survived this, the woman who'd hid in plain sight in the human realm would give him a piece of her mind. And right now, he prayed for Lex's condemnation. Would welcome it, for he feared he'd never hear her voice again.

He knelt and ran his knuckles along the cold blue-gray skin of Lex's jaw, his own jaw flexing. She wouldn't survive much longer out here. This had to work.

He closed his eyes and gently squeezed her shoulder, running his palm toward her hand and calling to his magic.

Nothing happened.

He blinked. "I sense no power."

Isle sighed. "As impatient as your father, I see. You must *envision* the magic flowing from Lexandra to you."

Garrin didn't want to take anything from Lex. She was already so frail. But she appeared much like she had before her mother melted the ice tomb by tapping into her magic. Presumably this didn't hurt her.

This time when Garrin closed his eyes, he visualized the essence of his power and the way it looked in his mind's eye.

And was slammed with heat and energy that ran from his scalp to his fingertips and down to his toes.

Garrin stood, his chest pounding with relief. He splayed out his hands and called to the snow.

And it obeyed. Compacting, melting. Forming stairs leading up, piling one on top of the other, higher and higher.

"Good," Isle said. "Now we leave this evil place."

CHAPTER

ELEVEN

Garrin picked up Lex. His arms weren't much warmer than her body after going without his coat for so long, but it didn't matter because they had a way out.

He ran up the ice stairs—and found Zirel standing there, half-naked and holding a handmade rope.

Garrin frowned. "What are you doing?"

"Attempting to rescue Amund so that we could rescue you. What has happened?" Zirel looked from Garrin to Isle standing beside him.

"Zirel, meet Isle Meinrad, Lex's mother."

"Mother?" Zirel said.

Isle looked down her nose. "Put on clothes, child, or you will freeze."

There was no time to explain to Zirel all that had happened inside the ravine, and Zirel must have realized that too, because he quickly began to unknot his clothing. He looked across to where Amund lay stranded. "What about him?"

"I'll retrieve him," Garrin said, and gently set Lex down.

With the help of new ice ledges that extended farther than the old ones, Garrin reached Amund in one swift leap, though the ledge cracked ominously on his descent.

Amund was in bad shape. He opened his eyes, and the effort appeared difficult. "Leave me. Get the girl to the kingdom."

"There is hope, my friend."

Amund shifted, and Garrin helped him roll over.

There was no way Amund could rise, so Garrin sat him upright then slung the burly Fae over his shoulder.

He used his powers to reinforce the ice ledges, including the section that had cracked, and extended them farther than he'd originally dared. He wouldn't build a bridge and risk complete failure, but if he was quick, two ice ledges and a strong leap should give him enough momentum to make it across with Amund on his back.

Garrin was more tired than he'd been in his life, but the jolt of power he'd drawn from Lex was more than he'd dared hope for. He didn't understand how he could draw from her ability to charge his powers, but he'd wonder about that after he'd gotten Lex to safety.

He secured Amund more squarely on his shoulder and took off toward the edge of the ravine at a run. He planted his snow boot on the ice ledge and leapt.

His toe had just made it over the ice ledge on the opposite side when Amund slipped from his grasp and went tumbling into the snow.

Garrin rushed over and knelt beside the soldier. "Are you all right?"

Amund nodded, his breathing labored.

Garrin lifted Amund and brought him to where the others stood with Lex. "Amund cannot walk."

Isle's mouth compressed. "Unless you plan to get my

daughter out of here using a snowstorm, let us hope Amund's abilities are more useful."

Isle was definitely related to Lex. No one spoke to Garrin with such fearlessness. "Amund is a portal creator—when he is healthy. And when Zirel is strong enough, he can heal others."

"Zirel first, then," Isle said, rubbing Lex's gloved hand as though to warm it, while her own body shook from the cold. "You've left my daughter on the brink of death, Dark Prince." She glared. "For which you will pay."

Garrin didn't fear Isle's wrath. He feared losing Lex. And not because his people needed her. He cared about her. If something happened to Lex, Garrin wasn't sure he could forgive himself.

He gestured for Zirel to move closer to Lex.

Isle instructed Zirel on how to regain his abilities, and like Garrin, the Fae faltered at first. But not for long. After a couple of attempts, Zirel straightened, his face flush with power.

Zirel leaned over Lex and placed his hands on her temples, above her heart, and lastly, he ran them down her arms and legs, exchanging the power she'd given him to heal her.

Lex's skin went from pale blue to just pale. Finally, her eyes opened.

"Zirel?" she said. "Why aren't you wearing a shirt?"

The rush of relief that filled Garrin was like nothing he'd experienced. If he'd lost her, he didn't think he could bear it.

He moved to her side. "How do you feel?"

She shifted slightly. "Like I could sleep for a month." She raised her hand and delicately touched his cheekbone with the tips of her gloved fingers. "Are you okay? You don't look well." And then she peered past Garrin. "M-Mom?" She shook her head and her eyes watered. "What…? Am I dead? What's going on?"

A wash of guilt ran through him. "You are not dead."

She blinked several times. "Am I hallucinating?"

"No, darling." Isle moved closer and gripped her daughter's hands, smiling. "I am here. I'm sorry for not warning you about what was to come. Had I known I'd be trapped in ice for so long… Well, I would have come up with a different plan."

Lex went to hug her mother, and sank back, her eyes crossing. "I'm dizzy."

Isle pulled Lex closer and wrapped her arms around her protectively. "There, there. All will be well."

Zirel tugged a shirt that he'd rescued from the knotted rope over his head. It was torn in several places, but the Fae fabric would help to keep him warm. "Lex is weak. She may need to be carried the rest of the way."

"But she will live," Garrin said, needing to hear the words.

Lex's eyes went wide. "Live? What the hell?"

"She will live," Zirel agreed.

"Are you sure?" Lex said. "Because now that I think about it, I feel like crap." She rubbed her temples and looked around, her gaze landing on her mother again. "Mom, what is going on? You were dead." Her voice quavered. "I saw it, didn't I? The avalanche? But Jas said I wasn't there…" She shook her head as though confused.

"Not dead," Isle said. "*Sleeping,* one could call it, until I was reunited with you and Jasper." She looked around. "Where is he?"

Lex sent Garrin a cynical look.

"I left him in the Earth realm," Garrin admitted.

Isle dropped her daughter's hand and stood. "You what?"

Both Lex and Isle were intent on making him explain himself. It was an odd experience. "We sought the prophesied one, and Jasper got in the way."

Isle moved close enough that her toes nearly touched his. He cocked his head, curious at her temerity. "I don't care whose son you are." She pointed at him. "How dare you take my child from her guardian?"

"Guardian?" Lex said, trying to stand and getting nowhere. "Uncle Jas?"

"Not your uncle," Isle said, still staring at Garrin. "That was what Jasper told you until I could return. With your powers...it was safest to hide you."

Lex's face tensed. "I don't have powers! And *you* should have stayed with me, Mom. Do you know how awful things have been?"

Isle flinched, and Garrin did too. He was partly responsible for her troubles. "No one suffers more than a mother kept from her child," Isle replied. "The king came after me, but not before I had Jasper hide you until I could return."

Garrin paced nearby. "Why would my father do this? It is madness."

"Yes, it is," Isle agreed. "Your father is an evil man, Dark Prince."

Zirel's eyes sharpened. He was fully clothed now, though much like his shirt, his coat was torn in several places. He must have attempted to lengthen the durable Fae fabric by tearing it. "The prince deserves your respect, madam."

Isle's smile was bitter. "Indeed? What do you know of the son of Casone?" She scanned Zirel. "You are not royalty. Your magic is useful, but you do not possess our strength."

"I have fought and bled alongside our prince as he risked his life for our people's freedom."

Isle laughed. "The Dark Prince is fighting for your freedom, is he? Oh, that is rich." She studied Garrin. "I wonder, have you any idea what your father is up to? He had the entire kingdom brainwashed the last time I breathed fresh air."

Garrin sighed. For all he knew, these were the ramblings of a madwoman who'd been entombed for two hundred years.

Isle stared out at the land. "Casone couldn't kill me without bringing down more punishment from the angels. So he did the next best thing; he entombed me in ice and made me impossible to find." She looked at Garrin. "Your father is the Ice King, just as you will be one day."

TWELVE

Lex was staring at Garrin in confusion, and he didn't know how to comfort her.

"Garrin, is what my mother says true? Did your dad do this to her?"

A burning sensation filled his chest. There had to be some truth to Isle's words, or she wouldn't have said them. "For as long as I can remember, I've been tasked with freeing our people. That does not sound like a king bent on harm." Isle's tale was filled with holes. There had to be a better explanation. "Others have fallen into the Great Ravine. Why did you not reach out to them the way you did us?"

"They weren't my daughter, now, were they? They hadn't her powers, and thus, they couldn't help me, nor I them. I was as helpless as you in the ravine. Until Lex gave me back my powers."

Isle knelt beside Lex. "Daughter, I will explain everything. For now, we must get you out of here." She looked at Garrin. "If your father still rules Dark Fae, it is not safe for

Lex to return to the kingdom. Will you risk her life at the hands of the man who imprisoned her mother?"

A pulse pounded at his temple. No—no, he would not.

"Garrin doesn't care about me," Lex said, rubbing her eyes as though the whole conversation had exhausted her. "He dragged me here because of some power he thinks I have."

Lex had been unconscious while Isle and the others had used her powers. She had no idea of what she was capable.

And she was wrong about him not caring. But he'd taken her from her land and forced her somewhere she never wanted to be. Why would she believe anything he said?

"She is correct," he finally said. "I intended to bring her to Dark Kingdom to save my people."

Isle stomped a few paces away. "I assume your father put you up to this." She threw up her hands. "My child! Your father wishes to use *my child* to save him from the mess he's made."

Garrin crossed his arms, his patience growing thin. "Dark Fae have lived on the precipice of life and death in a land that is forever winter. Only through our magic have we managed to maintain enough food. I assure you, my father wishes to better the lives of his people."

"His people or himself?" Isle tilted her head to the side. "Have you never wondered *how* Dark Fae became isolated and left in permanent winter?"

"They say the land is naturally magical and that the magic has grown, blocking us from leaving."

"Yes," Isle said. "Magical. And it only grew unbearable after your father committed a terrible crime." Isle walked through the snowy mountaintop, her feet sinking into the powder. "You and your mother weren't alive when the magic befell us; nor was I. But my father was. And he passed his knowledge to me." She stared at him. "My father was killed in one of our many wars. Or so I was told. I wasn't allowed to mourn his body. The soldiers were burned in a mass burial pyre above the ice-covered earth."

"Many have perished in the wars," Garrin said. "It is a tragedy, but not uncommon."

"You think so?" Her tone implied she did not. "Most females clamored for a chance at the king's side, but my father did not like this king. He didn't want his noble daughter to become a target. He followed orders, but there was no law that said he must hand over his child to the royal court. To make certain I didn't befall the king's clutches, my father and mother went so far as to hide my existence—not an easy feat when you're of royal blood. But they managed it. And then my father died in battle, and my mother died soon after under suspicious circumstances."

Isle wrapped her arms around her torso, her skin turning pale—from the story or the cold, Garrin couldn't tell. "The secret of my existence was revealed to the king. By whom, I do not know. It could have been any number of people. Either way, the king learned of me, and then my parents were gone. Soon after, your father sought me out."

"He brought you into his harem?" Garrin's stomach turned. He'd always wanted a sibling, but he couldn't imagine a worse scenario than Lex being his sister. Not with the way he felt about her.

Isle wrapped her cloak more tightly around her small frame. "He would have liked to be my lover. But it would have served no purpose. I already carried Lex in my womb."

And just like that, he could breathe again. Lex wasn't his sister.

"I stayed as far from the castle as I could," Isle said,

"living with friends of my parents. Friends who catered just enough to the court, but no more. Many watched over me and Lex once she was born. Yet Casone still discovered that I knew the truth about his first queen."

Garrin emitted a light groan at the absurdity. "There was no first queen."

She stared at him, her gaze hard. "Wasn't there? Even more damning, a dozen or so years after Lex's birth, your father tried to hide his darkest secret—one more harmful to him than the slow death he'd ordered on his first wife. But he discovered I knew that one as well. From that point on, my life was over. Casone silenced all who were aware of his secrets. Like he did with my parents. Like he did with me."

"Finding you in the ravine only proves you crossed my father," Garrin pointed out. "It doesn't confirm the notion that the king changed our history to suit his needs. You know very well he cannot lie to his people."

"Not lie," Isle said. "He manipulated the truth, as we all have at times." Her eyes narrowed. "The elders retain our past. How many remain, or have they died off in your lifetime? When I was a child, we had hundreds of elders. But by the time I reached my majority, over half were gone. I dare not think how many are left."

"A handful," Garrin said, dread filling him.

Isle crouched, with her hands clasped to her head, staring blindly at Lex. "Our history gone in one generation?" She looked up at Garrin. "Your father would have made it appear an accident or a natural passing. But at no time in the past have we suffered such losses. The elders protect the codicils and texts that are thousands of years old. There wouldn't have been time to train others in the dead languages, let alone teach them how to interpret the information. What will become of us?"

Garrin swallowed. To lose so many elders in such a short period was unprecedented. And also not discussed in his father's court. The crown had moved on, content to let their history die. And it no longer seemed like a coincidence. "Why did my father leave you in the ravine?"

"I planned my escape with Lex once I heard your father was coming for me." She choked out a humorless laugh. "Though not well enough. Casone found me, and you know how that ended. My only saving grace was that I had sent Lex ahead. Your father didn't know of her powers at the time, and I couldn't risk him finding out. But he must have known..." She wrung her hands. "He wouldn't have sent you otherwise."

Garrin racked his brain, thinking back to his father's every political move these last two hundred years. "He did not know of Lex's powers. My father only knows of the prophesied one." Unless what Isle said was true, and his father held secrets...

If there was truth and not simply madness to Isle's words, Garrin must be very careful with Lex inside Dark Kingdom. No one could know who she really was. Not until Garrin determined the threat. "No one will question Lex's presence in our land."

Isle huffed in exasperation. "And how do you figure that?"

Lex was malnourished and thin, but awake, her gaze bouncing between Garrin and her mother. If she hadn't wanted to go with him to Dark Kingdom before, he could only imagine her hesitance now. "Your daughter is full Fae. Her strength is the same as the rest in our land, and she will blend in."

"Fool," Isle said, and Lex moaned, either from the conversation or exhaustion. "She is like no one from this land. Which is why she was hidden so carefully until the time in which I could protect her from your father." She pointed at him. "And on that note, she cannot use her powers in Dark Kingdom."

He had no intention of asking Lex to practice her magic until it was safe, but he wasn't used to being told what to do by anyone except the king. "That is why we sought her. And how she and I were saved from our cold fate at the bottom of the ravine. If she is the prophesied one, she is the only Fae capable of freeing our people."

Isle squeezed her eyes shut. "If she uses her powers near the castle, the king and his minions will find her. How do you propose to hide her?"

Lex stared at him and raised her brow, as though curious about the answer as well.

"By making her a female of my court," he said.

Isle visibly bristled, her mouth agape. "You wish to make her one of your harem? My parents didn't lose their lives and I didn't lose hundreds of years of mine only to see my child end up as a courtesan! She will become a part of your court over my dead body."

Lex's mother was a frustration he did not need right now. "If that is what you wish."

"Stop!" Lex shouted. She glared at Garrin and attempted to rise—and fell back on the snow. "There is no way in hell I'll become one of your-your *women*, Garrin."

He quirked his eyebrow, admiring the fire in her eyes. Lex already was his woman. When he thought back to their first encounter, she'd been his from the very beginning. He just hadn't realized it.

Zirel had healed Amund, and Amund was finally on his feet.

"How do you feel?" Garrin asked, ignoring Lex's comment for the moment.

"Tolerable," Amund said.

Fae soldiers didn't complain. Which meant Amund wasn't well at all. "Strong enough to create a portal home?"

Amund looked off in the distance. "Not all of us at once, and not in one leap. The disruptive magic here causes my portals to be less precise. Once I'm off this mountain and away from the ravine, I will be able to find the kingdom quickly. Two, maybe three portals to the castle from there. I'll need to eat before returning for the others."

"Did you hear me, Garrin?" Lex said, her voice an octave higher.

Garrin rubbed his jaw and held back a smile. Lex was much improved if she was raising her voice to him.

"My daughter doesn't go anywhere near Dark Kingdom, son of Casone," Isle said. "I am not so weak as you. I have slept a very long time. And I am better at using Lex's powers. Don't think I won't use them against you."

Garrin picked up his pack. "Amund will take me and Lex to the castle. You and Zirel will stay here until he returns."

"Absolutely not!" Isle said at the same time Lex shouted, "What?"

He slid his gaze to Lex's slight form, stiff with indignation. "If there was another way, I would not take you from your mother. You must understand, I do this for your safety as much as for my people."

She hobbled to her feet, though her balance was unsteady. "You do this for yourself! You care nothing for me or my family."

Garrin would like for that to be true. It would make his duty easier to tolerate. He flicked his gaze to Amund, and it was enough to communicate his wishes.

The portal creator nodded.

"This is the way it must be," Garrin said.

Before Lex could utter another word, Amund grabbed her from behind, and the three of them were inside a portal.

THIRTEEN

Lex was in a closet. A damn closet! How dare Garrin take her against her will? *Again!*

He was going to get a piece of her mind. Just as soon as his overbearing, princely butt returned.

He and Amund had dumped her in the room, demanded she stay put, and then left.

She wanted to strangle them.

Lex felt around for some way to illuminate the space because, of course, there was no light. If Garrin hadn't insisted she remain quiet for her own safety, she'd be screaming her head off right now. It was creepy as hell being in the pitch-dark, and though her anxieties had improved in this craptastic land, for some reason, she wasn't yet immune to small, dark spaces.

Lex sank onto her bottom and seethed for what felt like forever, debating whether to listen to Garrin and stay put or go in search of him. She was somewhere inside the Dark Kingdom castle—the one place her mother had insisted Garrin not take her. So, of course he'd taken her straight here, because he was on a mission to piss them both off.

She dropped her head back against the wall. Her mom was alive, and Lex still hadn't wrapped her mind around it. Her mother's story was overwhelming, but having her mom back was the greatest gift. She had someone else besides Jas who cared whether she lived or died.

Maybe she'd make it out of this place alive?

There were times while traveling the Land of Ice she was certain they'd all die, and apparently, Garrin had feared it too. When she'd woken to find her mother there, she could have sworn he'd been worried about her. And then he'd taken her from her mom and dumped her in a closet.

Who knew what would happen now? It was a tough call with Garrin running the show. Even her mother couldn't control him. And her mom, now that Lex was near her again and remembering more, was pretty strong-willed.

Lex had forgotten the details of her mom, but with them face to face, flashes of memories had returned. Her mother's favorite fruit, the noise she made in the back of her throat when she was annoyed. Only Lex couldn't remember this place. Not the castle and not Dark Kingdom. She also had no memory of her father. Maybe that would come back too?

Lex couldn't hate Garrin too much. He'd brought her to her mom. And really, she didn't *hate* him. He was frustrating and arrogant, but he was also protective and pretty damn cuddly at night for a giant Fae soldier who liked to boss people around. The man even smelled good without bathing; it was inhuman. Then again, he wasn't human, so...

All Lex knew was that if Garrin didn't get his unwashed butt back here, she was going to lose her shit.

She pressed her fingers to her eyes and tried to remain calm.

Thirty or so minutes had passed when Amund finally returned to the closet. Along with Garrin and her mother.

"I've informed the palace guards that I will visit my father once I've cleaned up." That was Garrin's voice, and he was right beside her.

Lex inched to the other side to give him space in the dark—and ran into her mother, who ran into Amund.

"Lexandra," Garrin said. "I don't know if you've noticed, but we are inside a closet."

"I see sarcasm is alive and well in Dark Kingdom," she whisper-yelled. The small room, which had been pleasantly warm a moment ago, instantly heated with the addition of two huge Fae and her mother crowding it. "Get me out of here!"

Garrin covered her mouth. "Fae have heightened senses, and guards are not far away."

Lex breathed in the scent of him because *dammit*, he still smelled good. And then she bit his finger.

He shook it free. "Why would you do that?"

"Because you're under the impression you can control me!"

Her mother snickered beside her.

"Silence, pet," he said. "We must wait until I can determine how best to introduce you to my court."

"Pet?" Lex spat. "Did you just call me *pet*?"

"You did it now, prince," her mother said. "It seems I didn't need to be around for my daughter to grow into a strong woman."

Lex glared in the direction of her mother's voice. "Strong, Mom? Really? Jas has practically been holding my hand these last few years because I'm terrified of everything. And it's all because you led me to believe you'd been killed in an *avalanche*."

"That was poor judgment on my part," her mother admitted. "Jasper insisted on a backstory for why you had no mother in the Earth realm. And then our reunion was delayed."

Lex's mind sputtered. *Delayed?* "That is putting it mildly." Lex sensed Garrin flinch beside her, and she lowered her voice. "Why in the hell didn't you come with me and Jas in the first place?"

"Many sacrificed to hide you in Dark Kingdom. I had put dear friends in a troubling position. I was attempting to shield them when the king found me. As it turns out, I have no idea if they lived or died. And you were never on your own. Jasper was with you."

"Silence," Amund said. "Someone approaches."

Lex squeezed her lips together, but she couldn't hold back for long, fear replacing good sense. "They'll know we're here!" she said. "They'll sense us—our Fae energy, or whatever you call it."

A warm finger touched her lips, smelling of pine. *Garrin.*

Lex closed her eyes and tried to breathe.

"They are gone," Amund said and let out a sigh. "The castle is full of soldiers. Unless they have my skills, it will be difficult to predict our precise location. They knew we entered because of the Presence Charm, which is why His Highness alerted the guards of our arrival. When the prince has not returned to his quarters, they will count bodies and track us."

"Unless someone senses a second royal among us, and they send everyone in search of who it could be," Garrin said bitterly.

Isle made a sound. "Don't look at me, Dark Prince. I

may be royal, but I had my powers magically downgraded centuries ago to avoid your father. They won't detect me."

"This is true," Amund said. "She doesn't present with your power level."

"In that case," Garrin said, "Lex is safe for the moment, and I must leave and visit the king and queen."

"You mean, your father and that interloper you call Mother?" Isle snorted.

A pinched sound came from Garrin's direction. "I fear the isolation has taken your sanity, mother of Lexandra. Ailith, the queen, has always been my mother."

"Not always," Isle said sharply.

Lex sensed the tension radiating off Garrin. "Mom, why are you doing this?"

Isle squeezed Lex's hand. "If we are to keep you safe, the prince must know all the dangers."

"Explain," Garrin said, his tone forbidding. "If my mother didn't give me life, how do you account for my existence?"

"The angels made your father pay for his crime with this frozen land. And by not providing him a child born of his wife, nor of any of his harem. You are illegitimate."

"Absurd," Garrin scoffed.

Her mother had to be wrong. It seemed like something that would be insanely difficult to pull off. Then again, Casone had hidden the truth of his first wife, so anything was possible.

"I won't betray your true mother by sharing her identity," Isle said. "Not after all she did for me. But you would do well to be leery of the current queen. I've never understood her intentions."

Lex couldn't tell how Garrin was feeling. His expression

appeared blank in the dim light, as though he were holding in his emotion.

"What is your plan to keep Lex safe now that we are here?" Isle said. "No one will believe you went in search of the prophesied savior, only to bring home a female of no import."

"I will tell them she comes from the Land of Sun."

"The land of... You mean Sunland?" Isle harrumphed. "I see. You mean to call Earth by one of its Fae names so as not to lie, when you know very well that everyone in Dark Kingdom will believe she is from Sunland here in Tirnan. You tell a lie without lying. Did you gain that skill from your father?"

"Do you have a better idea, Mom?"

Lex prayed her mother did, because pretending to be one of Garrin's many girlfriends in some harem did not sound fun. It sounded like a great way to humiliate herself.

Garrin and the other Fae were hot. Even Lex's mom was beautiful, with amber eyes and clear, tan skin that was darker than Lex's. Fae seemed to age slowly, her mother easily passing for a woman in her late twenties.

Isle dropped Lex's hand and made a sound of disgruntlement. "We could attempt to return to the Earth realm—"

"No," Garrin said firmly. "I won't risk Lex's life again."

"—but," her mother said, her face pinched at the interruption, "the Dark Prince is right. Tapping into your magic to get us by is one thing. Traveling across the entire Land of Ice would be dangerous without your ability mastered. At the very least, the portal creator must rest and regain his strength before we attempt it."

Lex closed her eyes. Amund looked drained even after

she'd supposedly juiced him with magic. "That could take days."

Garrin smirked, which Lex caught in the dark because his expressive eyes sparked with mischievousness. "Which means you are my *girlfriend*, Lex, as they say in the human world. Until we come up with a better plan for keeping your presence discreet."

"The hell I am!" she said at full volume.

His eyes flared and he looked quickly out the door before shutting it silently. Garrin peered over her head at Amund. "We must leave before she alerts everyone."

"Agreed," Amund said in his deep rumble.

"Take her to my ladies while I speak with my father," Garrin said.

Amund grabbed her arm lightly.

"Wait." She looked at Garrin. "How can you leave me again?"

Irrational though it might be, Lex didn't like it when Garrin wasn't with her. She'd grown used to him. *Stockholm syndrome,* she thought, and shook her head.

His mouth quirked. "Getting used to having me around, are you?"

Her eyes narrowed. "No, you arrogant prince. I just don't like being kidnapped and then neglected."

He was still smiling when his breathing seemed to catch. He leaned closer, all signs of humor gone. "Amund, do you see this? Her eyes..."

Amund inched closer too.

"Hey!" She swatted at him. "What's wrong with you two? Ever heard of personal space?"

Amund straightened and looked at Garrin. "Her eyes have a light glow."

Isle sighed. "Of course they do. I told you, she is like no one else."

And then Garrin's hand burst into flame. Well, not burst. It was more like the flicker of a cigarette lighter. Only blue.

"I thought we were being incognito?" Lex tried to blow out the flame. "Put that thing out before you burn the place down."

But Garrin and Amund weren't listening. They were too busy staring at her face. And down her body. And then at each other.

"Shite," Garrin said.

"She has changed," Amund said. "No longer Fae."

Garrin tore his eyes off Lex to glare at her mother. "What is she?"

"I told you, prince, she is like no one. Now make good on your promise and keep my daughter safe. And get me out of here. If Casone discovers I'm inside his castle, we'll have bigger problems than we already do."

Isle squeezed Lex's hand. "The king has never seen you. With me away, you have a chance at hiding in plain sight. I won't risk you coming with me and rumors surfacing that you're my daughter. If I'm caught before we escape, at least you'll have a chance at survival. As long as no one knows you're my child."

"Mom, you're scaring me more than I already am. You won't get caught. And what is wrong with my eyes, you people?" Lex patted her face. "I haven't gotten good sleep, so I probably look like a nightmare... Wait, what do you mean I'm not Fae?"

"You are Fae," Isle said. "But also, more."

"How much more?" Garrin asked.

Memories of her mother were coming back to the point

that Lex felt her mom hadn't been gone all that long. That Isle wasn't a perfect stranger to her, but... "Mom?... *Who is my father?* I don't remember him at all."

"Later, darling. For now, do as the *Fire Prince* says. Don't think I didn't notice you have an ability with fire as well, son of Casone. No wonder the king sends you on his errands. You are as powerful as he, only he cannot control fire."

Lex felt her mother's hand on her shoulder. "You will pretend to be his girlfriend. For now."

Garrin swallowed. One of those nervous swallows. The kind Lex never saw him do because the darn Fae didn't get outwardly nervous the way humans did. Until now.

"What's wrong with you?" She snapped her fingers in front of his face. "Why are you suddenly afraid of being my boyfriend? You were gloating a moment ago."

"The girl's energy level..." Amund said, shaking his head. "How can this be?"

Garrin blinked as though waking from a dream, and his jaw hardened. "I don't know. But one thing is clear. She has come into her true being. And we must find a way to hide it."

FOURTEEN

One thing was certain: Garrin couldn't introduce Lex to his court. Not with her power level presenting greater than any Fae in the land. Not all Fae could detect power levels with precision the way Amund could, but some did.

They had minutes—seconds, perhaps—until the king's soldiers discovered their whereabouts. Garrin hadn't time to talk to his father first. He needed a glamour for Lex, and he needed it now.

Amund portaled them to one of Garrin's dressing rooms, and Garrin took in the familiar surroundings. Ornate mahogany furniture brought from the Earth realm several hundred years ago filled the space, along with colorful tapestries woven by his people. The tapestries hung from tall ceilings and looked crisp, as though they'd been recently beaten of dust. They depicted springtime in Dark Kingdom before the land became frozen. The scent of magic burning in the massive hearth was sharp and metallic, bringing back memories of the last time he'd entered this room, before he'd journeyed to the Earth realm. A great many months had passed, and yet the room appeared untouched.

Satisfied the chamber was safe, Garrin turned to Lex—and his heart nearly stopped beating.

Her heavy winter hood had fallen back, and locks of dark golden hair tumbled down her chest. Long hair—longer than before—and shimmering like the sap from an allon tree. Her cheeks were no longer hollowed and pale, but rosy with golden hues, her lips full and plump.

Garrin couldn't catch his breath. Lex was radiant. And far too beautiful.

Amund rubbed a hand down his face. "I must return to the closet," he said absently, staring at Lex as though thunderstruck. "I'll take the mother of Lexandra somewhere safe."

"Yes," Garrin said on a sigh. "Feed yourself before you return for Zirel."

Amund peered once more at Lex with a look of wonder, then stepped through the glimmer of a portal and left.

Lex's eyes were the first thing Garrin had noticed inside the hallway of her dormitory. They were a beautiful golden-brown at the time, but now they sparkled with life in the color of rich amber, so clear and bright that they glowed.

How would he protect her when she stood out so much?

She moved slowly about the space, studying the tapestries. "Is this your bedroom?"

He strode across the chamber to a large wardrobe and shoved clothing on hangers aside. A Fae without Amund's ability wouldn't detect anything unusual about Lex's power level. But once they saw her glowing eyes and beauty... "You must hide in the wardrobe, or your presence won't be secret for long."

Lex glanced at the wooden cabinet. "You've got to be kidding me. They'll still know I'm here."

"Most won't question whom I've hidden. Should someone enter, best not to arouse suspicion by revealing your glowing appearance." When she didn't move, he sighed. "Your mother told you to follow my orders."

Her face turned molten. "My mother hasn't been my mother for many years, and even Jas doesn't tell me what to do anymore. Or have you forgotten that I'm a grown woman?"

Garrin snorted. "I assure you, that is the last thing I will soon forget." He'd tamped down any desires he experienced for Lex while they traveled, and he would do so now. All his focus must be on learning the truth about his father and keeping Lex safe.

He slowly stepped closer. "Please. For now."

Lex blinked several times as though flustered. Then her mouth twisted in annoyance and she strode to the wardrobe and stepped inside, sending him a scathing look before she closed the cabinet door.

A second later, she opened the wardrobe and tossed out two winter coats—one she'd worn through the Land of Ice, the other Garrin's coat he'd bundled her in before they crossed the ravine.

Not five seconds later, a light rap sounded at the chamber door.

Garrin looked to ensure Lex was secure and shoved the coats behind the wardrobe before crossing the room.

Anyone with heightened ability would know he'd hidden someone, but as long as they didn't see that she was different, she would be safe.

He opened the door a crack and let out a mental sigh of relief.

A woman with light green eyes, tan skin, and long, wavy dark hair stood on the other side, and Garrin knew her well. "Amund sent me," she said, and tried to look past him.

He stepped aside for her to enter and closed the door behind her. "I have a request, Percilla. My friend needs a glamour."

She quirked her eyebrow. "Indeed?"

Garrin strode to the wardrobe and opened it.

Percilla's mouth parted as she took in Lex. "My, she is special." This was not a question.

"And it must not be known. Do you understand?"

She nodded immediately. "Yes, my prince."

Lex studied Percilla and stepped out of the wardrobe, her expression leery. "Who is she?"

"Someone with the skill to hide your true nature," Garrin said.

Percilla waved her hand haphazardly across Lex's body. "What does my prince wish? A different hair color, eye color?"

"Reduce her beauty and make her power level appear Fae."

"Beauty?" Lex said.

"Indeed," Percilla replied. "Most beautiful. And if you wish to hide, your unusual power level must also blend in." She smiled reassuringly. "I will make it look normal. Right now, you are too bright. You shine like a star."

She turned to Garrin. "Are you certain you do not wish for the king to see the gift you have brought us before I hide her?"

"Lex is a gift some would use against us," he said. "The king and others will be informed as soon as it is safe. To share knowledge of Lex overly soon would lead to punishment," he added, and Percilla flinched.

His courtier made one final sweep of her hand across Lex's body and stepped back. "It is done."

Garrin narrowed his eyes then grunted. "She is still beautiful."

"But her power level is normal," Percilla replied. She cocked her head. "I reduced her beauty, as you requested. What you see shines from within and is harder to mask."

Lex's brow pinched. "This is the weirdest conversation ever. And that's saying something after what I've been through these last months."

Garrin suspected Lex had been undervalued in the Earth realm, which solidified his belief that humans lacked intelligence. Lex had always been striking, and now she was more so.

Perhaps her beauty wouldn't be such an issue. After all, she'd need to be attractive if his father was to believe Garrin had chosen her for his court. Beauty and power were the only qualities his father prized in women.

Garrin strongly disagreed. After meeting Lex, Garrin had decided that a woman with a strong will and kind heart was more to his liking.

Percilla bowed and quickly made her exit.

Lex watched her leave, then turned to Garrin. "Are all Fae women as gorgeous as her? You were kind of an ass, by the way. She was doing us a favor."

"It is her job to support her prince."

"Does everyone support you? Are they your slaves?"

Garrin shot her a look. "Of course they are not slaves. My work protects the realm. The attendants know this, and they do not ask questions. It is in everyone's interest to protect you from danger if I say it is."

Zirel entered the room, saw Lex, and stopped abruptly in his tracks, his jaw unhinged.

Garrin glared. "That was fast, even for Amund. Particularly given my express instructions for him to eat before he returned for you."

"He ate before he came for me, and I healed him once he arrived."

"And Isle?"

Zirel glanced at Lex and back to Garrin. He shook his head lightly as though to clear it. "Isle is with my mother."

Zirel's family weren't noble, and they did not reside within the castle walls. They were also annoyed with Garrin's father for some grievance or another. Hiding Isle among Zirel's family was as good a choice as any.

Zirel continued to stare at Lex. "What, ah, what has happened?"

The woman Garrin believed to be a stubborn Halven was no Halven at all, nor was she Fae—that was what had happened. She was more than Fae. And powerful, if her new appearance was any proof.

"Magic hid Lex's true nature," Garrin said. "Likely a spell. The full extent of the spell broke once we entered the kingdom. One of my attendants has placed a glamour over her power level and dimmed her beauty."

Zirel's head swiveled to Garrin. "This is the diminished version?"

LEX CROSSED HER ARMS. Zirel, Garrin, and Amund had been acting weird ever since the closet. "Someone, get me a mirror so I can see what I look like."

"Lex," Garrin said. "It isn't only your face. You cannot see, but it is all of you. You radiate strength and beauty."

She frowned, and Garrin's gaze zeroed in on her lips, causing her stomach to flutter.

Damn prince and his Fae hotness. How was she supposed to keep a clear head when he looked at her like that?

Zirel cleared his throat, breaking the moment.

"Are you trying to flatter me?" she said. "You've already dragged me to this freezing place. What else do you want?"

Garrin let out a sigh. "This is not merely about your abilities and the initial reason we brought you here. It appears you have...returned to yourself. Physically, at the very least. Your powers may manifest more fully as well."

"What does that mean, I've returned to myself?" Lex looked for a reflective surface.

"It means," Zirel said, while Garrin peered away, seemingly unhappy about the situation, "your true nature has been hidden from the world. You are not only an incredibly attractive Fae, but your eyes glow in a way that is more than Fae."

Lex let out a bark of laughter. What was wrong with them? "You both know better than anyone that I haven't showered with more than one of Garrin's ice loofas in months." She pointed forcefully. "No one can match your looks, and certainly not me. *You* still smell good, which is just wrong. Men shouldn't smell better than women."

Both Fae turned abruptly to the door. "They will be here soon," Zirel said.

And what was scarier? Lex heard the sound that had caught their attention too.

Others approached from a distance Lex shouldn't be able to hear from, but she could.

"Go," Garrin said to Zirel. "I'll deal with the guards while you take Lex to my court. Her beauty will stand out, but it will also explain why I've brought her here. Tell them she is from the Land of Sun and that I've chosen her for my bride."

"Your what?" Lex said. "I thought I was your girlfriend."

"Intended, girlfriend, bride—it is one and the same. You must be more than one among my harem or my father will grow suspicious."

Lex narrowed her eyes. "But I'm not your fiancée, and you can't lie."

"Whether or not the ceremony occurs is to be determined—therefore, it isn't a lie."

Lex started to speak, but Zirel picked her up bodily and swept her through a side door she hadn't noticed.

He set her down abruptly, and the door closed behind them.

She dusted off invisible dirt in sharp movements. "Stop manhandling me."

He shrugged.

She looked around the large, ornately decorated room that appeared to be something straight out of another century, the ceilings at least twenty feet in height. The walls were made of gold, or what appeared to be gold, with polished stones creating stunning mosaics, including the one on the ceiling. And not only images of the snowcapped mountains she'd been subjected to. The mosaics showed imagery of forests and green hills, and people pushing carts of food. And battle scenes. Grisly battle scenes were depicted on one of the walls, with beautiful men and women attacking each other using swords and magic-flecked hands. "What is up with this place? Garrin said we were going to a castle, but I've never seen pictures of castles that look like this." She pointed to a prominent figure at the center of it all. "Is that..."

"The king," Zirel said, and peered out a door. He lifted his arm and gestured for her to come closer. "They are waiting."

The door Zirel stood beside was massive. Larger than any she'd ever seen. Then again, Fae were extremely tall, so tall doors probably came with the territory.

Lex had been called a giraffe back home because of her height. But her mother was tall, and Garrin and the others were even taller. She wasn't a giraffe. She was simply Fae and built like one. Which, sadly, now made sense.

"I'm not ready. What if I panic in front of Garrin's court?" She'd grown comfortable around Garrin and his men, but in front of an entire castle of Fae? Not likely.

Zirel sent her a gentle look. "You are not the same person you were at the beginning of this journey."

She shook her head. "You say I look different and that my power level has changed, but I feel the same inside."

"Who you are and who you will become is something to be discovered. But you will not succeed by hiding away."

Damn Zirel and his wisdom. Lex closed her eyes and let out a breath. He was right, and it was super annoying.

With her chin held high, she passed over the threshold and walked into another massive interior room. Only this one was crowded.

Over two dozen women in long gowns, their wrists and necks covered in jewels, stood inside the room, staring at her. These women were stunning, with hair in every shade, from pale blond to black, and every skin tone in between.

Lex had managed to keep her pulse steady upon entering the room, but it kicked up now.

"What is this?" one of the women said. She was a tall

redhead with bright blue eyes, who scanned Lex from head to toe with a snarl on her face.

One by one, the women took in her appearance—and didn't seem to like what they saw.

Garrin and Zirel had to be wrong. She should have checked herself in a mirror before agreeing to this.

"Lex, I am pleased to introduce you to His Highness's royal harem," Zirel said.

At the same moment, Amund returned through one of his portals. "You are a part of the prince's court now, where you will live," he added.

Lex smiled shakily at the strange women and murmured to Zirel and Amund, "You've lost your bloody minds if you think I'm living here."

CHAPTER

FIFTEEN

"What is the meaning of this?" one of the women from Garrin's harem said. She was taller than the others, with a regal bearing and light brown skin, her blonde, wavy hair striking in contrast.

"Good day, Cora," Amund said. "This is Lex, the prince's intended."

Gasps erupted, and several women lunged forward, lips curling in disdain, only to be held back by others.

Lex inched closer to Amund and Zirel. These women wanted to attack her? She'd seen Fae women in full battle gear in the mural. Lex was no match. She smiled stiffly and said, "Get me out of here," from the corner of her mouth.

"Silence!" Amund said, and the angry voices petered out.

Cora's brown eyes narrowed. "You've been gone a long while, Amund. And now you are one of the prince's closest confidants and bring...this person?"

"The prince expects the utmost care for Lex," he said

without explanation. "Should he hear of anything less, there will be repercussions."

Lex glanced at Amund. What was up with the threats? First Garrin with glamour lady, and now Amund with Cora. Lex wasn't entirely against *this* threat, as she'd like to continue breathing, but the conditions inside the castle were harsh for those with less power.

"I'm not safe here," she murmured. "They're going to tear me apart." A flash of pink caught her eye. "That blonde in the pink dress looks ready to pounce. Don't you dare leave me."

Amund pursed his lips. "They are disgruntled."

She swiveled her head and stared. "You think? It's a shitshow."

Lex hadn't been competition to human women, and she wasn't competition to these women either. But for some reason, they didn't see it that way.

Cora snarled. "This is whom His Highness chose for his intended?"

"Yes," Amund said, and Lex winced.

Of course Cora didn't believe Garrin had chosen Lex above them. No one in their right mind would. Lex was going to kill Garrin for this.

"It seems rather...abrupt," Cora said.

Amund hesitated. "Lex is special."

Lex snorted. "Special" as in, "can't wield magic like other Fae." He told the truth, but he left a whole hell of a lot out.

Cora's gaze moved over Lex's face and focused on her eyes. "Clearly."

What was everyone seeing in her eyes? This woman couldn't see Lex's power level, could she? Lex wasn't exactly sure what a power level was, but the woman who'd waved her hands over Lex had assured her that she looked normal.

Cora smiled stiffly. "Greetings, Lex. From whence do you hail?"

"The Land of Sun," Amund said, telling a lie without lying. According to her mother, Fae would assume he was talking about some place called Sunland in Tirnan.

Cora narrowed her eyes, taking in Lex's clothes. She wore the same items Garrin had given her when they arrived in the Land of Ice, but now her clothing felt too short and tight, like it no longer fit. "Welcome to His Highness's court."

Lex swallowed. "Thank you."

Cora snapped her fingers, and four women peeled off from the others. "Provide Lex with"—her lip curled—"new attire. What she wears is not suitable for the palace." She tapped her jaw with a long, graceful finger. "You come from the kingdom they call Sunland?"

The Land of Sun? Sunland? Lex was going with it. She tried to say, "Yes, I'm from Sunland," but the words wouldn't leave her mouth—were stuck as though trapped in her throat.

And then realization dawned. Lex couldn't lie anymore —*because she was Fae*.

Crap!

Along with losing whatever magical spell that kept her real appearance "hidden," as Garrin put it, she'd also lost her ability to lie like a human.

Lex smiled awkwardly, hoping it was a good enough answer.

"Very well," Cora said. "We will find something more appropriate for you to wear in His Highness's royal court."

These women weren't naked, per se, but what they

wore wasn't the look Lex typically went for. Garrin's court, *harem*, whatever, wore nearly sheer gowns that clung to their curves and showed off the beautiful skin of their arms. The dresses came in all colors, and some sparkled with jewels, but most were simply super sheer and sexy. Like the women themselves.

Lex wasn't sexy. And they wanted her to dress like them? "Are you sure I'll be warm enough?"

Cora blinked. "Warm?"

"She isn't used to our climate," Amund said hastily.

"Ah." Cora smiled. "Sunland is assuredly warmer than Dark Kingdom. The castle is plenty warm. You needn't wear your"—she waved at Lex—"over-things."

Meaning Lex's long-sleeved shirt and pants designed to stave off the cold inside a stone castle surrounded by ice and snow. No, they wouldn't want her wearing *that*. They'd rather put her in gauze. Lex sighed.

"If that is settled, Zirel and I will leave," Amund said.

"What?" Lex eyeballed both men. "I mean, are you sure? Wouldn't you rather stay here with me and the ladies?" She shot them a death glare.

The corner of Zirel's mouth quirked up, the jerk, and Amund said, "I am needed by His Highness elsewhere." He turned to the room at large. "A pleasant day," he said, and the women repeated it back like a trilling chorus of fairies.

And, Lex supposed, that was exactly what they were. Except not the small kind. These Fae were six foot at minimum, with incredible bodies and blinding beauty.

Amund and Zirel strode to the other side of the gallery that could host a two-hundred-person wedding and left.

They were leaving her. *Alone.* With all these strangers.

Lex's palms began to sweat. How was she supposed to survive inside the den of she-wolves?

G ARRIN ENTERED HIS PARENTS' rooms, followed by guards who'd found him seconds after Zirel absconded with Lex.

His father stood before a ten-foot window that looked onto the courtyard several hundred feet below. He spun around at the sound of Garrin entering. "Son." He grinned broadly, small lines framing his gray-blue eyes.

His father had always been a handsome man, but the years were beginning to catch up, his hair now white, with deeper lines shadowing his eyes and brow.

Casone Branimir's face pulled into a slight frown. "I hear you were unsuccessful in finding *the one* the prophecy spoke of, yet you've returned with a different female?"

Garrin bowed, first to his father and then to his mother, who stood off to the side wearing a ruby gown, her light brown hair swept over one shoulder in soft waves. He could force a lie through his lips—but the amount of effort usually gave away the lie, and most Fae couldn't manage it at all. "I have indeed returned with a female," he said instead. "I plan to marry her."

Had Garrin informed his father he had a "girlfriend," the king would have laughed. But a future wife was something else entirely.

His father chuckled without humor. "Marry her? I haven't even met this woman. What is it about her that made you decide to attach yourself to her?"

Garrin glanced at his mother, unable to recall a moment when Ailith Branimir had appeared genuinely happy. His mother's light brown eyes and smooth, even features were still as stone, revealing no cheer in response to his future nuptials.

Ailith Branimir was a queen and expected to do things

differently. Not to mention, Garrin had been one of only two or three children who'd grown up in or around the castle. He had little maternal influence to compare her to. And he'd never paid attention to his mother's warmth or lack thereof. Until now. Isle had created doubt in his mind where none had existed before.

The king often tried for children with his court females, spending as much time with them, or more, than he did his wife. Though it was the Dark Fae way, Garrin wondered if his father's mission to produce heirs hurt his mother.

Lex wanted to return to the Earth realm, and Garrin was heir to a kingdom. She would never become his bride, and yet he didn't like the idea of her with another man. His mouth twitched. She would certainly give him an earful if she didn't want him with another woman. "Lex is special. She is also clever and willful," Garrin said in response to his father's surprise at him marrying.

"Willful?" His father laughed. "Have I taught you nothing?"

Garrin's mother glanced at her husband sharply, then turned her back, looking out the window he had abandoned.

"Willful women are powerful protectors," Garrin said, remembering Lex and her reaction to him fighting Jasper.

His mother's head turned slightly, as though she were listening.

All Fae were protective of children, given the challenges they faced in conceiving. It took centuries to sire even one child. But when Lex cared, she seemed to care with her whole being, and it intrigued Garrin. Though he'd rather she directed her efforts at him and not that Jasper creature. Or at future children he and Lex had, not that they would. But if Garrin did, in fact, make Lex his bride, he could only imagine how caring she would be to their children. Unlike Ailith Branimir.

His father walked over and squeezed Garrin's arm. "Just make sure you have your woman in hand."

Garrin's shoulder stiffened. If not for Lex and her magic, Garrin wouldn't be here.

"When will I meet her?" his father asked. "Has she settled into your court?"

"She has," Garrin said. "Though I hadn't considered a formal meeting. We've only just arrived, and it wasn't an easy journey." An understatement. Garrin flinched at the memory of Lex free-falling in the ravine.

His father nodded. "It never is. And yet every time you return to me, I am that much more grateful." He looked down. "I've thought about your travels. The risk isn't worth it anymore. Perhaps it is our fate to live as we have."

This was new. Casone had only ever been interested in escaping the Land of Ice. "Do you fear I will not succeed?" Garrin asked. "I assure you, it is my life's mission to find a way out for our people."

The king paced several steps away, his back to Garrin. "No, nothing like that." He turned and smiled. "I simply don't want to lose my only child."

The king glanced at his wife for the first time. "We've not managed to have another, and I worry... Perhaps you should hold off on your travels until your mother and I sire more children."

Garrin looked at his mother, who stood rigid, the hand that bore her husband's crest flexing. "You mean, until you have someone to carry on the legacy should I perish?" Garrin's tone held an edge. If they didn't find a safe way out of Dark Kingdom, eventually their people would no longer thrive. To give up now was suicide.

It had been hundreds of years and they barely survived as it was, living in structures that predated the ice, and patching them together when they must. And the food... To say food was scarce in perpetual winter was making light of the situation.

Few animals had survived the original freeze, and it took great planning to ensure the population wasn't depleted. The only greenery left were allon trees, the species as old and magical as Tirnan itself. And even those trees had to be defrosted with care to provide much-needed nutrients. It was a challenging life, and Dark Fae numbers had dwindled due to the harsh conditions.

And battles. Trapped together with no way out had led to many battles among his people.

Casone's eyes turned unyielding. "Even you must admit, what is a kingdom without an heir?"

"What is a kingdom without freedom? Without proper food?" Garrin said.

His father's chest rose and his face turned red. Then he waved off Garrin's comment. "Let us not speak of such things when you've only just returned. We have a wedding to plan, do we not? There is plenty of time to talk of future travels once you are settled with your bride." He winked. "Perhaps you will not wish to be gone so long with a new woman in your bed."

Garrin could very well imagine Lex in his bed, and it terrified him. For so long, he'd made women a distant second to saving his people. And now he couldn't take his mind off Lex.

He didn't enjoy withholding information from his father and mother, but until he could ensure Lex's safety, he must. "Perhaps," he said, in regard to remaining in Dark Kingdom.

His father nodded. "Don't wait too long to introduce us to the girl. Your mother is most anxious to meet her."

Ailith stared out the window, showing no signs of excitement or eagerness.

Servants had cared for Garrin when he was a child, but in public, his mother had clung to him and claimed him as her proudest achievement. The older he got, the more he realized how disingenuous her affection had been.

But her coldness this day was harsher than normal. Did his mother fear her position in the palace with a new princess of childbearing years in residence?

Garrin wished Isle hadn't sewn such doubt about his mother, because now that they were there, he couldn't rid himself of dark thoughts.

SIXTEEN

Lex lifted the fabric of the pale yellow, floor-length gown one of "Garrin's women" had pulled over her head. But it wasn't see-through the way she had assumed it would be. The fine material fit snugly when she swished her hips back and forth, with a billowy layer that flared out, giving the illusion of lightness without being light. The material was stretchy and comfortable for something so frail-looking. And surprisingly warm. Apart from her exposed arms and neck, her core was warm, and that was what mattered.

A young woman who looked about Lex's age held up a stunning pair of emerald earrings. "What do you think of these, miss?"

The refracting surface of the green gemstones caught the light and bounced off the walls. "Are they real?"

"Real?" she said, and started to affix them to Lex's ears. "They are from the palace jewels, my lady."

Lex was going to take a wild guess and assume everything from the palace jewel collection was the real deal.

Especially given the weight of the earrings. "They're beautiful. Thank you."

This woman was fairer than Cora, but her face was just as pretty, with a narrow nose and rosebud lips. "What's your name?" Lex said. "I never asked, and I just realized how rude that was of me."

"Not at all. My name is Em," the woman said, and smiled.

"Pleased to meet you."

"It is my pleasure, Lex. You are to be a princess! What an honor."

"Any woman would be proud to call Garrin her husband." No denying *that* truth.

Em grinned. "And he's chosen you! There are many who would love to be his wife. You are most fortunate."

Wife. Lex took a deep breath. It was all make-believe. Not real.

The feelings she had for him—when he wasn't being bossy—might be real, but her memories growing up were from Earth, no matter her changed circumstances, and Garrin was a Fae prince. He called her his fiancée, but she'd never agree to be one of his many women, and he'd never leave his land to live in the Earth realm. "Em, what about the others? Are they disappointed Garrin—ah, *the prince*— will marry another?"

Em looked over her shoulder as the women in the large room scurried about. Some wore elaborate gowns for the evening, while others chatted happily amongst themselves, fluffing pillows on couches and pulling massive curtains back to draw in light from the vast white landscape.

Her brow puckered. "A few are displeased. They hoped to be chosen by the prince. But the others are happy to be among his women."

"You mean after the wedding, he'll still…"

"Oh, yes," Em said. "It is the prince's duty to provide more progeny for the kingdom. 'Tis a shame the king has not been able to sire more children." She brightened. "But his queen is not so old. There is still time. And there is the king's harem. They work hard to help him produce a child."

Lex choked. "I'm sure they do."

If Garrin was hundreds of years old, his mother had to be much older than that. And she could still bear children?

Not to mention, Garrin planned to continue sleeping with these women after he married so he could produce a soccer team of kids. Dark Kingdom castle was seriously messed up.

Even if this weren't all pretend, there was no way Lex would agree to marry Garrin…

Who was she kidding? She'd consider it because she was attracted to him, Stockholm syndrome or not, but never under these circumstances, with women waiting in every wing. In fact, she couldn't imagine a worse fate than loving someone who didn't love you back.

Em held a mirror in front of Lex's face.

And Lex's eyes flew open. "Holy shit!" She grabbed the mirror and angled it this way and that. What the hell had happened to her?

She'd glimpsed herself in mirrors once or twice when she first entered what appeared to be a communal dressing room of sorts, with dozens of wardrobes and lounge chairs. Her hair was longer and looked damned good, given the ordeal she'd been through. But then they'd plunged her into a copper bathtub, and that was the last she'd seen of herself until Em finished primping and dressing her.

Lex touched her cheeks, which were plumper somehow. And her lips, that had always been too pale, were now a deep rose hue. She shook her head slowly, hardly recognizing herself. Even the edges of her face were smoother, less angular, and more symmetrical.

She'd always been tall and slender, but now her waist cut in more, giving her an hourglass figure.

"I don't understand," she said.

"Miss?"

Lex glanced at Em and swallowed. "Nothing. Don't mind me. I didn't realize how well the dress would fit." She tried for a smile, but her lips felt stiff, her mind racing.

It was her in the mirror, and yet not.

She glanced at her hand, the skin now plump. But more importantly, it didn't shake. Oh, her heart beat faster than normal, but she'd not experienced any of the telltale signs of a panic attack since she entered the kingdom.

Garrin hadn't lied; she'd changed. And it wasn't only from Zirel's magic, which had brought her back to consciousness, or the sunny yellow dress. She'd gone through a physical transformation, yes, but also something mentally transformative as well. She wasn't as anxious or fearful as she would normally be.

"Is everything all right, miss?" Em asked.

Lex couldn't speak, her face frozen at the shock of it all. "I don't know."

Em stepped back and tapped her delicate chin. "The dress is a lovely shade on you, but I can get you another if you like?"

Em didn't get it. She hadn't known Lex before she arrived in Dark Kingdom. "No," Lex said. "This one is fine."

She looked around the large room and flinched. Because everyone had stopped what they were doing and were staring at her expectantly. "What's going on?"

"Oh!" Em exclaimed, and smiled. "The prince is on his way. They are anxious to see his reaction to you in your gown. They also wish to know if your union will be a love match." She grinned brightly.

What in the hell? Of course it wasn't a love match. How was Lex supposed to pretend otherwise?

The women chattered excitedly around her, moving furniture out of the way for ease of flow.

Watching them anticipate Garrin's arrival made Lex's stomach cramp. Maybe it wasn't a love match, but she had grown attached to Garrin, traveling and sleeping beside him for months. Even if she wasn't his real fiancée, she couldn't help but feel nervous with all the female attention he received. "Do they always get this excited when he's home?"

"Oh, yes," Em said. "It's been so very long since the prince has been in residence. Every one of us wants to be with him."

"Be with him? You mean...*be* with him?"

Em nodded and shrugged unapologetically.

"It doesn't bother you that he has a fiancée?" Lex asked.

Em seemed to consider the question. "No... However, as part of the court, we are not allowed to bed other men. And that gets lonely."

"You can't have a boyfriend?"

"Boyfriend?"

"A man you see outside the palace?"

"Oh, no, miss. That is impossible. What if one of us were to get with child? The royal family must know it is the prince's child, and there is no way to ensure that unless we are faithful to the prince."

Lex stared blankly. There were several ways to determine paternity in the human realm. But this was Tirnan, where medicine didn't exist because Fae lived for-freaking-ever. Besides, who needed a doctor when you had magical healers? "How long have you been a part of the prince's court?"

Em looked up as though calculating. "About a hundred years."

Lex's eyes bugged out. "You've been alone for a hundred years?"

Em waggled her head. "Give or take. But I'm never alone." She peered happily around the room. "There are so many of us. We keep each other company."

Too many, Lex thought. "Do you ever drive each other crazy?"

"Often." Em laughed. "But we find ways to entertain ourselves."

Before Lex could ask what the ladies did in their free time, because it had to be interesting, Garrin walked in.

Lex's jaw dropped. *Holy hell.*

Garrin had showered and shaved, the tips of his hair still wet. The thick stubble, which had grown thicker as they traveled, was gone, and his hollowed cheeks were no longer sunken with circles under his bright blue eyes. He'd clearly eaten, probably the same food Lex mindlessly wolfed down during her bath. Or maybe Zirel had healed him more now that Zirel's powers were fully returned?

Garrin wore a navy-like uniform, with gold-embroidered sleeves and collar that fit his tall, muscular frame to perfection. He looked fit and healthier than he had mere hours ago, and he was mesmerizing.

No wonder these women wanted to jump him.

Lex pressed her hand to her belly to stop it from

quaking and straightened her spine. *He's just a man. Just a really freaking beautiful man.*

How could she fault the women for wanting Garrin? *She* wanted him, and she didn't really want him. Lex would never live to be at Garrin's beck and call.

But damn, she saw the appeal.

CHAPTER

SEVENTEEN

"Greetings," Garrin said to the room, his gaze landing on Lex. Heat filled his eyes, and Lex's breath froze in her chest.

He was really good at the fake fiancé thing. Those eyes were giving her an excellent idea of what it would be like to be desired by Garrin Branimir. And she was not immune. Combine that with her confused feelings when it came to him after their travels, and her face heated.

Garrin crossed the room and lifted Lex's hand, his warm fingers sliding to the tips of hers. He placed a light kiss on her knuckles. "Hello."

"Hi." *Smooth.* She gave herself a mental head shake. "You cleaned up nice."

"As did you." His gaze skimmed her body.

Shivers raced down her spine and her belly wobbled. With food in her stomach and a warm room, her body was no longer in fight-or-flight mode and had time for less convenient reactions, like attraction. "So, future *husband*, what now?" she said quietly, though she wouldn't doubt others had heard.

Garrin was her fake fiancé, as well as boyfriend to some thirty women. And that seemed about right when it came to her luck with men. A handsome man finally looked at her, and he didn't have a secret girlfriend—he had *dozens*.

"Has my court treated you well?"

"Don't I look well?"

He scanned her body in another heated stroke, and her mind scattered to the four corners of the universe. "Indeed, you do."

She cleared her throat and said quietly, "Is there some-place we can talk that doesn't contain a roomful of women waiting to jump your bones?"

Garrin chuckled, the sound like pure seduction, damn him. He placed a hand on the small of her back and escorted her out of the communal dressing room and down a corridor of what appeared to be bedrooms. He stopped at the last door and gestured for her to enter.

This room wasn't as large as the others she'd been in, including Garrin's dressing room, but it was huge in Earth terms, with kelly-green wainscoting, tall glass windows looking out onto the snow and ice landscape, and a two-story ceiling decorated in ornately painted murals of entwined lovers.

Lex glanced at the lovers, and her face heated. Fae were not modest by any stretch of the imagination. "How did you build this place in what equates to the Arctic?"

Garrin looked around. "This was built long before the land became permanent winter. Believe it or not, we used to have seasons, with allon trees as abundant in Dark Kingdom as they are everywhere in Tirnan. I never saw it, personally. It has been winter since before I was born."

Garrin crossed the room and sat in a settee. He tugged his pants and crossed his leg over his knee. "Come," he said.

"What did you wish to discuss? Surely not the décor of Dark Kingdom castle."

Lex walked over and, as gracefully as she could for someone used to wearing jeans and sweatshirts, sat beside him in her pretty dress. Though maybe she should have rethought the close proximity.

He smelled good. Better than he already had during their travels. And the attraction that made her stomach drop and spin was stronger now that she was inches from his large body.

Garrin's gaze stroked her face, his eyes snagging on her lips—and there went the flutters in her belly.

Lex cleared her throat. "What are we going to do?"

His gaze slowly rose from her lips and settled on her eyes.

Lex leaned back. It was either that or she'd instinctively lean closer. But in her totally not smooth effort to keep her composure, her thigh bumped his, and her skin zinged through the fabric of her dress.

His chest rose, and his eyes dropped to her mouth.

"What are we doing?" she said, swallowing her nerves and clamping her hands together.

She'd admired men from afar. Occasionally considered what it would be like to have a boyfriend. But she'd never wanted anything the way she wanted to get closer to Garrin right now.

"You left me in that lion's den, a-and that can't last," she said. "They hate me. Well, everyone except for Em. And I have no idea where you stashed my mother."

"Lion's den?" He lifted his eyebrow. "Your mother is with Zirel's people and safe. Are you feeling"—he gestured with his hand and looked down her body—"the fear you had when we first met?"

What? "You mean my anxiety?"

He nodded.

"No, actually. I'm not comfortable here, but I don't have the anxiety I usually do in new places. Which is weird."

"That is not so strange," he said. "You have shed powerful magic that hid your appearance on Earth. You are not the same physically or magically. It stands to reason that your emotions have changed as well."

"I suppose." Maybe somewhere deep down she knew something hadn't been right back home, and the social anxiety was a result of not being able to be herself?

"Either way," she said, daring to lean closer, "what is the plan? You can't keep me here."

Bad move, the leaning closer part.

"The plan," he said, his eyes moving from her cheekbones to her neck and back to her eyes, "is for you to master your magical ability when it is safe to do so and without calling attention. Without the magic, we are either trapped in Dark Kingdom or risk death trying to escape. The strongest of us might survive travel through the Land of Ice, but most would perish."

A shiver racked Lex's body. They would have died if her mother hadn't saved them. And she had only managed that because of some unseen power Lex supposedly had.

"If your powers are as strong as your mother believes," Garrin continued, "there is hope that one day we'll be able to leave without risk. And not only some of us, but all of us."

"You escaped," she pointed out. "Several times. How did you do it and survive?"

"Once. I made it through to the Earth realm only the one time, when I found you. I lost dozens of Fae soldiers over the years trying before that," he said gravely. "My life was put at risk repeatedly, even with careful preparation. I am stronger than most in our land, save my father, but I have limits. Which is why we need a portal that isn't affected by the magical barrier separating our land from the rest of Tirnan."

"The ravine is what stopped you?"

Garrin nodded. "Among other things."

"My mother said your father put her in the ravine. Do you still trust him?"

A shadow crossed Garrin's face. "I don't know what to believe. Your mother's story is confounding."

"Fae don't lie. And my mother is Fae. And for the record, it seems I can't lie either. I tried to, and it got stuck in my throat."

"And you are disappointed?"

"Yes! The ability to lie is one of the best things about being human."

Garrin smiled, then looked down and seemed to consider her words. "Your true energy level, physical form, and essence have returned. The rules that apply to Fae apply now to you as well."

She glanced away nervously. "About that physical form business. What's the deal with that?"

He set both feet on the ground and leaned on his fore-arms, making their heads level. "You don't like your appearance?"

"It's not that. I just...look kind of pretty compared to what I used to look like."

"You've always been beautiful, whether Fae or human."

For a moment, Lex couldn't breathe. They were alone. He had no need to convince outsiders of his devotion, and yet he'd said the words anyway.

No one thought her pretty in the Earth realm. In Tirnan,

well, she supposed the physical changes helped. But if Garrin thought her beautiful prior to the changes...

Before she could wrap her head around what he was saying, Garrin did something she never would have predicted.

He leaned over and kissed her.

And not just any kiss. Her *first* kiss.

Time stopped. Every breath, every sound, including her own heartbeat, magnified.

The press of his lips was soft yet firm, and he hesitated just a beat as though he didn't want to pull away.

Her blood crackled to life and the electrical sensation that ran down her spine whenever they touched hit her tenfold.

EIGHTEEN

Lex touched her mouth. "Why did you kiss me?"

Garrin froze. Why *had* he kissed her? Lex tasted like the finest sweet *brune*, her lips infinitely soft and pillowy. He'd been drawn to her from the very beginning, but now that she was sheltered and hale, he'd done what he hadn't dared do in the Land of Ice.

That one soft kiss had made his blood stir. Lexandra didn't know how desirable she was.

Only that wasn't what he said. "We are to be married. If our first kiss is to look real, we should practice without others around."

Lex's shoulders sank, and Garrin wanted to immediately take back his words. He hadn't lied, but he hadn't told the whole truth. He'd kissed her because he wanted to.

"So, my first kiss...was from a guy who *had* to do it?"

"First kiss?" That couldn't be. Lex was a beautiful woman, even before her true appearance was revealed.

"Yes, you jerk," she said, and swatted his arm.

He lifted his eyebrow. "Was that an attempt to injure

my person? Because I assure you, it caused as much damage as a butterfly flapping its wings."

"You saw what I looked like on Earth. I was a giraffe no one wanted to be close to." She pointed a finger at his face. "What you did is cruel."

He leaned closer, her light, airy sent tickling his nose. "Humans are fools. Believe me, kissing you is no hardship." He narrowed his eyes and thought back. "That Jasper creature wanted to be close to you."

Garrin's annoyance rose from thinking about the Fae who'd nearly prevented their escape. Jasper had put all of them at risk by surprising Garrin and his men inside the cave.

Lex's nose scrunched. "Jas is like a brother to me."

Garrin saw the way the Fae had protected Lex. And he didn't like it. Though he had to admit, grudgingly, that he appreciated Lex having a guardian on Earth until Garrin could reach her.

She might not see it that way, however. "I'm sorry that your first kiss wasn't with someone you care for."

Her mouth softened and she wouldn't meet his eyes. "I never said that."

"Then you are attracted to me as I am attracted to you?"

Her gaze shot to his. "You're very direct, you know that?"

He leaned closer, giving her time to move away. When she didn't, he touched the underside of her jaw and kissed her the way he'd wanted to moments ago, with his lips and tongue.

Lex's hands slid up his chest, and Garrin gently eased her closer until her body was flush with his.

The electricity that sparked whenever they touched turned white-hot. Every stroke of his tongue against hers had Garrin's primal instincts firing. Especially after she let out a light moan.

He trailed his mouth down her smooth neck, leaving soft kisses behind. "Lexandra," he murmured, shocked at the desire that turned his voice gravelly.

"I think I like kissing," she said. "Should have been doing this a long time ago."

He grunted in agreement. Then pulled back abruptly. "With whom?" The words came out sharper than he intended.

She dragged his head back to her chest, where he'd been kissing her decolletage. "With you. Stop talking and get back to that thing you were doing with your tongue."

Garrin grinned and resumed kissing and lightly tasting her soft skin, her scent drugging him into a contentment that probably wasn't wise.

"Much as I hate to, we should stop," he finally murmured, forcing his mind back to more prudent matters. "The king will not wait long before he insists on an audience with you." He kissed her jaw, then the corner of her mouth. Then he was tasting her again, the fire inside him building.

She pulled back, panting. "That's how you stop? By making my body shake with the need to be closer? And what's with that? Why do I want"—she stared at his clothes as though frustrated and waved her hand up and down—"all of this out of the way?" She looked at him skeptically. "Are you doing this? Making me want you?"

"No," Garrin said, and ran stiff fingers through his hair. "I don't know what's come over me."

Garrin had never allowed pleasure to come before duty. His search to find *the one* had been his sole purpose. He'd never felt the need to protect a woman more than his king-dom. Yet he was feeling it now.

"Your mother must be mistaken about the past," Garrin said. "But I agree with her on one point; until I know the truth about what transpired, we cannot risk your life. We must tread carefully where your powers are concerned. And that could take time."

She crossed her arms. "I won't stay inside that vipers' den. Your women want to eat me alive."

He raised an eyebrow, finding pleasure in her jealousy. "First my harem is the equivalent of Earth lions, and now snakes? I doubt that very much; Fae don't eat their kind."

Lex tilted her head. "What *kind* do they eat?" She covered her stomach. "Oh God, I ate the food without think-ing, and now you're telling me it was something weird?"

Garrin sighed. This wasn't going the way he'd planned. "I don't know what my court offered you, but our food is much like yours. You are perfectly safe."

"And the meat?"

Garrin glanced to the side. Their animals were not at all like Earth animals. "Perhaps we should discuss your ability further."

Lex's eyes widened, but she seemed to think better of it before asking more questions. She nodded, her pretty mouth burnished from his kisses.

His gaze snagged on her lips, and he dragged his eyes away. He had to focus on his purpose.

But it was no use, because he *felt* her. Imagined her back in his arms...

Garrin looked to the ceiling and clenched his jaw. He'd need better control if he was to keep her safe.

He leaned over and braced his forearms on his knees,

careful to not look at Lex's mouth and flushed cheeks. "Someday you will master your abilities, but not until we know there is no danger in doing so."

Her hands clamped together, fingers twisting. "I don't know what my ability is."

"Your mother said you magnify others' abilities. She said there was no one like you, but I've heard of individuals with similar powers. They are so rare that some believe them myth. They are called 'puppet masters' for their ability to pull the strings of other magic-wielders."

"I have no idea how I gave my mother her magic. I don't even remember it happening." She sat straighter and compressed her lips. "If I can do this, though, it would give me a leg up. Because I don't feel safe here."

He reached for her hand, wanting to do more but not daring. Garrin had a court full of women, and he would have protected every one of them, but he'd never considered any woman *his*. Until now. "No harm will come to you while I draw breath."

Lex slid her hand out of his. "You said that before, and we both almost died in the ravine."

Garrin swallowed. He'd overestimated his ability to protect her outside his kingdom's walls. He wouldn't allow it to happen again.

He rubbed his brow and grudgingly stood. "I must go."

Lex frowned and climbed to her feet. "Why?"

"Remain with the women in my court. They will protect you, as will my guards." He had made certain the women in his court were trained in battle, as every Fae should be.

She crossed her arms. "You expect your lovers to protect me? Have you lost your mind? Forget it." She turned away. "I don't know why I thought I could trust you. I'll figure out my magic, with or without your help."

~

OKAY, so she'd been rude. Lex was a willing participant of those kisses. What had she been thinking? The man had two dozen girlfriends!

Garrin's gaze softened. "Lex, I know this is different than what you are used to, but please do not attempt to conjure magic while I am gone. It is for the best. As soon as it is safe, I will let you know." He sighed. "I must leave now. You said Em was kind to you. Shall I send for her?"

Lex waved her hand, not looking his way. "Whatever." Most dangerous word in the female language, and Garrin seemed to know it.

He sighed. "Give me time. I will do what I can to make things right."

He hesitated, but when she didn't turn around, the sound of him leaving followed.

Tears burned her eyes, but she wouldn't allow them to fall.

What was wrong with her? The man had given her a peck on the mouth and claimed it practice. She should leave it at that. But the kisses that had followed didn't feel like pretend.

Lex paced the room, her long gown flowing behind her. She was in no position to become infatuated with Garrin Branimir, even if it was too late. At the very least, she couldn't act on her feelings.

A rustling came from outside, and then Em slipped into the room. "His Highness sent me."

And that was how Lex came to be stuck with Garrin's harem for the night. Fortunately, she only had to spend time with Em, who slept in the room with her.

"Do you have magical abilities?" Lex asked Em as they readied for bed.

The young woman looked over from folding what appeared to be a flimsy nightgown and set it on Lex's blanket. Did she expect Lex to wear that thing? "Yes, of course. We all have powers." She looked quizzically at Lex. "Don't you?"

"Oh." Lex coughed. "I do, but I seem to have lost my ability to tap into it."

"I suppose that can happen," Em said, though her furrowed brow said she didn't believe it. "I don't know anyone from Sunland. Maybe things are different there? It's most unfortunate, though."

"So unfortunate," Lex agreed. "Which is why I was hoping you could help me find it again."

Her mother didn't want her to practice magic, and neither did Garrin. Not until he'd assessed the danger. But without her magic, how was she to survive in a land like this?

For some reason, Lex trusted Em, who came across as guileless. And besides, what was one more Fae using magic inside the palace? Garrin had made sure her power level looked normal.

Em shook her head adamantly. "I'm no alchemist. They are most knowledgeable about magic, aside from the elders. You should speak to one of them."

"I don't know the alchemists or the elders. I only know you. Won't you help me?" Lex opened her eyes wide, hoping she looked innocent.

"I suppose I could try," Em said slowly.

Lex smiled. "Wonderful!"

A rap sounded at the door, and Em strode across the room and opened it. A servant carried in a tray of food. Or, at least, Lex assumed he was a servant. He didn't dress fancy the way Garrin and his soldiers did. He wore simple clothes in shades of brown and ecru, with fine tailoring but none of the embroidery and details Garrin's court clothes contained.

The man placed the tray on a small table off to the side and lifted a metal dome. The scent of roasted meat and spices filled the air.

Lex walked closer and saw a slice of meat and what appeared to be something made from allon leaves. The same darn leaves she had subsisted on for months.

She thought she'd never want another allon leaf in her life, but these were prepared with care and somehow more palatable-looking. The meat, though—she had no idea what that was. By the taste of it earlier, it wasn't chicken. Not beef, either. Something in between, and wasn't that a scary thought?

She was still starved even though she'd eaten her weight in food when they fed her hours ago.

Lex and Em sat cross-legged facing each other on queen-sized poster beds that took up half the room, with the tray of food on the table between them.

"How do you get your magic to come to you?" Lex took a bite of vegetables while waiting for Em to answer. The flavors burst on her tongue. A bit salty, with a chestnut aftertaste, but not bad. She took another mouthful.

"You mean calling to it?" Em's lips twisted as she chewed her food and considered. "It's rather instinctual. I suppose if I had to define it, I would say it begins with a tingling sensation."

A tingling. Nope. Lex didn't remember any tingling. Then again, she'd been out of it when she somehow gave the others back their abilities. "Is there anything else?"

Em shrugged. "I'm sorry I'm not more help."

The conversation moved to court clothing—all of it apparently flimsy for the younger generation—and they soon tucked themselves into bed, Lex wearing one of the nightgowns Em had set out.

A thought struck her, and she pushed the thick covers back and sat up. "How do you and the others stay busy while the prince is gone? You said you entertain yourselves."

After kissing Garrin so they'd feel comfortable *doing it in front of others*, Lex could imagine how these women preferred to pass the time with him around.

A sick filling gripped her stomach. Fake relationship or not, she didn't like thinking of him with anyone else.

"The prince is very busy," Em said. "When he is away, we entertain ourselves with battle play."

Lex's eyes widened. "What is battle play?"

Em rolled onto her side and faced Lex, her head perched on one hand. "This Sunland must be a very strange place. You do not practice your fighting skills?"

"Um, that would be a no."

Em's mouth held a silent O. "Well, perhaps you can practice here? The ladies and I find great joy in honing the battle arts."

What in the... That sounded like a terrible idea.

Then again, Lex wanted to be less dependent on others. "Sure," she said. "What could it hurt?"

NINETEEN

Lex took back everything she'd thought of the statuesque Fae females in Garrin's court. They weren't just for looks. They were ass-kicking ninjas.

"One more time?" Em said, in full battle gear, which included a giant sword she wielded like a twig.

Lex limped off to the side of the mat where Em had been teaching her how to use her own sword, because she had one now too. Forget for a moment Lex had never held a weapon before in her life—and the weight of the darn thing—the maneuvering alone was insane. And these women were pros, battle cries and all. "I think I'll sit this one out."

Who needed male soldiers when your court had long-haired killers in frothy skirts? No wonder Garrin felt assured of Lex's safety.

Lex's muscles ached, but every time she thought she'd collapse in pain, she regained her strength. It was the only reason she'd managed several hours with Em inside the gymnasium decorated like an empty Victorian ballroom.

The room had all the plasterwork and intricate detailing of the other rooms inside Garrin's court, but it was huge—like basketball-court-sized huge. There were ropes and weapons hanging from every wall, and mats that could only be compared to something she'd seen in an Earth gymnasium, except not made of vinyl. The material was probably made from the skin of the animals she ate that she didn't want to think about.

Zirel entered just as Lex eased her sore, but rapidly healing butt onto a bench. Since her "true self" had taken effect, her body healed faster than usual. And she could eat the same amount of food as a full-grown man and never have a food baby—which was a huge bonus.

"Lexandra?" Zirel said, scanning her super-cool new workout gear. She too sported the thick, clinging black pants, tunic, and fighting boots the other women wore. And she felt damn powerful, truth be told. He looked around. "You are training?"

Was it such a stretch of the imagination? Yeah, probably. "What did you need, Zirel?"

"His Highness suggested you join me on an errand."

Lex's mother was living with Zirel's family. He must be taking her to see her mom. "I'd be happy to," she said, and quickly rose to her feet, withholding detailed questions until they were out of earshot.

Moments later, Zirel led her through a narrow stairwell and handed her a heavy ankle-length coat. "Cover yourself," he said. "Your head and face as well."

Lex pulled the hood down over her eyes, making sure it covered her face, as instructed. Zirel hadn't explained why, but Lex knew what sneaking around looked like. She'd spent most of her life avoiding the attention of others. Not to mention, Zirel seemed to be taking her on a circuitous route out of Garrin's court and into a part of the castle where few people wandered. Even if one of Garrin's harem saw her, no one would recognize her with the hood covering half her face.

She held on to Zirel's arm or risked running into a wall. "Where are we going?"

"Silence," he said, and exited the castle from a side door.

Freezing air hit her face and snow crunched beneath her feet. They walked for at least fifteen minutes, moving through what appeared to be a village near the castle.

Finally, Zirel slowed.

Lex pushed her hood far enough back to see Zirel glance around before slipping through a frozen metal gate.

She managed to not slip down the narrow, icy walkway, thanks to her new battle boots, and Zirel knocked on a wooden door with a thin sheet of ice that had crawled halfway up the surface.

Lex pushed her hood off her head completely this time and looked around. They stood in front of a cottage that resembled an Irish farmhouse. With the exception of the roof, which appeared to have been patched with ice instead of thatch.

She'd been tracking stone foundations with her hood pulled over her eyes and only a few feet of visibility. From what she could tell, they'd made it to what appeared to be the outskirts of town, given the space between dwellings. "Are all the homes in Dark Kingdom this primitive?"

Before Zirel could answer, an elderly man opened the door. "Yes?" He was tall like the other Fae, but Lex hadn't seen someone this old since she'd arrived. He seemed to recognize Zirel and said, "Please come in."

Her escort ducked his head beneath the rounded doorjamb, and Lex followed close behind, stepping into a small room with a fire burning in a stone fireplace. The—farmhouse? hut?—wasn't exactly warm, but it was exponentially warmer than outside. She unfastened her coat but kept it on.

"She is this way," the man said quietly, and they followed him to the back of the house.

To find Garrin, standing over an elderly woman in bed.

Garrin nodded at Lex, his gaze lingering a moment before he turned to Zirel. "This is Mertha."

The errand wasn't about Lex's mom. This was something else entirely.

Zirel approached the woman's bedside, her body tucked beneath a thick coverlet. He raised his hands above her, and Garrin walked to Lex.

"What's going on?" she said.

He ushered her into the room with the fireplace. "Mertha is at the end of her life and unable to speak."

Lex looked in the direction of the bedroom. "I thought Fae lived forever?" Wow, and wasn't that nuts, because she was now Fae too.

"Not forever," Garrin said. "Mertha is nearly fifteen hundred years old, and the oldest of the remaining elders."

"Fifteen hundred *years*?" Lex said loudly.

"The elders live longer than most Fae. Without Mertha and others like her, history would be lost. Elders are scholars with powerful memories who document our history. Unless the king orders it not to be documented." His eyes glowed with intensity. "Do you understand what I'm saying?"

No one had ever accused Lex of being slow. "Mertha is one of the last elders you and my mom spoke of. What happened to my mother isn't in the records."

He rubbed his eyes, looking more tired than the last time she'd seen him. "I must be discreet, you understand.

But those I've spoken with have suggested things that align with your mother's warnings. I suspect more of our history has been lost to the passing of so many elders."

Garrin paced two steps away, his back to her. "There is good reason to believe your mother's claims against my father are true. One of the people I spoke with heard tales, seemingly more myth than fact, but perhaps myth is fact." He turned and faced her. "That is why I've brought you here. Those who might know more perished in battles long since passed. But Mertha and a few other elders I've not been able to reach would remember the truth. And not simply about your mother, but of the deep history of our land and my father. History that has been documented—and some that has not."

He walked to Lex, an urgent look in his eyes. "Only Mertha is close to her end, and it's come upon her quickly. Her husband says within days she lost her ability to stand. Over the last hour, she lost her ability to speak. It will not be long now."

Blood whooshed in Lex's ears and panic settled in her chest. "If she can't talk, what are we to do?"

"There is a chance that with help from you and Zirel..."

Lex blinked and looked through the door to the other room, where Zirel stood beside Mertha's bed. "You think Zirel can heal her? She's not sick, Garrin. She's really, really old. How can Zirel heal age? I mean, that's not possible, right? You guys can't really make yourselves live longer?"

"No, of course not. But believe it or not, Mertha is relatively young for an elder. And with age comes ailments, even among our kind. Your kind now, Lex, lest you've forgotten. With Mertha's rapid decline coinciding with our arrival—I'm afraid there are forces working against us. Against Mertha. Forces beyond her ailments."

"Someone is hastening her death?" Lex shook her head. "And you want me to heal her?"

"I'm among the most powerful Fae in the land," Garrin said, "and you gave me back some of my magic while you were unaware. What are you capable of while hale?"

"Nothing. I haven't been able to do anything since we arrived. I tried last night with Em. She said there's a tingling that happens when she does her magic. I don't know. But I haven't experienced it. The only tingling I've felt was when you and I... Well, it doesn't matter."

His eyes widened. "When I gave you your first kiss? The power surge Fae experience before our abilities manifest feels very much like what humans call endorphins. It's also very similar to sexual excitement."

Lex's face heated. "You can't possibly think—"

Before Lex could finish her sentence, Garrin pulled her close and brought his mouth down onto hers.

And there went the butterflies in her belly.

His hand slid up her arm to her shoulder and the tender flesh at her neck, where he gently stroked her skin. He lifted his head and studied her eyes. "Do you feel it?"

She frowned and snapped out of her lust haze. "Of course I felt it. Didn't you?"

A smile slowly spread across his lips. "It is the same sensation in magic or love. But unlike love, Fae can call to magic. Whereas the other cannot be forced."

Love? What was he talking about? "I could try to call to it, but I'm telling you, it probably won't work."

"I believe in you."

And he did. She could read it in his eyes. Damn him.

Lex took a deep breath and a careful step back, slowly removing herself from Garrin's arms, while still envisioning the feel of being in his arms. She walked silently into the bedroom where Mertha lay.

Strangely, she sensed Mertha was dying. Sensed a weakening energy drain more and more the longer Lex stood there. Mertha was a memory person, or some such. Lex could feel Mertha's magic now. Frail, but there.

This was awful. These were Mertha's last moments with her husband, and Lex was interrupting it because the kingdom needed Mertha's knowledge. But Garrin's actions weren't selfish. In fact, one could argue they were altruistic. He wanted the truth about his father to keep Lex safe and to help Dark Fae.

Lex sighed, closed her eyes, and focused on Garrin's kiss. From his soft but firm lips to the way his hand had gently touched her arm and run up her shoulder to the skin of her neck.

A shiver of attraction ran down her spine, and Lex homed in on the sensation. She imagined moving the energy farther out—away from herself. And then she focused on Zirel, and the healing energy that wafted off him. She didn't know why she hadn't recognized Zirel's ability before. Oh, she'd seen him touch to heal, but she'd not *sensed* him heal. Until now.

Zirel's ability was as tangible now as holding an orange in her palm. Lex mentally fingered the power texture, tossing it metaphysically in the air. And then she lobbed it at Zirel and pushed the power back at him.

He looked up, startled. Then Zirel quickly glanced down and placed his hands on Mertha's, who immediately took in a deep breath.

"Yes," she said.

Garrin rushed over. "Mertha, it is Garrin Branimir. What is it you wish to say?"

"The answer to your question is yes. Your father had Isle Meinrad entombed." Soft brown eyes fluttered open and looked at Garrin. "Your father..." she started, then gasped, seemingly unable to take in air.

Zirel placed his hands on Mertha and looked at Lex.

Lex reached for the energy she'd sensed a moment ago, but panic made her thoughts scatter, and she couldn't grasp it.

"...is why we are here..." Mertha said, air leaving her mouth on a long sigh, her chest stilling.

No. *No!*

Zirel placed his forehead on Mertha's chest as though to push whatever power he had straight into her heart.

He slowly lifted his head and shook it, his eyes pinched closed.

A choking sound erupted from the old man, and he reached for Mertha's hand and rubbed it. "Oh, darling." He dropped to his knees beside the bed and wept. Without looking up, he said, "That is all, my prince. She is gone."

Garrin's eyes were wide. He blinked and walked to the older man, touching his shoulder. "I am sorry, my friend."

The man looked up, appearing puzzled. "It is I who is sorry." He peered at his wife. "She was more than all the knowledge in this land. More than the petty squabbles between kings. She was a gift."

Garrin's gaze slid away, his jaw tightening. He walked to Zirel, and the two of them bent their heads together, murmuring quietly.

Mertha was gone? How could she be gone? She was just here. Lex had never witnessed anyone die, and it was as horrible as she'd imagined it to be.

She stepped closer and gently rested her hand on Mertha's ankle, closing her eyes.

A willowy strand of energy weaved out. Not something Lex could see or feel with regular senses, but she sensed it just the same. Her eyes flew open, and she stared at Mertha.

Mertha's chest rose. Infinitesimally, but enough that Lex leaned over the woman, waiting on bated breath for it to rise again.

Her husband had leaned closer too, as though he sensed the energy as well.

Mertha's eyes blinked open at the same time her arm rose and she flattened her palm to Lex's head.

"Aaah!" Lex cried out as a pulse of energy burst through her, lighting up the room and what felt like Lex's insides. She flew backward, landing hard on the stone floor.

Garrin ran over to Lex, and Zirel returned to Mertha, who was utterly still now.

Mertha's magic and life were gone. Lex knew—because Mertha had just pushed the last of her energy through Lex.

Along with her knowledge.

CHAPTER

TWENTY

Lex cradled her head with her palms, attempting to keep her brain from exploding with information overload.

"Are you okay?" Garrin said. "What happened?"

Lex winced. "Head hurts."

She couldn't explain what Mertha had done because she didn't know. But the old woman had most certainly done something.

Lex's brain was firing on all cylinders, as though every neuron worked at once, making connections Lex couldn't track. And some that she could.

She'd been here before. To Dark Kingdom. Memories swept through her mind of running through a snow-filled village on a sunny day. Being served food at a table with Jas and his family, though Lex had never met them before. Only she had. Many times. She just couldn't remember it until now.

And it wasn't only a few memories of her childhood that were returned to her, but several of Mertha's memories too. Lex processed the images of her past with ease, but Mertha's memories came in pieces, like a skipping record.

"What did Mertha mean when she said your father was why we are here?" If Lex could figure out Mertha's purpose in sending the information shock wave through her, maybe she could make sense of the visuals filling her head.

"I imagine she blames my father for why we are stuck in Dark Kingdom," Garrin said. "And the truth that has long been hidden."

"You trust Mertha?" she asked.

He gave a curt nod. So even Garrin was disturbed by all that had been discovered this day.

"Will you be all right for a moment?" he asked.

Lex nodded, and Garrin rose and spoke quietly with Mertha's husband.

After a moment, he returned to Lex and helped her stand, placing his arm around her waist. They made their way through the village and back to Garrin's court through back doors of the castle, if there were back doors in a castle. But Garrin didn't take Lex to her room. He took her someplace farther away, with Zirel following quietly behind.

"Is this your bedroom?" she said as they entered a massive chamber with two rooms just beyond, one that looked like the room she'd hidden in earlier and another that held the biggest bed she'd ever seen. And, of course, her first thought was of Garrin taking women to the bed that was large enough to sleep four. "I don't want to be here."

He'd admitted he felt the same pull for her that she did for him. But if they both wanted intimacy, what was to stop them from being intimate? And if they didn't stop, what would become of her? Would she leave this place with a broken heart? She certainly didn't see Garrin leaving Dark Kingdom and his court to be with her in the Earth realm.

His eyebrows drew together. "It is safe, Lex. We can talk here."

She shook her throbbing head, not caring that Zirel was listening. "You've been here with them."

"With whom?" He looked confused.

"Your girlfriends." She felt like an idiot, and yet she couldn't help the words coming from her mouth. Jealousy over a man wasn't something she'd experienced.

His face relaxed and he let out a sigh. "The women in my court aren't allowed in my chambers. They have their own rooms."

Was that where he visited them? She squeezed her eyes shut. It didn't matter. She had bigger issues to deal with.

"I would like Zirel to heal you," Garrin said gently. "You seemed to suffer great pain from Mertha's power."

"No," she said, and stumbled toward a couch. Her head hurt like a bitch, but she didn't want anything to happen to the information Mertha had given her. What if Zirel healed her and accidentally wiped her new-old memories—the ones she'd only just gotten back? Or the memories Mertha had entrusted to her? She couldn't risk it.

Garrin looked at Zirel and notched up his chin. A signal the other Fae interpreted, because Zirel promptly left the room and closed the door behind him.

Lex was just about to sink onto the cozy-looking couch she'd perched against when Garrin caught her by the elbow. "This way."

He led her into the bedroom, letting go of her arm briefly to pull back covers on the giant four-poster bed. "You must rest."

It was probably the only command from Garrin she

would gladly agree to, because her legs were about to give out.

Lex climbed onto the bed, and Garrin pulled off her boots and slid the heavy coat off her shoulders and down her arms.

He tucked her under the covers and sat beside her. Garrin's bright blue eyes appeared warm in this light, his gaze filled with so much concern.

"I remember," she said.

He studied her face. "Remember what?"

"Some of my past, here in Dark Kingdom. The memories I lost when they placed the spell on me and took away my magic."

"Was that what happened when Mertha touched you? She gave you back memories?"

Lex nodded. "Along with something else. She gave me *her* memories too."

Garrin gripped her arm above the covers, his eyes wide. "You must tell me what they are. They could provide the information we need."

"To accuse your father of betrayal?"

Garrin's eyes closed briefly. "Yes. All signs point to my father having betrayed his people. Mertha's knowledge could help free us."

Lex sighed in frustration. "That's the thing. I don't know what the memories mean. They're not a part of my past. They're snippets of images from Mertha's life, and it's like trying to put together puzzle pieces that have no meaning on their own unless you see them together as a whole. I couldn't describe them even if I tried."

Garrin's shoulders sank. "We must find a way, Lex. Mertha wouldn't have given you the last bit of her life's energy if it weren't important."

"I understand, but I'm so tired and my head is full to bursting." Her face felt hot with fever, and her temples throbbed.

He let go of her arm as though it was fragile, and his expression softened. "Rest. I'll make sure you aren't disturbed."

Lex slid her hand from the covers and quickly grabbed his sleeve. "Don't leave me."

Garrin was a womanizer. Maybe. She wasn't sure. He'd taken her from the only home she'd known in order to use her. But he'd also saved her life, brought her back to her birthplace, and returned her to her mother. He'd cared for her all those days in the Land of Ice, offering her a warm shower out in the middle of nowhere and even his last food. He meant her no harm, even if he hadn't said as much. And the way Garrin had kissed her earlier...

Lex wasn't the most experienced in that department, but Garrin touched her with a care and passion that spoke of emotion. Emotion he never uttered but that came through just the same.

Whether it was convenient or not, they shared a connection, and there was no one Lex trusted more in Dark Kingdom than Garrin. Not even her mother.

Now that Lex had some of her memories back of Dark Kingdom, she realized Isle Meinrad hadn't been the ideal mother. She'd often left Lex for long stretches of time in the care of Jas and his family. What her mother did during that time, Lex hadn't a clue. But it had affected Lex. She'd often felt lonely and abandoned, no matter how hard Jas had tried to cheer her up.

No wonder Jas had been her guardian on Earth. They'd grown up together.

Garrin reached for her hand and squeezed it. "You have my word, Lex. I will not leave you."

She felt his oath to her soul. And with that oath, the last of Lex's energy waned. She sighed and sank into a deep sleep.

Lex opened her eyes, but Garrin wasn't in the bedroom like he'd promised.

She threw back the covers, swung her legs off the bed, and looked down at the blush-rose dress she wore with what looked to be cut diamonds waterfalling down the length. It was beautiful, but what the hell? Someone changed her while she slept?

She hurried barefooted across the wooden floor to the door that led to the large chamber they'd entered from the hallway, but it too was empty.

Lex ran across the room and tried to open another door. It was locked, and her heart raced. She banged on the wood. "Garrin!"

No answer, nothing. Not even the sound of the wind whistling against the room's frosted-over windowpanes.

She paced to the fireplace, hands clenched. Garrin couldn't have been gone long. The fire hadn't died down.

And then she saw it.

A foggy haze creeping along the floor toward her.

Lex backed up until her shoulders knocked into the corner of the mantel. "Help!"

Her heart pounded in her ears as the fog whirled and coalesced, causing the hair along her arms to stand at attention.

The fog grew taller until a male figure formed—sometimes blurry, and sometimes in sharp relief. Except for the face. The face was a blank mask.

She couldn't see the color of his eyes or his hair, and espe-

cially not his facial features. But he wore a crown, and his voice rang clear.

"I see you."

Lex screamed.

Lex woke abruptly, gasping for air.

Garrin jerked upright from a chair across the room and ran to her side. "What is it?"

"How many kings are here? Do they all wear crowns?"

"In Tirnan? Three: New Kingdom, Old Kingdom, and Dark Kingdom. Sunland has never had a proper court, and New and Old Kingdom have changed power since I returned. A queen rules New Kingdom. A young woman about your age they say isn't even Fae, but Halven. The King of Old Kingdom was a soldier for most of his life. I don't know if he wears his crown."

"And your father?"

"My father wears a crown." Garrin grabbed her hand. "What is it, Lex?"

She looked around frantically. "Paper. I need a piece of paper. And a pencil."

Garrin crossed the room to a desk.

He brought back what she asked for, and Lex sketched out the shape of the crown on the man in her dream. The dream was important somehow. And it had felt real.

She held up the sketch. The drawing was of a triangle with a circle weaved into it. "Does the top of your father's crown look like this?"

Garrin's expression froze. "Where did you see this?"

"Your father knows who I am."

TWENTY-ONE

Garrin grabbed Lex's shaking shoulders. "My father knows you're here because I told him we are to be married, remember?" Garrin didn't know what had frightened Lex so, but his father couldn't have entered her dream. He hadn't that ability, unlike other Fae.

She shook her head. "The dream was real. How would I know what your father's crown looks like?"

"It's an angelic symbol. Perhaps you've seen it in the Earth realm."

Lex's small hands grabbed Garrin's and squeezed, squeezing a place in his heart as well. He didn't like to see her so afraid. "The man with the crown knows who and what I am. And I swear he was in this room."

Garrin pulled away gently and stood. "It can't be the king."

"Why not? What Mertha did—sending her last energy into me—that was impossible. My mother waking from inside a cave after hundreds of years and saving our asses, that was impossible too. But this"—she held up the sketch again—"this isn't impossible. Not when you consider what has happened so far."

She peered aimlessly as though searching her mind. "Your father is a magical being, right? He came to me in my dream like a phantom. You were gone, and the man in my dream was made of icy-cold fog. I couldn't see his face, but I had a clear view at one point of the shape of his crown."

"My father doesn't have the ability to project into people's dreams, but if he used alchemist magic..." Garrin didn't want it to be true. But the longer they were in Dark Kingdom, the more anything seemed possible. And the more dangerous it became.

"What if what my mother and Mertha said are true?" Lex said. "And now your father suspects me in some way. What will happen?"

An image of his father bringing down the full force of his power upon Lex flashed through Garrin's mind, and his heart sped up. "You can't stay here. Not in the castle."

"Where will I go?"

Garrin paced across the bedroom he hadn't slept inside in over a year, his travels taking him far and wide to find Lex. "I'll find someplace safe until we can leave Dark Kingdom."

He stopped and closed his eyes, calling to a guard in his court who read minds. He commanded the Fae to put together a small group of royal soldiers for an errand.

What Garrin didn't mention to the guard was that he intended to have the men remove Lex from the castle unseen.

"What if—" Lex started to say when a knock sounded.

That was fast. Garrin crossed the room to open the door.

Four castle soldiers stood on the other side. None of them the Fae Garrin had reached out to.

Garrin frowned. "What is this?"

"His Majesty wishes for you and the lady to join him and the queen for supper."

"A moment," Garrin said, and shut the door. He ushered Lex to the other side of the room and away from the guards' hearing. Speaking quietly, he said, "We must leave now." He rubbed his forehead, pressure building at his temples.

She nodded, but her eyes were filled with worry.

Another knock sounded, and Garrin's jaw tensed. "They are ambitious, these soldiers whom I've not met before." He wondered about that for moment, until he caught Lex's terrified expression. "Have you everything you need before we go?"

"Of course I don't!" she said in a low, forceful voice. "I'm still in this dress."

"There is no time to change. I only meant a shawl or some such."

Lex's shoulders relaxed. "I don't have a shawl, though I will say I'm not as cold as I should be wearing this gauze dress. But I doubt it will hold up to the outdoors."

"We'll find a coat on our way through the hidden passageways." He motioned for her to precede him into another room. "Amund hasn't returned, and he's still drained. The passageways are our best bet—"

Another knock sounded, but this time, the person on the other side didn't wait for Garrin to answer.

The king walked inside and took in Garrin's surprised expression—as well as his rapid exit at the other side of the room. "Going somewhere?"

There was enough information about Garrin's father to fear for Lex's life should she remain in the castle. But he couldn't fight the king *and* the army of men that stood behind him. There was no escaping. Not in this moment.

Garrin's only tactical maneuver was to feign ignorance. "You and Mother requested our presence at supper. We were just leaving." No need to mention he and Lex had been leaving the castle entirely.

His father's smile was stiff as he took in Lex. "Allow me to escort you." He extended his arm in the other direction.

"Of course." Garrin glanced at Lex with his back to his father and sent her a stern look he hoped conveyed that they must go with the king.

She swallowed and walked to the exit.

His father strode off, but fifty or so soldiers did not. The men surrounded them.

Garrin sidestepped the guards and gestured for Lex to precede him. "Gauze?" he said, attempting to keep the moment light when it was anything but.

She sent him a sidelong look. "Yes, prince. What is with the frothy gowns you make your women wear?"

She was doing a good job performing in front of the others.

His mouth twitched. Lex managed to give him grief even at a time like this. "It is tradition for women to wear such gowns around the castle. Does it displease you?"

She stared ahead. "It's more comfortable than I thought it would be, but not nearly as comfortable as my normal clothes."

"When we are finished with supper," Garrin said, conscious that every word would be noted, "you may wear what you are accustomed to in the Land of Sun."

She made a sound, and Garrin glanced over. "I didn't say I wouldn't wear the dress," she said, her chin tilted up. *Stubborn.*

He questioned every choice he'd made since finding Lex in the Earth realm, but he would never regret the time he'd spent with her. Lex would eventually return to her normal life. Perhaps marry... The thought put Garrin in a worse mood than the one he was in after his father's ambush.

Before long, they entered the royal quarters, and Garrin took in every guard, every servant he'd never seen before. He'd traveled for years, but he typically knew the royal soldiers.

In the time he'd been gone, many of his father's staff had been replaced. And that was not a good sign. It meant his father didn't trust them.

Soldiers and servants peeled from the walls, carrying trays or armory, depending on their role, and followed Garrin and Lex into the dining room, while their escorts remained outside.

There were more than the typical number of attendants inside the dining room, another sign that didn't bode well.

Garrin peered down the twenty-person table set for four. Large chandeliers were lit, and the walls were covered with pictures of kings and queens of millennia past, their various children depicted behind them. A king was no king without his progeny, even if that progeny numbered one or two over a lifetime. The only king missing from the walls was his father.

Casone Branimir had been waiting for more children that would never come. Garrin had considered it reasonable for his father's portrait to be withheld, assuming it a king's right to see if more children would arrive. But why not celebrate the one who existed? If Garrin were a legitimate heir, there was no shame in presenting the land with one child. Unless Isle was right, and Garrin wasn't legitimate.

His father stood with his back to Garrin and Lex, though there was no question he heard them arrive, not with the number of guards in tow. But while Casone remained with his back turned, his wife stared at Lex, mistrust etched along the edges of her oval eyes that would never be considered warm, despite their russet color.

"Your majesty," the king's head butler said. "The prince and his companion have arrived."

The king slowly turned from looking at a painting of one of Garrin's more virile ancestors standing in front of four children, to peer possessively at Lex.

A surge of adrenaline filled Garrin's chest.

He shifted closer to her. "Father, I'd like to formally introduce you to Lex," he said, careful not to give her full name. The name Lexandra was common, but not so common that it wouldn't stand out among his people. Lex had spent her youth in Dark Kingdom. It was best to tell the truth and no more. "She has made the arduous journey to Dark Kingdom and is to become my bride."

Without taking his eyes off Lex, the king said, "What is your surname, child?"

Garrin heard Lex audibly swallow. "Meinrad," she said, her voice shaky.

Garrin stiffened. There was no doubt his father would investigate who her parents were.

His father's brow rose. "An old noble name."

"Not where I'm from," Lex said.

Which was true. In the Earth realm, Lex's surname would have no noble bearing.

"Interesting." The king tapped a bejeweled dagger sheathed at his waist, and Garrin looked to the sides, preparing for an attack.

His heart raced. He had made a grave mistake. He should have never allowed Lex to meet his father. Should have fought off a hundred, two hundred soldiers, if need be.

He'd believed if he presented Lex as his future bride, it would distract long enough to get Lex out of Dark Kingdom safely. But there was no calm behind his father's intense green gaze. No warmth from his mother's brown one, either.

He'd watched as others attempted to come between his father and the throne and witnessed his father's calculated maneuvers for snuffing out threats. Some involved words powerful enough to dissuade, but most entailed lethal force. Before attacking, his father always tapped the dagger he carried at his waist, a precursor to what lay ahead.

Casone Branimir suspected Lex. Possibly from the moment Garrin had brought her into the kingdom. Or earlier.

A trickle of sweat slid down Garrin's back as the queen approached the mahogany table and gestured for them to sit. "Tell me," his mother said, "where did you meet Lexandra?" She smiled in Lex's direction, but the gesture, like his father's dagger tapping, made Garrin ill at ease.

"In the Land of Sun," Garrin said, and sipped from a crystal glass that had been set out. For humans, *brune* was potent, but Lex was Fae. The beverage shouldn't harm her.

She sent him a questioning look, and he smiled encouragingly. She must pretend to know *brune*, as everyone did in Tirnan. She lifted her glass and sipped, her eyebrows rising at the flavor or the strength, he wasn't certain.

"You were sent on a mission to find the prophesied one," the king said. "How did this meeting in Sunland come to be?" His attention moved to Lex. "Has my son mentioned our struggles?"

Lex set her glass down. Her gaze strayed to the king's crown, and she flinched. It was the same crown she'd drawn after her nightmare. "He told me you have no way of leaving the land," she said.

"Indeed." The king's eyes were curiously intent. "Though that's not entirely true, or you wouldn't have managed the trip. What else has my son said?"

Lex's shoulders straightened. "That he wishes me here." She held her hand out, palm up on the table, and Garrin blinked.

When he didn't immediately respond, she glanced at his arm.

For someone so new to Dark Kingdom politics, Lex was remarkably good at rearranging the truth. He placed his hand on the table, and Lex slid her palm into his.

"And what are your plans?" his mother said, eyeing the handholding with open hostility.

Lex's hand shook, and he sensed her panic. It seemed her ability to lie without lying had limits.

"I plan to show Lex the land and people, and to share our history," Garrin said. "We also plan to return to the Land of Sun for Lex to meet with those she left behind."

The king set down his glass with a heavy thud. "Return? You've only just arrived. Surely it will be years before your bride wishes to return to her homeland?"

"I have friends I missed," Lex said. She glanced at Garrin. "My fiancé was so dashing when we met, I'm afraid I didn't take time to say my goodbyes before we rushed here."

The king made a sound of disbelief. "Sunland is more hospitable than other parts of Tirnan. Regardless, crossing the Land of Ice isn't worth risking the life of our future princess. I'm told you both were haggard when you arrived, my son more so than his future bride. I see no reason for you to leave Dark Kingdom."

Garrin squeezed Lex's hand firmly in a silent plea for her to remain quiet. "As you say, Father." Now was not the time to call more attention to them.

"And when is the wedding to be held?" his mother asked. "Had I known there was cause for celebration, I would have planned a feast." Her smile was bitter. She smoothed her hand across the silk damask tablecloth. "You know how much time goes into our formal food preparation."

Garrin's shoulders tightened. He'd never seen this side of his mother. The cold side, most certainly. She was aloof in a way that put off most Fae. But the bitterness seeping off his mother's tongue was new. Or he'd just never noticed it before. "There's no need for a feast that uses up our larders. Lex is aware of the challenges we face producing food, and we have no wish to burden the people. We will hold a small ceremony."

Garrin sensed Lex's questioning glance, but he didn't dare look in her direction and let on his concerns to the king and queen. The longer they remained in the room, the more danger they ran into with their words and actions.

The king raised a hand, and several servants placed a first course of soup in front of them.

"Now, now," the queen said, then took a small sip from the bowl before her. "We must have a proper ceremony for our only child." She looked at Lex. "You will come with me this evening to choose a gown. I see no reason to wait."

Lex dropped his hand and pinched him in the waist below the table.

Garrin coughed lightly into his palm. "I fear we are both tired after our long journey, as Father pointed out. Wedding gowns can wait."

The queen peered at Lex. "Are you having second

thoughts? There is no undoing a royal wedding. Do make sure you value my son before you bind yourself to him."

"I value your son," Lex blurted, her skin coloring. "Very much." She glanced at Garrin, and he couldn't look away. Not from the declaration, and not from the sincerity in her eyes. She wouldn't have said it if she hadn't meant it.

"Well, then," came his mother's bitter tone. "There is no reason to wait, is there?"

"Every couple needs time to prepare, Mother," Garrin said. "I will inform you when Lex has had time to tour the land, meet our people, and adjust to winter."

The queen didn't flinch, but the hand that rested atop the table had balled into a fist. "Don't leave us waiting too long, son. It is your father's dream to have a second heir to the throne."

"Don't nag him, Ailith." The king wiped his mouth with a cloth napkin and stood. Garrin and the queen stood as well, followed by a startled Lex. "You will meet with me tomorrow, Garrin," he said, and moved swiftly to the exit.

Garrin touched Lex's elbow and escorted her toward the door as well, the food and drink abandoned upon the king's departure.

But his mother stopped them before they could leave. "A gift," she said, and extended a ring with a sparkling yellow stone secured in a basket-weave gold setting.

Lex's mouth parted and her eyes widened. "I-I don't know what to say. This is beautiful. But I have nothing to give in return."

Ailith slid the ring onto Lex's finger. "For my future daughter-in-law," she said, and walked away, sending one last sidelong look as she did. "I'm certain in time you will give me far more."

TWENTY-TWO

Lex watched the queen leave and clenched the hand that held what had to be the biggest freaking gemstone she'd ever seen. "Did your mom really just give me a ring the size of a bird's egg... Garrin?"

His face had gone pale. Once the queen turned the corner, he carefully placed Lex's hand with the ring on his forearm, as though to escort her away.

But that wasn't what he did.

Angling his body, he hid her arm from the soldiers who had maintained a steady presence behind them since the king's summoning. Then he slipped off the ring from her finger and tucked it inside his breast pocket. "A lovely gift from my mother." His expression held no happiness. In fact, the look on his face was so dire it sent tremors down Lex's spine.

This man had kept her alive through freezing conditions no human could survive—and now he was scared?

They made it to Garrin's quarters. The soldiers maneuvered on either side of the door, but they didn't try to enter.

Garrin closed the door and gently pulled her toward the

far end of the chamber. He backed her against a wall and leaned in, his forearm braced above her head, his mouth inches from her own.

Lex's heart fluttered and her breathing turned spastic. She'd been terrified around the king, who she swore had entered her dream with that awful crown on his head. But Garrin oozed charm, even when his handsome face was stressed. No matter the danger they were in, every moment with him was seductive.

"What's going on?" Lex couldn't begin to imagine how powerful something had to be to scare the Dark Prince.

His head dipped even closer until his lips brushed her earlobe. "Someone wishes to track your presence in our land. The ring is charmed."

Lex jolted. And not from Garrin's mouth on her ear— though that *was* distracting. "Your mother?"

He touched his finger to her lips and shook his head slowly as though reminding her to remain quiet. "I don't know," he murmured. "But the ring contains magic."

She peered up past his full lips to his crystalline eyes. How could she have ever thought them cold when they held so much warmth? "You sensed it?"

"Someone didn't want anyone to know the ring was charmed. The magic has been masked, but it's there," he said quietly.

"What do we do?"

Garrin swallowed, his muscular neck bobbing in a nervous gesture she wasn't used to seeing from him. "We get you out of here."

"That was already the plan after what we learned about your father," she whispered.

He shook his head slowly. "After meeting with my

father and mother… I don't know how, but they are several steps ahead of us. We must go immediately."

She reached up and curled her hand around his arm. "Don't you leave me," she said.

His gaze dropped to her mouth, and he looked away. He didn't speak for a moment, and then he said, "I'll do whatever necessary to keep you safe."

Lex frowned. "Garrin, I'm not kidding."

He touched her chin, his warm gaze tracing the outlines of her face. "Em will bring clothes more suitable to your tastes," he said quietly, though loud enough that the men stationed outside the door could hear.

She tilted her head and crossed her arms. "The clothes…? You're very selective about what you listen to."

He paced away and opened the door a crack, requesting for Em to come to his chamber. When he returned, he said, "I always listen to you, Lex."

"Since when?" She let out a harsh sigh. She was able to decipher the guards' murmurs and knew they heard her clearly too. "What are you going to do?" she whispered as softly as she could.

"Get you out."

"By myself? *Garrin*," she said.

He rubbed his brow, strain showing in his every move. "Do you trust me?"

She wanted to say "hell no," but that would be a lie, and she couldn't get the words past her lips. "Yes."

"Please do as I say." His expression was so earnest that Lex nodded. She couldn't contradict him when he was this stressed. She wanted to go to him—hug him—but his stance was closed off, as though he were preparing for something terrible.

A moment later, Em knocked on the door with an

armful of clothing. But thankfully, these looked more like the pants and long-sleeved top Lex had worn through the Land of Ice.

"Oh dear," Em said as she helped Lex change in the dressing room. "I've forgotten your coat." Her mouth twisted adorably. "Wait but a moment and I'll return with it."

"Thank you," Lex said, and finished pulling on the— leather? rubber?—boots Em had given her. These things were the most comfortable shoes she'd ever worn. She needed to steal herself a pair before she returned home.

Lex walked into the main room and noted that Garrin had changed into a similar outfit.

"Better?" he asked.

"Much."

He nodded, though his brow was furrowed as though he carried the weight of the world on his shoulders. He picked up a dagger, but as he attached it to his belt, he stilled. "That is odd."

Lex glanced down instinctively and smoothed out her top, which couldn't have fit her better if it had been custom-made. "If you're trying to make me comfortable, you're failing. What's wrong with my outfit?"

Garrin moved toward the door and opened it before any knock had sounded. And if Lex thought about it, she'd heard it too—the footfalls of several people approaching.

She wasn't used to the things her senses picked up, but she had better adapt quickly, because the Fae who stood on the other side of the door were terrifying-looking, with glowering faces, some of them covered from head to toe in robes.

What in the what? The men were in formation, as though preparing for battle. And that couldn't be right.

Garrin's father could have had them attacked earlier, but he hadn't, so why now?

"Where is Zirel?" Garrin asked an extra-tall Fae with light brown hair that stood straight up on top.

"The king requests that you return to his chambers."

Garrin's back stiffened and he moved to the side, blocking Lex's view of the soldiers—and their view of her. "I will attend my father in just a moment. You may leave."

"We will escort you to the king, my prince," the guard said.

"You misunderstand," Garrin said pointedly, as though trying to impart wisdom. "I have one errand, and then I will go to him."

Guards outside the door entered the room and surrounded Garrin, the air filling with something...the Fae energy Garrin and the others spoke of?

"What are you doing?" Garrin said.

The tall guard grabbed Garrin's arm. "King's orders."

Lex's heart raced. Panic she'd not felt in forever bubbled up, horrifying and familiar. "Garrin?"

He yanked his arm free, but when he raised his hand, no blue fire sparked and no ice formed.

His face crumpled in pain and multiple guards quickly surrounded him. One of the men wearing a dark auburn robe touched Garrin's head.

He collapsed, his eyes rolling back.

"Garrin!" Lex screamed.

The soldiers and men in robes lifted him and carried him out and into the hallway.

"No!" Lex closed her eyes and called to her powers.

Absolutely nothing happened. When she looked up, Garrin and the soldiers were gone, the sound of their rapidly retreating footfalls the only thing left behind.

She jumped to her feet and ran after them, but the door slammed in her face. And it was locked from the outside.

"Let me out!" Lex banged on the door, then clutched her head, which pounded worse than when she'd woken from the Land of Ice. She sank to her knees, her mind racing.

Moments later, Em walked in as though the door hadn't been secured.

Em appeared oblivious, looking down at something in her hands, the coat she'd promised hanging over her arm. "I found these gloves and thought you might wish to wear them in addition to... What has happened?" Em scanned Lex. "Are you all right, miss?"

Lex stumbled to her feet and grabbed Em. "They have him."

"Who?" Em draped the coat over Lex's shoulders, and Lex automatically slipped her arms through the sleeves.

"The prince. Palace guards took him." She couldn't trust anyone, but Garrin had entrusted Lex with Em. "It's not safe for me inside the castle, and apparently, it isn't safe for Garrin either."

"But he is the prince. Why would he not be safe?"

Lex gripped the girl's upper arms. "Em, will you help me?"

Em looked utterly confused. "You are certain it was palace guards who took the prince?"

"Garrin recognized them."

Em's gaze fell on a turned-over chair, her eyes growing wide. "Let us return to my room, where you can tell me what has happened."

"I don't know—"

Lex was about to say she wasn't sure it was a good idea

to show her face in the castle any longer, when the sound of heavy footsteps came from somewhere down the hall.

The soldiers might be farther away than she imagined. Or they could be right on top of them. "They can't find me," she said, her eyes pleading with Em's, whom she hoped was truly on her side.

Em glanced at the door and her mouth puckered. "Guards and two alchemists. I can hear their robes brushing the stone floor. How unusual…"

"Alchemists? That's what those monks are? Didn't you say they're Fae who understand magic better than anyone?"

"Among other things." Em ushered Lex into Garrin's bedroom.

Lex looked back. "Shouldn't we leave before they get here? We'll be trapped."

"Not trapped—liberated." Em pushed on a panel, and an invisible door opened to a hallway like the ones in the rest of the castle, with stone floors and arched ceilings, only narrower.

"What in the hell?" How did Em know about a secret chamber from Garrin's bedroom?

She shook her head. Did she really want to know?

"Not hell, miss—a secret corridor. Come." Em yanked on Lex's arm, and they ran down the hallway. "Everyone knows of the passageways. We must hurry before they get here."

"If that's true"—Lex looked back—"what's the purpose of using them?"

"Ages ago, they were used to pass secret messages and lovers." Em slipped inside an empty room and pulled Lex in with her. She shut the door behind them.

"Lovers? Isn't this a free-love castle? The king and prince have harems at their disposal."

"The men, yes." Em urged Lex out another door and down another long hallway. "The passageways are for the lovers of the women. This way." They raced around several more corners until they were in what looked to be the servants' section.

Lex caught her breath, her hand pressed to her chest. "Isn't it forbidden for women to have lovers?"

"Oh yes, miss. But..." Em shrugged.

Lex thought Fae regimented and old-school, like Garrin. Turned out, they might be old-fashioned, but they also broke their own rules. "You Fae are pretty naughty, aren't you?"

"Most assuredly." Em winked and opened another door, this one to the outside.

Cold air stung Lex's face, but the door they'd exited a second ago disappeared, smoothed over by ancient walls covered partway up with ice.

A secret portal? Only it wasn't like the ones she'd traveled through. It had already existed... There was so much to learn about magic. "Will the soldiers find us?"

Em wrapped her arms across her chest, shivering. She still wore the gauzy gown of the court women, while Lex had on proper winter clothes and coat. "Let's not find out. Where would you like to go?"

Lex pulled her arm out of one sleeve of her coat and held it for Em to slip into, the two of them huddling together. "I might be able to find a cottage Zirel took me to."

"You've been to the village?"

"We visited an elder named Mertha."

Em nodded as though she knew Mertha, or knew of her,

and they took off, running as quickly as they could while sharing the coat.

But the farther from the castle they made it, the more disoriented Lex became.

Inside the village, the cottages all looked the same, and everything was covered in snow. The first time she made the trip, she'd had her hood pulled below her eyes, relying on Zirel to escort her to Mertha's. Her lay of the land had consisted of what she could see from her knees and below.

Em and Lex were out in the elements now, with guards likely close behind. They wouldn't last long before they were discovered if they didn't find coverage soon.

"I'm sorry." Lex glanced ahead and behind them, and shook her head. It had started to snow, the moisture dampening her hair and blurring everything. "I thought I could find it, but I'm turned around and I don't know where we are."

Em sent her a shivering smile. "I do. We will go to the home of my childhood. It's not far."

TWENTY-THREE

Zedekiah, the king's head soldier, struck Garrin in the jaw with a sharp uppercut. "Where did you find the female, and who is she?"

Garrin spat blood onto the stone floor and narrowed his eyes. He glanced past Zedekiah—or Zed, as Garrin knew him—to alchemists hovering in the shadows. "At some point," he said casually, "the alchemists will tire of holding back my power. Have you considered what will happen then?"

Zed picked at his tooth with the blade he'd stolen from Garrin's belt. "I suppose I'll bring in more alchemists, should that happen. Though at the moment, I see no cause for concern." He leaned forward, his hot breath coating Garrin's chilled skin inside the frigid dungeon that his father reserved for the worst offenders. "You may be powerful, but not against the king's army."

It had shocked Garrin to find Zed in charge of torturing him. He'd known the soldier most of his life, and the sense of betrayal ran deep. "Who ordered this?"

"King's orders, as I said."

The king was ruthless, but he rarely left punishment to others, preferring to do it himself. Something was off.

The commander Garrin had mentally requested to sneak Lex from the castle was nowhere in sight. Lex had either escaped, or they held her trapped in Garrin's quarters while they beat him for information. Either way, the situation wasn't good.

Zed struck Garrin with a backhand to the face.

"Was that supposed to hurt?" Garrin willed his eye not to twitch, though it pulsated from the blow. "You never could fight without backup."

Zed snarled. "Laugh all you want, Your Highness. But I will get the truth from you one way or another. Answer now before it is too late. Where does she come from?"

Too late? What was that supposed to mean?

It didn't matter. Garrin would never tell of Lex's origins, now that his fears about his father and the past were confirmed. He couldn't believe it, but he must—he was imprisoned in his own dungeon. "The Land of Sun," he replied.

This time, Zed switched things up and punched Garrin in the stomach. A blow that brought tears to his eyes.

He coughed and gasped for air. "If my father is behind this, where is he?" None of this made sense. Not the torture on behalf of his father, nor the interest in Lex.

Contrary to other Fae rulers, Casone Branimir passed up female soldiers in favor of their male counterparts. He'd never been one to believe women powerful, and he wouldn't believe Lex a threat. Unless...

No. Her mother would never share Lex's true origins, not even if her life depended on it. It was possible—unlikely, but possible—that Amund or Zirel had betrayed Garrin. More likely, his father had investigated Lex's surname after she'd been unable to lie and connected her with Isle. Or perhaps the person who'd betrayed Garrin was no one he suspected. The castle seemed to always be one step ahead of them.

"You're beginning to annoy me, Zed. Tell me why you were given these orders or prepare to pay for years to come."

His jailer looked off distractedly. "I do not think so, my prince." His gaze slid back to Garrin, filled with something akin to regret. "My orders are to obtain the information, no matter the cost. No matter whom I torture. Including you."

LEX AND EM ran as quickly as they could above packed snow while attached to a single coat. The village was deserted, though light glowed from cottages built like the one Mertha and her husband had lived in.

They had just passed what appeared to be the heart of the village, with small shops lining a frozen road, when the sound of others approaching came from behind.

Em hesitated. "The soldiers will soon be upon us." She looked around, as though searching for somewhere to hide.

Lex glanced back. She couldn't see anyone, but she heard the crunch of rapid footfalls over snow as well. "Shouldn't we keep running?"

Now that she was healed, Lex could run faster in Tirnan. Heightened senses, the ability to run super-fast—it had to be a Fae thing. But sharing a coat while running slowed them down.

"We won't outrun them," Em said. "Come." She pulled Lex to the side of a cottage, hidden from the main road.

The footfalls grew louder.

Lex looked at Em. "What now? They'll see us any minute."

Em bit her lip. "I can make us invisible. Briefly," she quickly added. "But you must hug me close." Lex's confusion must have shown, because Em said, "It is my ability, though I'm not very good at Blending others. I can manage in a pinch, but we'll have to time it right."

Lex didn't hesitate; she hugged Em like her life depended on it. Which it did.

"Don't move, okay?" Em said, and closed her eyes.

A wash of Em's magic swept over Lex.

The soldiers were talking, and so close now that Lex could throw a pebble and hit one of them in the forehead. Her heart hammered in her chest, and she closed her eyes too.

"I sense them," one of the guards said.

"Where?" came the voice of another from what couldn't be more than a few feet away.

Em was doing it. The guards were right next to them. If they sensed Lex and Em, they should be able to see them, but they didn't. The only problem? Em's magic was waning. Her body shook as she attempted to keep them Blended, or whatever she'd called it.

Through her mind's eye, Lex saw Em's power drifting away and weakening.

Leave, Lex thought. Em wouldn't be able to keep them hidden much longer.

The guards were standing around, searching for what they sensed but couldn't see.

Lex had read the magic Em used when she made them Blend. Lex gripped Em tighter and focused on holding on to it.

Em's body stiffened, and Lex opened her eyes. Em was

staring wide-eyed, but she remained perfectly still. Then her eyes slid closed, and she redoubled her concentration, because the energy wasn't only coming from Em anymore but bouncing between the two of them.

Lex's power pushed Em's, and Em's boosted off Lex's energy in a synergistic dance.

The two guards who'd lingered finally gave up and moved on, but Lex and Em remained Blended until they could no longer hear the men.

Em pulled away. "How did you do that? You gave me strength—*magical* strength."

"Honestly?" Lex said. "I'm not exactly sure. I felt your power and pushed it back at you. We're lucky it worked, because I'm not very good at it, whatever it is."

Em's brow furrowed. "I've never heard of an ability like yours."

"It's a strange one, for sure, but we can talk about how weird I am once we get to your house. The guards will realize what happened and double back."

"They will," Em agreed. "They aren't daft. At least, not all the time."

And on that note, Lex shifted and moved in the direction they'd been headed, when Em gripped her forearm, stopping her.

"There is nothing strange about you, Lex. You have a unique ability, and that is to be celebrated." She smiled.

Which nearly moved Lex to tears. When was the last time she had a friend who wasn't Jas?

She couldn't remember. Certainly not in the Earth realm. A few of her memories of Dark Kingdom had returned, and the ones Mertha had sent Lex of her time in Dark Kingdom were hazy. She had played with children, but she didn't remember a close friend.

Lex glanced at Em as they continued running through rows of homes that grew larger and farther apart. "Thank you for being kind to me."

Em flashed her a smile and pointed at a spot in the distance. "There. That is my home."

Lex couldn't see the house clearly from where they were, but it appeared four or five times the size of the homes they were passing, and these weren't small like those in the village. "That's where you grew up?"

Em shrugged. "My parents are relatives by marriage to the royal family. Once we arrive, we'll be safe."

Lex wasn't so sure—not if Em's parents were related to Garrin's father, who couldn't be trusted. More importantly, Lex hadn't felt the least bit safe since they took Garrin away.

Would castle guards hurt their own prince?

TWENTY-FOUR

Garrin had been attempting to glean as much information from Zed as he could, but enough was enough. Too much time had passed since he'd seen Lex. He waited until his body was partially healed and then mentally reached out to his powers. They were muted, but the alchemists reining them in grew weak. Zed would send in replacement alchemists soon, and Garrin couldn't have that.

He froze the metal shackles binding his wrists and ankles and immediately froze the guards and alchemists where they stood. Nothing deadly, just enough ice cover to pin them in place while Garrin escaped.

Garrin stumbled toward the metal barring his exit from the dungeons. The surge of power it took to break his shackles and freeze the men had weakened him, but with the alchemists temporarily frozen, so too were their powers. With each breath, Garrin's body healed and his powers returned.

He lifted his hand and waved it across the bars, taking

the metal to subzero temperatures. A loud pop sounded, and cracks splintered the metal.

Garrin kicked the bars, breaking them apart. He ran out of the dungeon and down freezing basement passageways. When he rounded a corner, two familiar faces headed for him.

Amund and Zirel had their swords drawn, which they quickly sheathed after they saw it was Garrin.

His men had been beaten, their clothing bloodied and torn. "Where have you been?" Garrin asked.

"Indisposed," Amund said. "They thought to torture information out of us." Amund looked up as though the stone ceiling were made of glass. "We must hurry. They move in as we speak."

Garrin didn't care about the damned soldiers. He'd trained most of the newer ones before he left, and he knew how to avoid the rest. Though the fact there was so much turnover was worrisome. "Is Lex safe?"

Zirel kicked open a locked basement door to a room full of weapons and supplies. "I'm told she escaped with Your Highness's court female they call Em." He handed Garrin a sword and grabbed outerwear for the three of them.

Amund pulled on a coat as they ran. "Others travel through our land, and they move in Lex's direction."

"You know where she is?" Garrin asked.

Amund sent him a sidelong look. "You may have glamoured her, but her power level is distinct for those aware."

The glamour should have downgraded her power. "If you sense her—"

"The king's alchemists may too," Amund finished.

～

THE ROAD that took Lex and Em to Em's parents' house was lined with hundreds of partially frozen allon trees. A caretaker stood on a ladder and blew on the branches of one of the trees they passed, melting the ice with his magic.

Freed from their cold prison, leaves fluttered happily from one branch to another, as though butterflies dashing through a eucalyptus field.

Thanks to Mertha, Lex remembered the magic of allon. The leaves were in shades of purple, blue, orange, and pink, shifting from one branch to another, and yet she missed the variety of plant-based food she'd grown used to in the Earth realm. And fast food. She'd kill for greasy fries right about now.

"We're here," Em said as they climbed slippery stone steps to a home that wasn't quite a castle but far grander than most homes they'd passed.

If Mertha's place was an Irish cottage, Em's house was an Irish manor. Beneath snow and icicles, Lex could make out three stories of ornate stone walls, a dozen paned windows, and two massive chimneys bookending a pitched roof.

Em pushed open the ten-foot entry with her body and let out a sigh. She smiled at a liveried man rushing forward, wearing a red and black uniform. "Alaric, please bring us hot tea."

"Certainly, miss." He draped wool blankets over Lex and Em's shoulders and handed their coat to another servant.

Em walked down a wide hallway, and Lex followed her to a parlor with walls covered in red damask wallpaper and gilded mirrors that stretched to ornate black and gold crown molding. Em's house was filled with ornate antiques and decorated like the Dark Kingdom castle but on a smaller scale.

Lex sank into an upholstered wingback chair next to Em and a fireplace, and was soon handed a piping-hot cup of tea. She stared after the...footman? Servant? She didn't know what to call the helpers, but there were a lot of them. "It almost seemed like they were expecting us," she said to Em.

Em sipped her tea, shivering before she answered. "Mother trained the staff to be ready for any eventuality. Particularly if her cousin the king should stop by."

Lex gripped her cup. "*Cousin?*" She half stood, the blanket slipping off her shoulders. "You said they were related by marriage. You didn't mention anything about cousins. Your parents can't hide this from family. I should leave."

"Cousins by marriage." Em blew on her tea and twisted her mouth to the side as though thinking. "The castle guards are likely using spells and magic and interrogating everyone to find out where you've gone."

Lex wrapped her arms around her middle and paced in front of the windows, searching outside. "Why would you bring me here?" Fear lanced her chest. Had Em set her up?

Em quickly set her cup down. "It will be all right. They don't know where we are. We can't stay for long, but we can remain long enough to get nourishment and proper clothing."

"What about your parents? What if others learn they helped me? And now you're caught up in this too..."

"I pledged my oath to the prince. No one will question my loyalty after Garrin bade me care for you."

"Don't the king's wishes trump Garrin's?"

Em waggled her head. "In matters of war, certainly. But when it comes to court politics, it is more of a gray area."

Lex might have hazy memories of Old Kingdom, but her

knowledge of nobility was a giant blank. She remembered a small house, bland food, and playing with a couple of other children. She must have been poor in Dark Kingdom.

Something else Em said had caught Lex's attention. "What does it mean for a woman to pledge an oath to Garrin? Is he essentially married to all of you?"

Em tipped her head back and laughed.

Lex crossed her arms. "I'm glad my ignorance amuses you."

Em caught her breath and waved her hand. "It's not the same as a marriage pledge, though there is commitment. Once the prince pledges himself to you as his wife, it will supersede all others, with the exception of his commitment to his people."

But Lex and Garrin were never supposed to marry.

Regardless of what they were to each other, a court full of women pledging themselves to him made her ragey and possessive.

Lex continued pacing. "I shouldn't stay. I should find my mother and try to help Garrin."

Em stood too, glancing out the window. "The guards will double back and find us. We shouldn't tarry too long. Come," she said, and moved toward the door. "I'll have someone bring us fresh clothes, while I find my parents and gather supplies—"

Before Em could reach the door, the air shimmered in front of her and she froze, forcing Lex to stop behind her or risk running into her.

"What is it?" Lex whispered.

"Someone is entering my home through a portal. Father!" she yelled. And then Em was running toward the fireplace, where she reached for a sword that crisscrossed another above the massive mantel.

That was when all hell broke loose.

People wearing thick black winter coats and combat boots tumbled through the portal at the same time an older-looking couple ran into the room along with several servants.

The older woman wore a court dress, minus the flimsy material Garrin's harem sported, and leapt onto the arm of a settee. She bounced off the seat cushion and grabbed the second sword above the mantel in midair. She landed beside Em in a matching sword stance.

The older man who had entered the room casually set a snifter of what looked to be brandy on a tray one of the servants held and pulled out a dagger with a ruby hilt.

Holy hell. Shit was about to go down.

And then Lex got a good look at the soldiers in black who'd tumbled through the portal. "*Jas?*"

TWENTY-FIVE

Jas scowled at Em and her parents, who looked ready to slice him up. "Get out of the way, Lex!"

"For the love of God, Jasper, my friend Em is *helping* me." Lex looked past him to the group of men and women he was with. "How in the world did you get here?" And then Lex remembered the shimmer she'd seen before they arrived. "You came through a portal?"

Em's mother raised her sword. "An *illegal* portal. State your business or prepare to die."

Em relaxed her stance. "Mother, my friend Lex knows these people. Let's hear them out."

"Who in the devil is Lex?" Em's mother asked.

A younger woman with a mass of wavy reddish-brown hair stepped forward. "I'm Elena Rosales, queen of New Kingdom. This is Derek O'Brien and Reese Fisher. The tall soldier over there is Keen, ruler of Old Kingdom." She gestured to the black-haired woman with bright blue eyes. "Camille is a portal creator. She helped us travel from New Kingdom."

Em's mother looked Elena up and down. "Queen? Who is your mother?"

"Theodora Joelle Rainer. You can tack on Rosales to that, since she married my father and took on his name as well."

Em's mother made a harsh sound in the back of her throat. "Last I heard, the princess was imprisoned for bearing a half-breed."

Elena's shoulders straightened. "This half-breed stopped treasonous Fae from taking over Tirnan. A battle in which my mother lost her life."

Em's mother rested the tip of her sword on the tufted rug. "That is news indeed. I am sorry for your loss, but are you saying a Halven now rules New Kingdom? Powerful or not, that is too much to be believed."

"You don't need to believe it. We're not here to start a war. We came to assess the Dark Fae threat to our lands and to rescue Lexandra Meinrad."

Jasper's green eyes flashed with anger. "I should have slaughtered that bastard inside the cave when I had the chance."

Lex rubbed her forehead. How was she going to explain Garrin to Jas? "Garrin took me, but he's not the enemy."

"Garrin...the *Dark Prince*?" Jas asked. "We're getting you out of here, Lex. *Now*." Jasper surged toward Lex, but Em and her parents blocked him. They returned to their fighting stances, along with the servants, who'd pulled out their own hidden rapiers and daggers.

Elena held up her hands as though they were armed. Which was scarier than the household's weapons collection. If Elena had fought a Fae army and taken back a kingdom, Lex didn't want to know what kind of magic she possessed.

"Whoa," Lex said. "We're all friends here." She smiled shakily.

"Dark Fae are not friends with those from New Kingdom and Old Kingdom." Em's father's tone was ominous for a guy who'd remained silent until now.

Em turned to her father. "Dark Castle guards tracked us before we arrived, and Lex says they took the prince by force. We lost them along the way, but it won't be long before they find us. We were about to leave when the portal opened."

Em's mother pouted. "Without even a hello?"

Her father rubbed his chin. "What does Casone want with the young woman?"

Em's mother sighed and climbed onto the couch, shoving her sword back into place above the mantel. "Does it matter, my love?" She hopped down with catlike agility and stood beside her husband. "If my cousin is behind this, we must help. You know how insecure he is."

Jas shoved his sword into a sheath on his back. "That doesn't explain why the Dark Prince stole Lex."

Lex shifted her feet. "Actually, it does. Garrin brought me here to help his people. On our way to Dark Kingdom, we ran into my mother, who said the king is responsible for why Dark Fae are trapped in the Land of Ice. We had just confirmed it when Garrin was taken by the king's guards."

Jas tilted his head as though hard of hearing. "You mean to tell me the king's *guards* took the king's son? Now I know they've been lying to you."

Lex sighed. "Fae can't lie, as you well know. Besides, I was there and personally saw them take Garrin."

His lip curled in a snarl. "There are many ways to tell the truth. Who knows what you really saw? It could have been a setup."

Lex's mouth hung open. "And you think my mother is a part of it? According to Isle, the kingdom has been silenced by Casone Branimir."

"Your mother was supposed to retrieve you in the Earth realm years ago," Jasper said. "I assumed she was killed. But you say you've seen her?"

"She is very much alive. The king entombed her in ice. If not for my mother tapping into my power, both Garrin and I would have died in the Great Ravine and my mother would have remained there for all eternity."

At that, Jas swore.

Camille shook her head. "Many have perished in the Great Ravine."

"Where Lex wouldn't have been," Jas retorted, "had the Dark Prince not taken her from my protection."

Camille studied him. "Is that why you hate him? Because he bested you?"

Jas frowned. "I despise the prince because he is selfish and a mercenary for his father." He turned to Lex. "And your story doesn't explain why the king sent his soldiers after his own son."

"No, it doesn't." Lex walked up to Jas and grabbed his hand. "I know you don't trust Garrin, but he has taken care of me. I owe him my life."

"You owe him nothing."

God, her uncle was annoying. "Garrin knows where my mother is, Jas. I'm not leaving without her. Which means we must find Garrin." She would have fought for Garrin no matter what, but she didn't want her overprotective uncle to blow a gasket.

"If you're on the run from palace guards, we have to get you out of here first," the petite blonde named Reese said, and looked up at the Fae that Elena called Keen.

Keen's expression softened at Reese, his shoulder-length white-blond hair a sharp contrast to his chiseled face. "We will get her out, little one. Do not worry." He turned to the room. "We must go somewhere Lex won't be discovered."

Em and her parents looked at each other, then back at the group. "There is no such place," Em's mother said. "Castle alchemists will eventually find us no matter where we hide."

"Perhaps not." Em's father retrieved his snifter from the tray the servant held and took a sip. "The caves above the battlegrounds... Dark Fae of all kinds avoid them."

Em's mother squeezed her eyes closed. "The graves? Must we?"

Her husband lifted his shoulders. "They will find us there too, but it will take longer."

Em shook her head. "Mom, Dad—you stay here. The fewer of us, the smaller our power imprint. Better yet, Dad, take Mom and go in the opposite direction to visit friends."

"Your daughter is correct," Camille said. "Our chances of remaining hidden increase if there are fewer of us." She was older than the other women in Jas's group, who appeared closer to Lex's age. But given they were all Fae or Halven and aged differently than humans, who could be sure? Camille was incredibly beautiful, though, with bright blue eyes, much like Garrin's.

Lex's stomach clenched. The longer she was away from him, the more worried she became. That man hadn't given her an inch of breathing room before they'd arrived in Dark Kingdom, and now she couldn't hold on to him.

Camille tipped her head up abruptly. "Too late. They've found us."

Amund tracked Lex's energy level, and his portal deposited them at a home Garrin had been to as a child. It belonged to a cousin by marriage twice removed, or some such. The room they stood inside was familiar, with faces he recognized—but only one face mattered.

Garrin didn't stop to greet his cousins, or even properly assess the danger. He swept across the room to the woman whose presence consumed his thoughts. "Lexandra."

A tall human—no, worse, *a Halven*—blocked his way before he reached Lex. "I don't think so, buddy." The Halven had shaggy brown hair and a bulkier build than Fae, and he exhibited what Garrin believed to be a strong energy level for a Halven. Amund would know for certain. But all that mattered was that the Halven stood between Garrin and Lex.

Flames rose from Garrin's palms, and he was about to teach the Halven a painful lesson when a blond Fae warrior stepped between them.

"Derek," the blond Fae said. "If I'm not mistaken, this is the Dark Prince. You would do best to give him space."

Derek eyed Garrin. "Dark Prince, eh? He's light for a Dark Prince, don't you think? Though he is rocking black hair, and I don't think any of you Fae have that in our land. You're all pretty pasty."

"Except for me." A woman with black hair and blue eyes stepped forward. "Hello, Garrin."

Garrin glanced at Lex. He wouldn't be reassured until he could speak with her. "Do I know you?" he said to the dark-haired woman. He didn't trust these people, and after the dungeon, he'd lost his patience.

"We met a long time ago. I am Camille."

Her face was familiar, but Garrin didn't have time for this. He shouldered past Derek and reached for Lex's hand. A ripple of sensation flowed up Garrin's arm where they touched. He drew Lex close enough to see the gold flecks in her eyes and tucked her into the cradle of his body. He held the back of her head, relishing the sense of relief that washed over him. "Are you okay?"

Lex wrapped her arms around Garrin's waist. "Em helped me escape before more soldiers came." She leaned back and looked past him to the others. "These are my friends."

"Garrin Branimir is no friend of yours." It was the Fae who'd attempted to block their exit from Earth and forced Garrin and his men to rush into the Land of Ice unprepared. "He kidnapped you!"

"I will have your head," Garrin growled. "Lex could have died, thanks to your interference."

"If she had died, it would have been on *your* head, prince!"

"Jas, stop being an ass," Lex said, and moved out of Garrin's arms to his side.

"He's got you brainwashed, Lex. Don't you see it?" Jas lunged for Garrin, only to be held back by Derek and the blond Fae soldier.

"I'm not an idiot, Jasper. I know what Garrin did and why. Do you?"

Garrin wanted to take Jasper apart piece by piece.

Jasper's gaze flickered away. "It doesn't matter why. He's not to be trusted."

Lex looked at Garrin, and she squeezed his hand.

His chest loosened. The world could cave in around them, but Lex was safe and by his side. He could manage.

Amund—indifferent to the conversation—stared at Camille. "You are the other portal creator."

Instead of addressing Amund, Camille was looking at Garrin. "I am."

"Ooookay," Elena said. "And I thought New Kingdom was bad." She looked at the blond soldier. "Keen, it seems we had nothing to worry about. The Dark King is more interested in destroying his own people than ours."

"For now," Keen said.

"Well, I don't know about any of you," Elena said, "but I think we should do as suggested and get out before the king and his men show up."

Derek must have loosened his hold on Jasper's arm, because he yanked it away, but he didn't go after Garrin again. "Agreed."

Elena looked at an older man who was familiar. "We'll go to the caves you mentioned. Where people are buried."

The grave caves. Garrin looked down thoughtfully. "It is bitterly cold there. And the graves are haunted."

"Could be haunted." The older Fae rubbed his chin. "No one knows for certain."

"Not haunted," Camille said, but she didn't elaborate.

Garrin sighed. "It won't be the first place my father looks, which gives it merit."

Amund nodded. "Considering the size of our kingdom, we would have a few days before they find us. Unless they get lucky with alchemists. Lex's power level is—unique."

"Indeed," Camille said.

"It's a chance we'll have to take." Garrin looked around the room. There were more of Lex's friends than he realized. All were Fae or Halven. "We should leave."

Camille tipped her head up as though reading something in the air. "Roughly forty-five soldiers approach as we speak."

"Fifty," Amund countered. "On the outskirts of the village and rapidly making their way in our direction."

Camille's mouth twisted in annoyance. "Fifty if you include the half a dozen soldiers minutes behind the first forty-five."

Lex dropped Garrin's hand, her shoulders stiffening. "So, a hell of a lot of deadly Fae. Let's leave, but"—she sent Garrin a worried look—"I can't go without my mother."

Garrin looked at Amund, and Amund nodded. "Amund will bring your mother to the caves." He turned to Camille. "If you portaled this many people across the Land of Ice, which is unheard of, I'm assuming you can get us to the caves?"

Camille nodded slowly. "I can. We've all drunk from the tea of the Ancient Allon. Our powers are enhanced, along with the powers of the soldiers we left in charge. Though I hadn't anticipated the trip taking as long as it did. We spent two weeks traversing the Land of Ice on our way to Dark Kingdom. I will require days of rest if I am to portal everyone home."

The Ancient Allon grew through the center of Old Kingdom castle. All allon were infused with Fae magic, but not like the Ancient Allon. According to lore, it held the power of Tirnan. If Camille and the other had drunk from it, that explained their strength and the speed in which Camille had traveled here.

Garrin had questions for Camille and the others, but they could wait until he got Lex somewhere safe. "We leave now."

TWENTY-SIX

Servants handed Lex clothes and food before she stepped through Camille's portal—to a scene she'd hoped to never see again.

Lex was back in her worst nightmare. *Dammit.*

Dark Castle might be antiquated, but at least there were *people.* Out here, in the grave caves, no less, there was only ice and snow-covered mountains. Adding ghosts to the mix was just cruel.

Lex stood at the entrance to a massive cavity Garrin had blown a hole into—literally; he blew on it and the ice and snow that had packed the entrance melted away. "Are you sure this isn't one of the burial sites?" She inched closer to him.

The walls inside the cave were relatively smooth, with a dirt floor and rocks and stones along the inner walls. "This one was a barracks of sorts," he said. "Soldiers lived here during battles."

The place was huge, so Lex could imagine a bunch of seven-foot Fae soldiers hunkering down. Still, burial caves and deadly wars? "There isn't someplace else we can hide? A loyal friend's hut, perhaps?" she asked hopefully.

Garrin's jaw was tense. "I'm afraid not. I would rather you be cared for by my court, but after what Zed did...it's not to be."

"Zed?"

Garrin frowned. "He was the head guard who took me. A friend I've known all of my life."

Lex grabbed his hand. He was being betrayed on all sides. "I'm sorry."

Guilt washed over his face. "It is I who should be sorry. Much as I despise that Jasper creature, he had the right of it. I brought you into harm's way, and I'll do everything within my power to get you out."

Lex gripped his hand tighter. She didn't regret the turn her life had taken. And she didn't regret being with Garrin. In fact, she worried more about his plan for her to leave and what that would mean. Would he go with her? She also wanted to know why his father's soldiers had taken him away. "What did the king's guards do to you?"

His chest fell on a heavy sigh. "They asked me questions."

"What questions?"

He waited for Keen and Derek, the tall men carrying blankets and other rations from Em's house, to pass. "It's not important. Your mother was right about my father; that is all. We must get you out with the help of your friends."

That sounded an awful lot like Garrin didn't plan on going with her. Which didn't sit well. Not well at all. They were in this together. But before Lex could say as much, out of the corner of her eye, she saw Camille slump over a large stone.

Lex rushed over, and Garrin followed. "Are you all right, Camille?" she asked.

Camille tilted her head up and smiled wearily. "I am fine, only tired. The Ancient Allon enhances my powers, but carrying power-heavy Fae and Halven across a kingdom after traversing the Land of Ice is draining."

Garrin called to Zirel, and the healer ran over.

"Can you help her?" Lex asked.

Zirel shook his head slowly. "I cannot give her back her magic. Only time can do that. But I can ease her exhaustion." Zirel placed his hand on Camille's back and rubbed up and down.

She relaxed for a moment, then suddenly looked up, her gaze intent on something beyond the entrance of the cave. "Two Fae are about to emerge. It could be Amund, but I cannot be certain. Too drained..."

Garrin shoved Lex behind him and unsheathed a sword attached to his back—right as Amund stumbled into the cave, followed by Lex's mother.

"Mom!" Lex rounded Garrin and embraced Isle. The hug wasn't as familiar as it should be, but Lex drew comfort in knowing her mother was safe.

Isle stepped back and glared at Garrin. "Did I not tell you?"

Garrin put away his sword, his expression a mix of frustration and anger. "You were correct." He scanned the people inside the cave. "Now that we are all here, it is time we hide our presence." He waved his hand across the entrance of the cave, and a wall of ice and snow formed, enclosing them inside. His gaze darted between Lex and the wall as though he were realizing too late his mistake. "Does the barrier bother you?"

Garrin had witnessed her anxieties one too many times

during their travels. But she didn't experience the same panic she once did. She was never going to be a fan of snow, but it no longer caused her fight-or-flight response to go into hyperdrive. "I'm okay."

"We're all okay," Isle said sarcastically. "Now, can we get back to what you learned, Dark Prince? What is your father's plan?"

Em walked up to Lex right as Garrin was about to answer. "It is cold, and we should change."

Lex met Garrin's gaze, but he said nothing.

Was he really not going to answer in front of her? "Did you discover the king's motives?"

Garrin sent Lex a soft smile. "Go with Em. She will show you to one of the inner chambers."

Lex's mouth parted in disbelief. She glanced at her mother, who'd turned her back to Lex.

Were they truly going to keep her out of this?

The cave was freezing, and Lex was shivering because neither she nor Em had changed out of their wet clothing before they left for the caves. It turned out sharing a coat only offered partial coverage from the elements. That didn't mean she wanted to leave the conversation. But Garrin simply waited.

Isle walked over to Camille, and Camille's expression softened with affection.

Neither Isle nor Garrin were going to talk. At least, not with Lex around. "I know what you're doing," she said to Garrin. "If I'm the one in danger, I should know the facts."

Garrin gave her a small nod. "Understood."

Did he? Did he truly?

Lex was stronger in Dark Kingdom, and she wanted to be a part of the solution and not stuck in the shadows anymore. But her mother was angry at Garrin and blamed him for everything, and Garrin hadn't been acting right since the king's soldiers whisked him away. Lex wasn't going to get anything out of them if she pushed now.

She shot a warning look at Garrin, signaling that this conversation wasn't over, then followed Em out of the main cave and down a low, narrow passageway where a half-dozen offshoots of deeper caves existed.

"This place is a labyrinth," Lex muttered as she hunched to avoid a silvery stalactite.

Em looked around. "I've never been here, but my parents have spoken of it. The quicker we leave, the better."

Lex and Em chose one of the smaller offshoot caves and changed into clothes similar to what Lex had on, only dry.

Lex shivered at the warmth of clean, dry fabric. "I've never felt anything so good."

Em flung the soaked dress she'd been wearing disgustedly to the side and tugged out two heavy coats from the bag she'd been carrying. "You won't need this inside the cave. Our clothes are enhanced to keep us warmer, but keep the coat near."

"In case of what?"

Em bit her lip. "If we need to leave suddenly, you won't want to be outside in the elements without it."

Lex clutched the coat to her chest. "Good point."

"Do not worry. The prince is a master strategist. In his short life, he's helped the king maintain power through two wars and survived many trips through the Land of Ice. He will ensure we get you out safely."

"What about you, Em? If the king knows you've helped me, which he must at this point, you're in danger too."

Em smiled. "You've met my mother and father. There's a reason my parents are related to the king and haven't lost their heads. They are ruthless, and the king is indebted to them."

"Indebted how?"

Em frowned, her gaze turning inward. "That I do not know, but I know it to be so. I fear my parents may have helped the king in ways that haven't always been in our people's best interest."

Lex thought about that a moment. "They might not have had much choice."

Em nodded. "Perhaps. Even so, I'm at your service."

Lex touched Em's arm. "You're my only friend, Em."

She shook her head slowly. "Not true. You have a friend in the prince. More than a friend. He is much changed since he came home. I've never seen him devoted to any woman. And he is devoted to you."

Lex didn't know about *devoted*, but there was something between them that grew with each day.

"Come," Em said. "Let us return so you can discover what the king is up to."

"Exactly!" Lex said. "Why did you pull me away during a crucial conversation?"

They started down the cave's narrow inner corridor. "More will be disclosed if they do not fear worrying you," Em said. "And we can always pry it out of the others later."

Lex stopped and stared at her friend. "You're very devious."

Em laughed. "Indeed. All those years spent in the prince's court."

Lex looped her arm through Em's, and they continued through the cave maze until they made it to the larger cavern where the others were getting organized. Except for Garrin and Isle, who were glaring at each other.

"Oh, no. What are they doing now?" The antagonism

between Garrin and Isle wouldn't do. They needed to work together if they were to leave together.

Em frowned. "Don't underestimate your influence on the prince. He will listen to you." She released Lex's arm and tipped her chin in Garrin's direction. "Go to him."

"I don't know about influence, but I'll do my best to keep those two from brawling."

Lex took a deep breath and approached Garrin. Her mother sent Lex a tense smile and walked away. "I see you're getting along well with my mom."

Garrin's brow furrowed. "Ah, I see. You are jesting."

"Why are you and Isle fighting?"

Garrin absently brushed hair off her shoulder, the back of his warm knuckles skimming her neck and sending shivers down her body. "Your mother is a fine person, but her experience with my father has tainted her opinion of me. I do not blame her."

"Won't that be a problem? What if something goes wrong? How are we going to safely get out of here if none of us trust each other?"

"It matters most that you and I trust each other, yes?"

Warmth suffused her face at the intimate look in his eyes. "Yes."

A long moment passed before Lex realized she and Garrin stood so close that she could feel the heat blasting off him. And that it had grown quiet inside the cave. The others, attempting to look busy, glanced every now and then in Garrin and Lex's direction.

Garrin's gaze slid down her body, his expression distracted.

Her stomach wobbled and she stepped back a few inches. She cleared her throat. "How long can we stay here before your father finds us?"

He scratched the stubble along his jaw that had begun to grow. "A few days, at most. Our magic isn't as sophisticated as your human GPS, but your power level is unique. It won't take my father long to discover where we are."

Not for the first time, Lex realized how much danger she was putting them in. "First of all, I'm not human. Second, when have you used GPS?"

Garrin picked up a round stone and weighed it in his hand. "The Earth realm has many useful tools. I used everything at my disposal to find you."

"Aren't you worried your dad will find us before we can leave?"

"We have no choice but to wait until Camille has rested. Chances are that between her and Amund, and their ability to detect magic, we'll be long gone before anyone finds us."

Lex's shoulders loosened. "That's good. What should we do in the meantime?"

Garrin gathered more rocks and set them in a large circle at the center of the cave. "We plot our escape. Nothing can be done to save my people in our present state. We must leave the Land of Ice and my father, and beg assistance from another kingdom. There are others like Amund and Camille, with the ability to create portals, but not many. And none as powerful as what my people need to escape Dark Kingdom."

He set another stone in the circle and looked at his work. "Thousands live in Dark Kingdom. I'm afraid of what my father would do if we left anyone behind. We need a way to get everyone out at once. And right now, I know of no way." Garrin frowned.

She hadn't missed that he'd said "our escape." Lex placed her hand on his arm. "We will find a way, but are you sure everyone will come?"

"Most wish to move freely between our land and the other kingdoms. And Earth. There are those who wish to venture off this realm."

"Is that a good idea?"

Garrin looked at her, his gaze sultry. "Certainly not."

Lex swallowed. She might be Fae, but it was still new to her. As far as she was concerned, she was extremely vulnerable to this man's magnetism. What sort of havoc would beautiful Fae let loose on Earth cause?

A hell of a lot. Halven—there would be a shitload of new Halven.

But then Lex thought of Elena and Derek, and Keen's girlfriend, Reese. They were half Fae, and Lex felt inferior beside their confidence and capability. Maybe more Halven wasn't such a bad thing.

Garrin glanced across the cave at Elena as though reading Lex's mind. "It is useful that the Halven queen of New Kingdom and the Old Kingdom king are among us. I'm told they detected me and my men entering their lands on my way to find you, and Jasper asked for their assistance in getting you back. Presumably, they wished to know what Dark Fae were up to and if we were a threat. Which my father most certainly is." He let out a long sigh. "Now I must convince their courts of a truce with Dark Kingdom. Elena is not popular among her people, and Keen is only newly crowned. A deal must be brokered before the kingdoms will allow Dark Fae into their lands."

He looked at the circle he'd created as though insuring its symmetry, then back at her. "I don't know how much you recall of our history, but brokering a deal with those who have traditionally been our enemy will not come easily. Dark Kingdom rulers were inhospitable even before we were locked away." He dusted off his hands on his pants.

"Perhaps someday I can return with an army and deal with my father. No matter what, Dark Fae must come first."

That sounded an awful lot like he was going to shelter her from danger and put himself in it. This was her land too. Her kingdom. And she felt a profound urge to rid it of tyranny. "We can determine the specifics later," she said, and his mouth turned down. "What did you learn about your father?"

"Enough to know he will do anything to get his hands on you." Garrin stepped closer and towered over her. "I will never allow that, Lexandra."

Truth be told, the Dark King's influence over the land was scary. Garrin had indicated Fae kings and queens needed support from their followers, and yet Casone Branimir had manipulated his kingdom and pulled the wool over the eyes of most everyone.

"It's not safe for you to fight your father. The soldiers and men in robes who took you are loyal to him."

Garrin lifted an eyebrow. "I allowed them to take me because I wanted to draw attention away from you. And to discover who controlled them. For now, the soldiers are loyal to my father, but my father has betrayed them too, if everything your mother says is true. I would be no better than my father should I allow him to continue as he has."

Zirel walked up and dragged a heavy hand down the top of his head. It had been a long day. "The camp is set up, my prince. We should rest for a few hours."

Garrin moved toward the entrance and waved a hand over the ice and snow he'd sealed the cave off with earlier, thickening it and darkening the cave further.

"And that is why he is the Ice Prince," Isle said forbiddingly.

Lex turned to see her mother standing across the circle

of stones, staring at Garrin. She looked at Lex. "I sense the attachment, daughter, but never trust the Dark Prince. He is his father's son."

Garrin stood off to the side, speaking quietly with Zirel and strategically lighting small, suspended balls of blue fire around the cave. Keen and Reese walked up to one and raised their hands above it while continuing their conversation. Jas snarled at Garrin's blue fireballs, but he moved closer to the heat too.

Lex turned toward Isle. "You're wrong, Mom. Garrin is nothing like his father. He cares about his people."

"Garrin has been his father's mercenary since he was a boy. When the time comes, he will not turn on the Dark King."

Lex's memories of Dark Kingdom were as solid as swiss cheese. She remembered bits and pieces, but nothing concrete. Certainly nothing about Garrin and the royal court and his mercenary past. Even so, she didn't believe what her mother said. And that felt wrong, continuing to disagree with a mother with whom she'd only just reconnected. So she walked away, not wanting to give in to her mom's antagonism.

Lex was squeezing her hands, concerned about her mother's distrust of Garrin, when he walked up to her.

"Everything okay?"

She nodded. "Thank you for keeping us warm."

He glanced around. "I wish it were more. For now, this will have to do." He waved his hand to the side, and a large fire roared inside the circle of stones he'd built.

Light flickered off his handsome profile, and her resolve strengthened. He might be an Ice Prince, as her mother said, but he was an Ice Prince who created fire. He wasn't this cold shell of a person Isle believed him to be.

Her mother stood just outside the central firepit, arms crossed, studying Lex and watching everything that passed between her and Garrin.

Garrin caught Lex looking at her mother. "What has happened?"

Lex huffed out a sigh. "Isle believes you'll hurt me."

His brow furrowed ever so slightly. "Is that your opinion?"

She held his gaze. "You would never hurt me."

He let out a deep breath and reached for her hand. "Nor will I allow harm to come to you." He looked around at the others talking quietly in small groups while Camille slept to regain her portal abilities. "Will you rest a while with me?"

Lex swallowed. Rest, as in lie down? Next to him?

What was she thinking? She'd slept beside Garrin for weeks. This was no different.

Only it felt different. Now that they were in Dark Kingdom, Lex was not only strongly aware of her physical attraction to Garrin, but also her emotional connection to him as well. Lying beside each other alone left room for those feelings to manifest into something more.

Camille was passed out in a corner, and Zirel and Amund quietly talked near the entrance of the cave. Jas and the others had moved to the central firepit and sat around it in quiet discussion. "Where should we go?"

Garrin led her toward the back of the main cave, down the narrow passageway, and to the alcoves where Lex and Em had changed. He gestured to one of them. "Here?"

Lex entered, and Garrin walked to the back. He took off his coat and splayed it on the hard ground. His gaze grew hooded. "I would like to hold you, if that is all right?"

"We don't have to pretend to be engaged. You don't

have to pretend to-to like me," she stammered. "Everyone here knows who I really am."

He studied her. "There is nothing fanciful about my feelings for you. You know that by now, yes?"

"Do I?"

He looked away. "I took you from your home and nearly got you killed, not to mention the danger you face inside my kingdom. I suppose you wouldn't." He stood and moved to her, gently pulling her closer. Lex was tall, but Garrin was easily a foot taller. "I should have predicted my father's spies inside the castle. I know how his mind works. I am sorry for the trouble I have caused you."

"Spies?"

He glanced at the entrance of their small cave and beyond, where the others resided. "Not Em, as far as I can tell." He tilted his head. "You know, she has asked to be your lady. She no longer wishes to be a part of my court, but a member of yours."

Lex laughed. "Court? I'm not royalty."

He gave her a slow, leisurely look that ended on her mouth. "You are a queen in my eyes."

"That was super cheesy." She licked her suddenly dry lips. "Are you trying to seduce me?"

"Only if you want to be seduced." His finger grazed her jaw, causing a flurry of sparks inside her chest.

"I might," she said in a breathy voice. What was the Dark Prince doing to her?

Garrin waved his hand at the entrance, and an ice partition formed, blocking off the smaller cave.

She felt it. The magic that rushed through him when he drew on his powers and touched her at the same time. "Wow."

"The shield is thin and can be taken down at any time. I thought we might want a small amount of privacy."

Her eyes returned to his face and his mouth inches away. "Privacy is good. My surprise wasn't at the ice wall, but at the magic I sensed when you made the barrier."

He studied her face. "It is good that you are getting better at sensing your ability. At some point, you will have mastery of it, but I'm afraid that won't be soon enough for our escape." He gently pushed a lock of hair from her face. "Camille will regain her abilities by tomorrow or the next day, and between her and Amund, we will get you and your friends out of Dark Kingdom."

Lex frowned. "My powers were supposed to help your people. I feel useless."

He shook his head. "You cannot help anyone if you are harmed."

"There has to be a way."

He cradled her face with his hands. "Anything that pits you against my father, I will not allow."

The heat from his palms was intoxicating. "You're very bossy, you know that?"

"I am very protective of what is mine." He leaned down and softly kissed her, his lips lingering above hers.

Her heart thumped in her chest, and she leaned up and returned the kiss, pressing her body closer.

Garrin tilted her head and took her mouth fully. He tugged at her chin and parted her lips, his tongue taking possession in a way that had her body trembling.

Body trembles? Could she be any more virginal?

Garrin pulled back. "I won't let anything happen to you." He looked intently into her eyes. "You understand that, yes?"

Lex nodded, but she really felt like shaking her head.

She didn't understand why Garrin desired her. She was powerless and, thus far, had been more burden than help. Her mother said he wouldn't put Lex above his people, but that seemed exactly what he was doing. "What if I decide to protect you?"

He kissed the corner of her mouth. "That is not how it's done here."

She tilted her head back, but he leaned closer, focused on her lips, undeterred. "Why not?"

Garrin continued to pepper the sides of her mouth and chin with light, seductive kisses. "Because Fae men take care of their women."

TWENTY-SEVEN

Garrin covered Lex's mouth, drugging her with his kisses. Not that Lex was complaining. "Fae men take care of their women, do they?" she managed to get out.

His lips slid to her neck. "Always."

"Em and the other women in your court seemed pretty competent at protecting themselves."

"They are." He nudged her chin up with his nose, giving him better access to her neck. "I trained them."

Warmth filled Lex's limbs and her mind went blank. When she caught her breath, Garrin's hands were sliding down her sides, his palms causing heat to flare up wherever they touched. "I'm not a part of your court," she said. "I'm not one of your women."

"You are my *only* woman."

She was done for if he kept talking like that. "You sleep with other women too," Lex said, trying to keep her head on straight and remember her place in all of this.

His expression turned to one of chagrin. "Not all of

them. And not in years. I've been too busy searching for you."

"But you would have slept with them if you could have."

"I could now. I choose to be with you." He guided her to the ground and the coat he'd laid out. "You're the only woman I think about. The only one I wish by my side. My father raised me to believe it my duty to expand the royal family. Until I met you, I saw no reason not to. But my father's actions have caused my mother a great deal of pain. I see that now. I will not hurt you. Not for anything. Not even for duty."

His eyes were dark inside the cave, his pupils nearly covering the iris. But she sensed his sincerity.

She pecked him on the lips. "I would mind, you know. If you were with another. But I do admire your court women. They are brave." She glanced up at the ceiling. "Maybe a little too obsessed with you, but I can't blame them. I might be slightly obsessed too."

"Only slightly?" Garrin resumed kissing her neck and nudged the top of her tunic until his soft lips pressed against the tops of her breasts, his hand cupping the bottom. "*Hmm.* We'll have to work on that. I want you as desirous of me as I am of you."

Lex exhaled on a shaky breath while her heart pounded in her chest as though she were sprinting. No need to unnecessarily stroke his Fae ego, though. "I could be persuaded."

"You are so beautiful... And so mine."

Lex looked down skeptically. "You keep saying that."

He laughed. "You doubt it? Human women are strange. I've never given this much attention to another, and yet you question my feelings?"

Presently, she was pushing her chest into his palm, so clearly, she wasn't stressing about it. Still… "First of all, I'm Fae, in case you've forgotten. Second, attention is one thing. Emotions are another."

His talented fingers continued their delicious torture of her breast. "Do not doubt my feelings for you, Lexandra. Whether we give in to desire or not, you are mine."

~

GARRIN WOULD WAIT centuries to be with Lex. Thankfully, it appeared he wouldn't have to.

Lex sank her fingers into his hair, pulling his head up from where he'd been showering her decolletage with attention and delivered a kiss of her own. "You're mine too."

Garrin fit himself more fully over Lex, his hands running over her body, kissing her with a passion he'd never experienced. He ran his nose along the soft skin of her neck, moving his lips up and across her cheeks and seeking her mouth. Until a surge of energy filled him, and a loud crack sounded.

Garrin had just lifted his head when ice rained out from behind. He threw his arms over Lex.

"What the…" Lex wiggled and tried to escape his hold. "What just happened?"

Garrin looked back and saw the faces of their friends, their chests rising and falling as though they'd run at the sound.

The ice seal he'd created at the entrance of the small cove to provide privacy had burst into a thousand pieces.

The crook to Amund's mouth indicated he knew exactly what Garrin and Lex had been doing. "Is everything okay?"

Garrin rolled off Lex until he crouched in front of her, his protective instincts revved. "Yes, but…" He looked at Lex. "It seems Lex's powers are growing."

"*My* powers?" Lex was sitting up and staring at him now.

"Did you not feel it?" he asked.

She blushed. "I felt…something."

His lips twitched. "The ice wall should have held. Most cannot detect when another uses their ability, let alone define that energy and re-create it. Earlier you said you sensed my power when I made the wall. I felt you push the energy back at me before the wall shattered."

"But I wasn't trying to do anything." She bit her lip. "I might have *touched* it when we…"

Garrin waved off the crowd. "You may go."

Isle remained, ignoring the command. "She sensed your power and mimicked it, breaking apart the ice. What I wish to know is why you felt it necessary to put up a wall separating my daughter from the rest of us? Are you attempting to ruin her?"

"Oh my God!" Lex said. "I'm an adult, Mom."

Isle huffed out a sigh. "You are a powerful Fae who could rule a kingdom. You must think of your future."

Lex scrambled to her feet. "I don't want to rule a kingdom, Mom."

Isle murmured something about *back in her day*, but she cut off her words. "In any case," she said, and stared at Garrin, "my daughter consciously drew on your ability like a true puppet master."

Lex shook her head. "I wouldn't exactly say *consciously*. I wasn't thinking about taking down a wall."

"But you felt Garrin's power—were 'touching it,' as you said?"

Lex glanced at Garrin, and another blush swept her face.

Isle caught the exchange and rolled her eyes. "You can use your senses to manipulate others' powers." She paced the alcove, and Garrin's annoyance grew. He wished to be alone with Lex, not lectured. "You simply don't understand what you are capable of."

Garrin's eyes narrowed. "How do you know so much about Lex's ability? Few in our history have ever possessed it."

Isle straightened, her chin tilting up in the same manner Garrin had seen Lex do. "I've known of my daughter's power from when she was very young. I am her mother; do you truly believe I would not understand it? And no one is capable of puppet mastery the way Lex is."

He looked at Lex. "You would have shown signs at a young age. We all do. Do you have memories of your ability?"

Lex shook her head. "Nothing. My memory is spotty at best."

"You don't need to," he said. "In time, we'll do everything we can to recover your memory." Garrin would get to the bottom of the magic Isle had used to keep her daughter in the dark. His parents had their faults, but any Fae capable of wiping her child's memory and abandoning her could never be innocent. "For now, we will focus on your power if you are beginning to draw on it. It should be safe here, away from the castle."

Isle stepped forward and grabbed Lex's hand. "Darling. What were you doing when you drew from the Dark Prince's powers?"

Lex looked at Garrin. "Uh..."

"We were talking," Garrin said. "Intimately."

Isle glared at him. "I can imagine." She turned to her daughter. "But what were you feeling?"

"Mom, I'd rather work with Garrin on this."

Isle dropped Lex's hand and took a step back. "I see."

Lex stumbled forward. "Please don't be offended. It's just that I've spent a lot of time with Garrin."

Isle's gaze slid to his. "That is what I'm afraid of."

TWENTY-EIGHT

True to his word, Garrin had held Lex as they grabbed a few hours of sleep. And that was all they'd done.

What in the hell? Now that her hormones had been activated, why did people decide to show up and ruin the moment? Lex had wanted to investigate these new sensations Garrin brought out in her. Only she'd accidentally shattered their privacy wall during her exploration.

Somehow, Garrin had managed to pass out after the entire cave caught Lex and Garrin in a compromising position. It had felt amazing to be held by Garrin as night turned to dawn, but whatever happened to men not being able to think of anything besides sex? Instead, it had been Lex who slept fitfully, aching to do more than sleep, and now that they were awake, she was still thinking about it.

Lex sat around the large firepit with Garrin and the others as they plotted their escape. But not everyone was plotting. Some were preparing in other ways.

The sound of swords clashing rent the air as Amund

deflected a strike from Em while eating Allon bread from her parents' house.

Em glared at the food in Amund's hand and thrust forward with more force. "Keep it up, portal maker, and I'll cut you into ribbons."

Amund took another bite. "Still waiting for you to give me a reason to use two hands."

Lex tilted her head toward Garrin beside her. "I've never seen Em upset."

Garrin glanced up from the pebble and dirt map he'd been creating with Zirel. He took in his former courtier and Amund for the first time, and his brow lifted. "I don't know Em as well as some of my other courtiers, but she's not known to anger easily. I wonder…"

At that moment, Em must have reached her limit for patience because she growled like a wild animal, levitated, and roundhouse-kicked Amund on the side of the head.

He stumbled and shook his head.

Lex stood abruptly, along with Garrin and Zirel. All eyes in the cave were on Em, who was back on solid ground and smirking at Amund.

Garrin chuckled. "Told you not to tease my courtiers."

A smile slowly curved Amund's lips, and he threw his food aside. "No more playtime. Now we fight."

Apparently, that was when the real fighting began. Because Em started hopping all over the cave, jumping off walls, levitating for brief moments, and deflecting Amund's quick swordsmanship.

"Umm…should we worry?" Lex said.

Garrin had resumed his mapmaking. "She can handle him."

"I'm talking about Amund. Em looks *pissed*."

Em made another impressive leap, kicking off the wall

and the ceiling before doing a backflip and landing on the ground.

Lex's jaw went slack. "Since when can you levitate?" she said to Em.

Em was crouched, waiting for Amund's counterattack. Her face scrunched. "I can only do it for a second or two, the same as my other ability."

"Does everyone from Dark Kingdom have multiple powers?"

"Many do." This from Keen, who stood across the cave observing Garrin's meticulous mapmaking, commenting on strategy from time to time. He lifted his chin in Zirel's direction. "Healer and partial empath." Then across to Jas. "Glamourist and illusionist."

Jas snickered. "I made you plain-looking on Earth, but even then, you attracted attention. I created illusions of you tripping and knocking into people to put others off."

Lex held up her hand. "Are you telling me the reason girls in college hated me is because you made them see things they weren't actually seeing?"

Jas sipped a jug of *brune* someone had smuggled in. "Precisely. The men were less deterred, so I got more creative with them."

Lex's jaw dropped. "I hate you. No wonder I had no friends... Wait, what did you show men?"

Jas looked up as though sifting through his metal Rolodex. "One particularly ardent male started trailing you incessantly, so I showed him you picking your no—"

"You did not! What the hell, Jasper?"

"You have my respect," Garrin said to Jas.

Lex's gaze darted between the two men. "I have PTSD from students ostracizing me, and you're happy he kept men away?"

"Certainly," Garrin said without looking up.

She smacked him in the arm, and he grinned.

Lex turned to her mother. "Did you have anything to do with this?"

Isle stared at the fire. "It was necessary."

Jas frowned at some move Garrin had made on the map. "You may not like my methods, but it was how I kept you hidden on Earth."

Lex wrapped her arms around her knees. Necessary or not, she was going to be scarred for the rest of her life thanks to her loving family. "Did you take away my powers too?"

Jas looked up. "I'm good, but I'm not that good. Your mother enlisted alchemists for that part."

Isle straightened her back, her chin squared. "Someone at the castle owed me a favor."

Garrin set down his map markers. "You didn't think it would put your daughter's life at risk asking for help from a castle alchemist?"

Isle glared. "No, prince, I did not. The alchemist was in love with Camille. At the time, he was also extremely angry at your father and would have done anything for her and her friends."

Lex sensed anger boiling off Garrin. Interesting though the conversation was, tempers were rising. "What about your power, Keen?" She'd ask her mother more about that alchemist thing later.

Keen grinned. "I have the power of telepathy."

"You can hear our thoughts?"

"Indeed," Keen said, and grinned, a twinkle in his eye.

"Oh. *Ohh.*" Crap. Images of Lex and Garrin before everyone had walked in on them last night crossed her mind, and her face flushed. Was Keen reading her thoughts and how much she desired Garrin?

"Yes," Keen answered.

Lex sat up straight. "Stop that!"

Garrin stood, his bright eyes pinning the Old Kingdom king. "Mess with my woman once more, and it will be the last thing you do."

Reese lifted her head and yawned after a nap she'd been taking on Keen's shoulder. "Lover, you are being super annoying right now."

"Me annoying? Never," Keen said.

"It isn't polite to embarrass people," she said. "Don't make me teach you a lesson." Reese stood and started walking toward the back of the cave, her expression mischievous.

Keen's gaze trailed Reese, and the apples of his cheeks turned red. He slowly stalked her as she giggled and disappeared down the corridor.

"What just happened?" Lex murmured.

Garrin crouched and added another pebble to his map. "Reese can make people feel whatever she wants." Garrin chuckled. "She used it to distract him."

Lex's eyes went wide. Was he talking about what she thought he was talking about?

Lex leaned over until she was inches away. "What sort of distracting?"

Garrin stared at her mouth, his nostrils flaring lightly. "Can you not guess?"

"I might need more lessons, since my boyfriend fell asleep on me last night."

He dipped his head closer and nuzzled her neck. "I wasn't sure if it was too soon. And your mother's threat of death was a deterrent."

"You're afraid of my mother?"

He pulled her closer until her hip touched his side and continued nuzzling her neck. "I do not wish to get on the bad side of the mother of my girlfriend."

"She already hates you by nature of your paternity."

He leaned back, and a disturbed look crossed his face. "I suppose that is true."

Lex clung to his muscular arm. "She doesn't know you. She still believes you're like your father."

"He is like his father," Isle said, clearly listening in on their conversation.

Lex shot her mother a glare.

Garrin tucked her hair behind her ear and cradled her cheek with his palm, forcing her to look at him. "Would you like me to stay awake tonight?"

Lex glanced in her mother's direction, but she'd finally gotten the hint and walked off to talk with Camille. "Only if you want."

He leaned over and kissed her softly. "I want."

INSTEAD OF RETURNING to their love cave, Garrin insisted on finishing details of their escape plan. Not exactly romantic, but he was trying to keep them alive, so *point taken*.

Lex joined Em and Amund to get pointers on how to fight—and to try something she'd thought about earlier. "Do that levitating thing again, Em. Only do it when I say this time, okay?"

Em glanced over while blocking a blow from Amund. "Why?"

"I want to try something."

Em sidestepped a slashing sword maneuver by Amund,

then made a vicious cut at his body, which he managed to deflect. That was how all their attacks ended—a hairsbreadth from severing a limb.

"For the record, watching you two is stressing me out."

Their movements were fast as hell. Faster than the battle practice Lex had witnessed inside Garrin's court. But in this battle play, Em seemed to be giving it everything she had.

Energy wafted off Em, so much so that Lex could easily detect it. Not so much Em's power level, which only Amund and Camille were good at reading, but the cocktail of energy that made up her unique magic. And the magic she used to levitate was different from what she used to Blend.

Lex saw her window of opportunity and yelled, "Now!"

Em leapt into the air and levitated. Only this time, she didn't fall a second or two later. She remained rooted on invisible strings powered by Lex.

Em's arms swung in the air, and she nearly dropped her sword when her natural landing didn't come.

Lex blinked, her eyes burning, unable to hold the magic.

A few seconds later, Em landed on the ground, her sword at her side. She looked over in surprise. "Can you boost my magic and someone else's at the same time?"

Lex's hands shook as her mind relaxed and she regained her strength. "I don't know." The amount of concentration it had taken to hold Em's magic was intense.

She glanced at Garrin, but he was already staring at her. And he wasn't alone.

Everyone in the room was staring. The only person who didn't appear surprised was her mother, standing off to the side with a smug look on her face.

"Do it again." Em bent her knees in a ready stance.

"Reading your power and pushing it back at you took

mental energy, Em. I don't know if I can do it right away. Pretty sure I can't hold you there and boost someone else's power at the same time."

Isle stepped forward. "You can, if you split your mind."

Had she lost it? "I'm a decent multitasker, but I'm pretty sure I can't do that," Lex said.

"As a human, no, but you are no longer human, daughter. Only your memory tells you that you are."

Garrin sent Isle a cutting look. "And who is to blame for that? You wiped her consciousness, leaving scraps behind."

"I did what any mother would—I saved my child's life. From *your* father, Dark Prince, if you recall. Even if my daughter had been fully grown and capable of her magic, she could not have stood against the Dark King and his soldiers."

Isle paced the cave. "There was a reason I hid, and not simply because I was of noble blood and Casone would have wished me to be a part of his court. I feared your father finding Lex and discovering who she was. Of him discovering *what* she was."

Lex pinched her eyes closed. What was her mother talking about now?

Isle stopped pacing and leveled a look at Garrin. "Regardless of my desperate actions, your father figured it out. When, I do not know. I thought I had hidden us well, but I worry now it wasn't me Casone wanted the day he buried me. Zirel's kin said the Dark King heard tale of my daughter—and of her father."

Garrin's brow furrowed. "Who was her father?"

Lex huffed out a breath. "Whoever it was, he wasn't in my life."

"Of course he was," Isle said. "He simply was not of this realm, preferring to watch over you from afar."

"A human?" Garrin shook his head. "Impossible. Her power is like none in our land. We've already determined she isn't Halven but full Fae."

Isle raised one eyebrow. "No, not Halven."

Garrin's jaw clenched. "Speak plainly. There is no other realm besides Tirnan and the Earth realm."

"Is there not?" Isle slowly looked around the room. "There is a realm from which we all hail. From which our forefathers came."

Garrin blinked, and his gaze shot to Lex. "You mean to say she...she is..."

"My husband Kushiel was sent down to condemn the Dark King. Lex's father was an angel."

TWENTY-NINE

Garrin shook his head slowly. "Impossible." Or was it? Lex's eyes and their glow. Her unusual power...

"Is it impossible?" Isle said rhetorically.

"Angels no longer come to our realm. They haven't for thousands of years," he said, attempting to place logic where there was none.

"Until your father committed a most heinous crime," Isle spat.

"What crime?" Garrin shouted, his patience dissolved.

Isle moved beside Lex, who was staring at her mother in shock. "Your father hadn't produced a child after hundreds of years of marriage to his first wife, Dark Prince, so he sent her away. In the middle of winter."

Garrin looked down, trying to interpret her words. "He sent her to live with others. It isn't compassionate, but there was no crime committed."

Isle chuckled darkly. "Not to live with others. He sent her to live in the Land of Ice on *her own*."

Garrin looked up and blinked. "To fend for herself?"

"Casone ordered it a crime to the crown should anyone assist her. Her body was found many months later," Isle said, stone-faced. "No one can survive the Land of Ice in the middle of winter without support. His noble-born wife was no exception."

Garrin couldn't believe what he was hearing. "You speak of the murder of an innocent woman, Isle Meinrad. Of the murder of a royal ordained to lead our land."

"Indeed." Isle gripped her daughter's hand, and Garrin frowned. "And now you know why I must protect Lex from you and your father at any cost."

Not from him. Never from him.

Garrin looked around the room. "Who else has heard this?"

Each face was more blank than the last. Until Garrin reached Amund's hulking frame. "I have, Your Highness. Nothing for certain. And only amongst Newlanders. Nothing from our land."

Camille carefully stepped forward. Garrin hadn't noticed her partially hidden behind the others. "What Isle says is true."

All eyes turned to Camille, even Isle's, whose look of surprise could not be masked.

"I was acquainted with your father before I escaped Dark Kingdom," Camille said. "The rumors of his ruthlessness in siring an heir are true. I never knew his first wife, but I knew y-your...mother."

Camille's whole body shook, whether from lingering weakness or the topic, Garrin didn't know. "The angel Kushiel punished Casone, as Isle said, for what he did to his first wife by placing powerful magic over the land, preventing Dark Fae from leaving. I wasn't alive at the time, but it is whispered to be true."

History lessons and texts swam through Garrin's mind. All of them missing evidence of what Isle and Camille said. "Why would an angel punish our people? If my father were to blame, why not harm or destroy him?"

Camille folded her delicate hands at her waist and looked down. "There is no greater punishment for Casone Branimir than failure. It is said that by making him responsible for his people's misery, Kushiel served him his greatest sentence."

Garrin felt the blood drain from his body. His father's pride was a powerful thing.

If what they said was true, it would make his father a monster. One who callously murdered his first wife and silenced all those who knew about it. "My father couldn't get away with such a past without lying."

"Your father re-created the past in a farce that isn't truth nor lie," Isle said. "The truth lies in the details, which have been hidden. What is left is what Casone wants everyone to believe. And now, here we are." She flung out her hand at their surroundings. "The Dark King wanted Lexandra, daughter of my husband who punished him, and you have spoon-fed her to him. Your father will have her destroyed."

"I'm not afraid," Lex said, and held Garrin's gaze. "Okay, that's not entirely true. The king scares the crap out of me. But I'll fight with you. Someone has to stop your father."

His nostrils flared, and he stared at Isle. "Why didn't you mention any of this earlier?"

Her chest rose on an angry inhale. "If you recall, I told you not to take Lex to the castle. You didn't listen. I do not trust you. Why would I tell you more than you needed to know?"

Lᴇx ᴡᴀᴛᴄʜᴇᴅ Garrin run stiff fingers through his hair, his expression a mask of anger. "You told me not to take Lex to the castle," he said to her mother, "but you failed to mention why. Lex had just survived a near-death experience in the Land of Ice. Without details of the king's perfidy, the castle was the logical escape."

Energy filled the room, and goosebumps rose on Lex's arms. Garrin was pissed. And the room felt it too, because bodies shifted in what appeared to be preparation for a fight.

"There's a lot of heat in here," she said. "Why don't we all just take a breath?"

Garrin's death stare on Isle didn't relax one bit.

Lex moved in front of him and ran her palm up his chest until she touched his jaw with her fingertips.

His eyes dropped to her face and lingered. After a moment he said, "Dangerous trick, Lexandra."

"Trick?" The only thing dangerous in the cave was Garrin's banked anger.

"Your touch," he said, and gripped her fingers, tucking her close. "I cannot resist it."

Amund re-sheathed his sword, which Lex hadn't noticed him pull out, and walked toward Garrin. "There is much mystery surrounding your father's reign. Many wars. Many noblemen killed in battle or gone missing. It isn't only Lex's memory that has missing pieces."

Garrin eased Lex to his side, still holding her. "Nothing has changed. We will get Lex out of Dark Kingdom and deal with my father later."

And then Amund asked the question Lex had feared. "And if we fail? Your father has managed to hide secrets from his people for centuries. If he finds us before we are able to leave…"

Zirel joined Amund's side. "He's right. We must plan for a worst-case scenario."

Garrin looked at Camille. She was on her feet, but she still looked awful. "Has your magic returned?" he asked.

She shook her head. "I will need a couple of nights' rest at least. I fear what would happen if I tried to portal us now and we became stuck."

"Amund?" Garrin asked.

"I could get us there," Amund said slowly, "but it would take months, like it did the first time. And if all of us grow depleted during the extended trip…"

Garrin sighed. "We have more people and only slightly more food. We'll wait and leave as soon as Camille is able."

"What about my power?" Lex said. "I doubt I could portal anyone, but I might be able to help Camille regain her ability."

Garrin looked down, considering. "Your mother helped us tap into your power at the ravine. It is worth a try."

Lex had no idea what her mother had done to give Garrin and the others back some of their powers, but if Lex could bring back even a fraction of Camille's portaling ability, it would be worth it.

"Do not underestimate my daughter, Dark Prince," Isle said. "She is more powerful than all of us combined."

Lex's face heated, and she looked at Garrin. "Ignore her. She's delusional."

He smiled softly. "I do not doubt you will someday become more powerful than all of us."

"So you're not too much of a man to let a woman best you in magic?" Which was hilarious, because Lex could hardly use her abilities for more than a few seconds.

His lips twitched. "It will not hurt my ego."

"That's because your ego is enormous."

He laughed. "Perhaps."

Camille stepped forward. "Though it hasn't manifested fully, Lex's power is bottomless." She looked at Amund, and he slowly nodded. "It is—" Camille opened and closed her fists, seemingly trying to come up with words.

"Vast like the oceanic tide of Tirnan—never-ending and surging with energy," Amund said.

Em looked at Amund in surprise, and Lex had to admit, his description was uncharacteristically eloquent. Only... what the hell?

Like her memory, Lex's power was spotty at best. "I can't control it."

Camille waved her hand slowly in front of Lex. "Even so, it is there, waiting for you to command. Kushiel bestowed upon you a great gift."

It would be easier for Lex to believe she'd been fathered by an angel if she'd actually met the man.

Garrin stiffened beside her, and she looked up.

"Powerful magic can be misused or used against oneself," he said. "You've not had decades of practice like the rest of us."

"Speak for yourself," the Halven named Derek said. "Maybe some of us don't need decades to master our abilities. Elena and I"—he looked at the woman beside Keen— "and even Reese over there have only had our magic for a year or two. Yet Elena stopped a disease from destroying your world. Never underestimate a powerful will."

Garrin's jaw shifted. "I listen to you only because you came to help Lex and we need all the soldiers we can get, but don't cross the line, Halven."

"This again?" Derek shook his head, his shaggy brown

hair falling in tousled layers around his handsome face. "You people really need to get over your prejudice toward the half-breeds of the realm. We're here to stay."

Lex caught Garrin's eye. "He's right. You once believed I was Halven. Did you think less of me then?"

"You were always different," he replied. "But I won't see you harmed."

"And I won't be. You have a plan. We'll stick with your plan, and in the meantime, I'll try to help Camille."

He hesitated a moment, then nodded. "Lexandra will practice her skills. The rest of us will coordinate travel across the Land of Ice. It will be grueling, but less deadly with Camille's assistance."

Lex mentally flinched at the idea of another trip across the Fae equivalent of the Arctic. But even that didn't surpass the fear of a narcissistic king after her. She'd take the Arctic with Camille and Amund's portaling abilities any day.

She glanced at Garrin, and her mouth twitched. It was cute how he thought he decided whether she practiced her powers or not, but she let him believe he did because it doused that stubborn temper of his.

Garrin stepped away and pulled Camille aside, murmuring something that had the portal creator growing paler than she already was. But she nodded in response. Then Amund and Zirel, along with Keen and Jas and a few others, crowded around Garrin.

Isle approached along with Camille. "I will show Camille how to draw from your power."

Lex nodded and practiced reading the portal creator's magic. If she had to describe it, she'd say it was light, like smoke. She focused and pushed it at Camille the way she'd done with Em and Zirel's magic.

It worked. Sort of.

Camille's head sank, dark crescents shadowing her eyes. "I sense Lex's power, but I cannot absorb it the way I should."

Isle touched her friend's shoulder. "Are you certain you cannot draw more?"

Camille shook her head. "I could portal all of us off this mountain, but not very far. If I slept…"

"Sleep, friend," Isle said, and escorted Camille to a quiet corner inside the cavern.

Lex gave them space, and Elena, who'd remained quiet all this time, approached her along with Keen's girlfriend, Reese. "You will want to know our abilities as well. The more powers you are familiar with, the better prepared you'll be."

"In some ways, your and my powers are similar," Reese said. "We both use others to inflict the most harm."

"Or help," Elena said. "Not everything is about harming."

Reese grinned. "Most of the time it is."

Elena sighed in exasperation. "Thanks, Reese." She shook her head. "Everything will be fine, Lex. But it can't hurt to know more magic."

Lex nodded. "I'd like that. I want to understand what I'm doing, just in case."

Elena sent her a soft smile. "Just in case."

CHAPTER

THIRTY

While Camille slept, everyone in the cave bided their time, with a lot of tension filling the room. And this time it wasn't merely physical sparring.

Keen and Jas glared at each other from across the firepit Garrin had constructed. Only they weren't saying anything. "What's going on?" Lex asked. "Why do they look angry?"

Garrin had finished his escape strategizing with the others, which mostly involved survival skills for the Land of Ice, and now lay beside her next to the fire.

He hitched his weight on one elbow. "Keen is reading Jasper's thoughts."

"They can talk to each other?"

"Not exactly. Most telepaths cannot send messages. Keen doesn't seem to like what Jasper is thinking."

Lex blinked. "But they came together. Aren't they friends?"

Garrin snorted. "Keen is from Old Kingdom and Jasper is from Dark Kingdom. There will be no friendship."

She shook her head slowly. "That is ridiculous."

"It is our way in Tirnan."

"Elena and Keen are friends, and they rule different kingdoms," Lex pointed out.

Garrin scratched his jaw. "That is peculiar. I assume Keen feels no competition with the Halven."

"Excuse me," Elena said from across the cave, where she was practicing roundhouse kicks. She put her hands on her hips and said, "I'm plenty powerful," punctuating it with a lightning strike that scorched the cave wall.

Smoke filled the air, and Lex's ears rang.

"That's my girl," Derek said, before returning to his conversation with Zirel.

Lex huddled closer to Garrin. "You better watch what you say."

Garrin grinned, seemingly comfortable in the cave filled with magic and mayhem.

Across the fire, Em appeared only mildly surprised by the indoor lightning strike. Amund murmured something to her, and she turned her shoulder away, frowning.

"What about them? Em isn't Halven and they're both originally from Dark Kingdom. Why don't they get along?"

Garrin waved his hand over the fire, causing the blaze to pulse. "That is simpler in nature. Amund wants my courtier."

"You mean *my* courtier. Em is a part of my nonexistent noble court now."

He chuckled. "I stand corrected."

Em had been a part of Garrin's harem... "Does it bother you that another man wants Em?"

Garrin frowned and blinked several times. "It does not bother me in the way you suggest. I'm not certain Em wishes to have Amund."

Lex studied the two. "She's ignoring him, but I don't

know; there's something there. I've never seen Em angry, and Amund really brings it out in her."

Garrin nodded. "I agree. There is lust involved."

Lex laughed, and Em's gaze shot to them. "I wouldn't have put it that bluntly," Lex said, "but yes, that's my sense as well. It's weird, though, right? To like someone, but to fight it?"

Garrin shrugged. "Fae women are strong. He might have offended her in some way, and now she won't give in to the attraction. Who can say?"

Em crossed her arms. "Stop talking about me," she said, seemingly forgetting she was speaking to her prince.

"If Amund offended her," Lex said, "she shouldn't be with him." Lex winked at Em, who shook her head and glanced away.

A warm finger trailed up Lex's back, setting off sparks down her spine. "Is that what you think, Lexandra? I once offended you too. Do you believe we should be apart?"

Her pulse raced and she drew in a breath. Damn him. "Of course not. Fine, I'm no good at understanding attraction."

"You are new to lust. I will teach you." He grinned enthusiastically.

She shoved him, but he barely budged. "Maybe I will teach *you*."

His smile faded and his eyes sparked. "I would like that. Shall we begin?"

Before Lex could respond, Derek walked over. "You mind?" He looked at Garrin and gestured to one of the side caves. His girlfriend Elena was already inside, arranging their heavy coats on the ground.

Derek walked in behind Elena, and Garrin waved his hand at the entrance, sealing it off from the main corridor with a translucent ice wall that didn't show shapes, but let in light.

"What happens if they need to escape quickly? Won't they be trapped?"

Garrin stood and stretched his arms above his head, a peek of lightly tanned skin and toned abdomen showing beneath. "The ice is nothing the Halven couldn't break through when he chooses."

"Thank you," Derek shouted.

Lex tried not to stare at Garrin as he pulsed embers in other parts of the cavern, heating the space while everyone slept, but his power was hot, literally and figuratively, and she couldn't help admiring him.

"Come," he said, holding out his hand. "We should rest."

Lex gripped his warm palm. It was late, and Keen and Reese had already peeled off into one of the cavern's other internal caves.

Garrin sealed off their small space too, and the faint sound of Reese laughing filtered out.

Lex blushed. "This is quite the love nest."

Garrin squeezed her hand, studying her eyes. "Shall we adjourn to our own? We'll find one that is more private."

Jas and Zirel were passed out near the large fire, while Amund stood guard. But Isle was awake and watching them from across the firepit.

"Give me a moment," Lex said.

She crossed the cavern to her mother and sat beside the fire, the embers dancing in magic-filled shades of blue. Devoid of wood and kindling, this fire was silent. "Please don't be mad at me."

Isle's lips pursed. "I am not upset with you, Lexandra. Merely frustrated. I had no choice but to modify your memory and leave you with Jasper. It was either that or allow Casone to get his hands on you. The angels only know what that fool would have done. I dare not imagine. I couldn't reach your father, and I did what I had to."

Lex bit the inside of her lip, treading carefully. "I understand you did what you had to when I was younger, but I'm a grown woman now."

Isle studied her. "Jasper said you are a splendid student, though you keep to yourself." Her amber eyes grew shadowed. "I'm sorry for what the magic and memory loss did. I had no idea you'd suffer from a human mental disorder."

"Anxiety. And it was partly from memories I had of you dying by avalanche. But Jas's presence helped. If it makes you feel any better, I no longer suffer from anxiety. Not since I came here and, well, changed."

Isle's throat bobbed, and she nodded. "You didn't suffer from it before you left. I wouldn't expect you to have it now that you've returned."

Lex touched her mother's shoulder. "Whatever suffering I've experienced, it's brought me to you. It brought me Garrin too. And as much as I appreciate what you've done for me, it's time to let me spread my wings." That sounded like a bad angel pun. "Figuratively speaking."

A sad smile crossed her mother's face. "You're like your father in more ways than you think. You're a peacekeeper, and you are incredibly stubborn."

"I think I get some of that stubbornness from you."

Her mother sent her look that said she was not amused. Her eyes grew watery. "I realize you're no longer a child, but that doesn't mean I wish to lose you again." Her eyes narrowed on Garrin.

"I'm not going anywhere, Mom. But I *am* with Garrin."

Isle's mouth pursed as though she tasted something

sour. "Why the Dark Prince? Jasper is perfectly suitable. And not really your uncle, if you hadn't figured it out."

Lex winced. "Jasper is like a brother to me, and the thought of being with him is truly disturbing."

A snorting sound came from Jasper several feet away. He held a fist to his mouth and seemed to be holding back laughter.

Apparently, he was no longer dozing.

Lex sighed. "What made you fall in love with my dad?"

"Your father is, well...your father."

Lex rolled her eyes. "Helpful, Mom, thanks. So, what you're saying is it was nothing you can put your finger on. That's partly how it is for me and Garrin too. More importantly, he has believed in me more than I believed in myself from the moment we met."

Isle eyed her skeptically. "You like the prince because he is dangerously handsome. But his father—"

"Is not Garrin. And yes, Garrin isn't hard on the eyes, but he's more than a pretty face. He—" Lex would have said he loved her and challenged her and protected her. But she didn't know Garrin loved her. He'd never said as much. She only felt it.

Isle's eyes softened. "Are you sure you can trust the Dark Prince?"

"Yes. Now can you please trust me?"

Isle hesitated a moment, then reluctantly nodded.

It was a huge concession, and Lex wasn't about to take it for granted. She'd do what she felt was right in the end, but she preferred to have her mother's support. She hugged her mom, the gesture more comfortable the more time they spent together. "Thank you. Sleep well, Mom."

Lex stood and walked to Garrin, careful to tiptoe around the others.

He reached for her hand and led her to the small alcove in the far reaches of the cavern where they'd rested earlier.

They entered, and Garrin put an ice wall in place for privacy. He walked to his coat still left on the ground. "Is everything okay with your mother?"

Lex followed him blindly, tired after her conversation with Isle. "She's still uncertain about you."

He took her arms and drew her close. "I don't want to come between you and your mother."

"You won't." Lex reached up and kissed him, trailing her hand down his broad chest, a surge of renewed energy filling her.

He closed his eyes. "Lex, you don't know what you do when you touch me."

The corner of her mouth turned up. "I may never have done this before, but I'm not entirely naïve."

"Aren't you?" He trailed his fingers between her breasts, his hand flattening on her stomach the way she'd touched him.

Lex's belly clenched. When her heart calmed, she looked into his bright eyes. "Maybe I am naïve. I'll need more demonstration."

THIRTY-ONE

Garrin's eyes glimmered in the soft glow filtering through the translucent ice wall. "I want to show you everything, but are you ready? Perhaps another—"

"I'm a twenty-one-year-old virgin with not only the hottest guy I've ever known, but also a man I've come to care deeply for. You're kissing me and touching me and setting my body on fire. I want this."

It was precisely what Garrin needed to hear. Even so... "Are you certain?"

"Yes, now stop talking and more of the rest of it."

He quirked his brow and slowly drew her top up her stomach, his knuckles grazing her soft skin. "Okay?" Lex nodded, and he pulled her tunic over her head and tossed it to the side.

Her teeth started to chatter as he kissed her brow, making his way toward her lips. "Cozy as our love cave is," she said, "it is nowhere near warm."

"Allow me." Garrin eased her down on top of his coat and leaned over her.

Lex cuddled into his body. "Mmm, this was how I stayed warm all those weeks traveling across the Land of Ice."

Garrin thought back to their treacherous journey and the reason he'd meticulously planned their return trip. He'd been so fearful of losing Lex that he hadn't thought about keeping his distance, often tucking her against him at night.

"I haven't begun to warm your body." He ran his hand up and down her back and over her soft curves, sending heat to her limbs with his magic.

Her eyes widened. "Oh, now that is a nifty trick. A perk of commanding fire?" She glanced at his hand on her rear. "You're very thorough."

He took her mouth with a fiery kiss that set his own blood racing. "Tell me to stop and I will." He moved his hand over her thigh, warming her.

A soft, breathy gasp escaped her lips. "If you stop, I'll singe you with your own power."

His mouth pulled into the beginnings of a smile, and then he stilled. "Can you do that?" The wonders of Lex's power were never-ending.

She grinned. "While you strategized our survival in the Land of Ice, I might have practiced creating a fireball or two with Elena and Reese." Her mouth twisted and she glanced up. "It looked more like a spark, but just you wait. I'll get there."

If his father knew what she could do—

Lex ran her hands over his chest, causing heat to simmer beneath his skin.

His mind went blank and he looked down at her beautiful face to her neck and lower. "Perhaps we can test it out later when we're not busy," he said. "They say the best way to stay warm is skin to skin."

Lex laughed, and he frowned. "Is there something funny?" he asked.

"That is the oldest pickup line in the book. Even I've heard that one."

He sent her a crooked smile. "I may have heard it in the Earth realm a time or two."

"Did you seduce many humans with that one?"

He nuzzled her neck. "You're very cute when you're jealous. I didn't partake in what the human female who delivered the line offered. I was too busy searching for you."

"Such arrogance."

"So you've told me. Shall I take off my clothes?"

She glared at him as though trying to decide if she should argue. "Yes, but do it slowly."

Garrin reached over his shoulder and eased off his tunic the rest of the way. He sensed his hair sticking up in the back, but he didn't bother to smooth it. Because Lex was staring at him with lust in her eyes, which caused desire to pulse through his veins.

She swallowed and cleared her throat, scanning him from head to waist. "You Fae are well built." She ran her fingertips over the muscles of his shoulders and chest, setting off fireworks beneath his skin.

Garrin inhaled, his breath catching when her fingertips reached his lower abdomen. "Some more than others."

"Again with the arrogance," she murmured, but she seemed to be enjoying herself, because her next words were, "Maybe you should take off your pants? You know, to keep my lower half skin to skin."

"You're using my line."

"Do you have a problem with that?" she said distractedly as he unfastened his pants and pulled them down.

Garrin felt the shiver that ran through Lex's body.

"This only works if you're naked too, yes?" He kissed her mouth and placed his hand over her heart.

"My fingers are numb," she said, staring at his manhood.

Garrin didn't wear human underwear, and Fae men were larger than human men. Everywhere. "Your shock at my masculinity is understandable."

Her gaze lost the distracted look, and her mouth twisted. "I've seen naked men. Not up close and personal, but I've watched nature channels, for goodness' sake. And none of those men were built like you. Good heavens, give a girl a moment, will you?" she said, her gaze returning to the part of him that was straining toward her.

Garrin eased down her body and looked up at her with hooded eyes. He unbuttoned her pants and slid them down her legs, kissing her thigh and lifting her leg to kiss her calf, his tongue darting out and touching the back of her knee. "Take all the time you need."

Lex's eyes widened. "Moment's over—keep going."

"Indeed." Lex's skin was incredibly soft, with the intoxicating sweet scent of *brune* and wildflowers.

He looked up, and her face scrunched as though she were perplexed. "You're very good at this."

"Shh, I'm working." He discarded her pants off to the side and inched up her body, taking his time and kissing her as he went. He kissed the crease between her leg and sex, and Lex's breath caught. He glanced up. "Anytime you wish me to stop..."

"Why would I want you to stop?"

"This is your first time. I don't want you to do anything you're not comfortable with."

She let out a breathy sigh as he kissed her breasts through her bra. "Pretty comfortable. Don't stop."

LEX RAN her hands over Garrin's body as he unclasped her bra one-handed.

Fae women didn't wear bras, so she really didn't want to know where he'd learned that trick.

Her breasts were larger now, her body taller and slightly different after the magic that hid her true self had dissipated. And Garrin worshiped every inch of her until she was shaking with want.

She felt his body, hard and warm against her chest—his erection against her thigh—but he didn't press forward. He kissed her mouth, her neck, her stomach, and finally began to slide down her panties with talented, sensual fingers.

Lex's heart pounded, and she arched toward him. She didn't realize until now how much she'd craved Garrin. This was the man she'd waited for all her life.

He shifted and centered himself at her entrance.

"Wait." She pressed her hand to his chest. "What about birth control?"

He kissed her jaw and ran his nose over her cheek, sending a shiver through her. "Fae don't reproduce easily. It takes hundreds of years to sire a child. The chances we would conceive this day are nearly zero."

Okay, she'd heard something like that. It made sense. Still, it had been programmed into her that you never had sex without protection, and now her brain was battling Fae conception problems with Earth's birth-control practices.

Lex kissed him and ran her hands down his back, pulling him closer. "Fae don't carry diseases, according to Elena, who fought the only known one. But pregnancy? You don't understand how much it's been hammered in my brain as a human to never have unprotected sex."

He lifted his head. "But you've never had sex."

"Exactly! I don't know what I'm doing, and I feel like we should use birth control."

Garrin flinched. "That is an appalling notion. However, if it pleases you, there are...*precautions* I can take. Given my potency in everything, it would not surprise me to get you with child the first time."

Lex frowned, then jerked his head down and kissed him, nibbling the corner of his mouth. "I can see how well those precautions worked, since we are allied with *several* Halven."

He slid his hand along the side of her breast. "Not all Fae are as gentlemanly as I."

Garrin didn't rush things, even though Lex was ready to explode. He touched her with practiced hands and kissed her passionately until her desire bordered on frenzy. And then, in slow increments, he entered her.

Lex stared into Garrin's fathomless blue eyes. His mouth was tense, and she leaned up and kissed it. "Are you okay?"

"I'm trying to go slowly, and it is a lesson in patience."

Nothing he did hurt her. "Don't go slow."

She didn't need to tell him twice. He dropped his head and moved deeper until he was fully seated, which should have blown her mind, given his size, but she felt too good to think clearly. He was kissing her and moving, and her body clenched his.

He ran his hand over her breast and down her stomach until he touched her where they connected.

Soon Lex's head tilted back, and her breathing increased. The sensation he elicited made her feel out of control.

And then her body convulsed and she moaned, falling from the highest high she'd ever experienced.

Lex clung to Garrin as he kissed her and balanced his weight on his elbows, continuing the rhythmic motion like before, only less controlled and more urgent.

He pulled away, and a low moan of pleasure vibrated from his chest as he touched himself and found his release.

Lex felt the loss of him immediately.

After a moment, Garrin rolled to the side and pulled Lex with him, tucking her close to his heart. "I wish to be with you always, Lex. To protect you as long as you will have me." He leaned back and looked down at her. "You're the only woman I've loved and ever want to love."

Her breath caught. She touched his jaw, the growth of stubble tickling her fingers. "I love you too. And don't think I won't protect you back."

He laughed softly. "Given your inclination to disregard my orders, I wouldn't expect anything less."

Lex snuggled against him, her limbs more languid than they'd ever been.

Soon she sensed the telltale signs of him falling asleep, his breathing low and measured, his body twitching every few seconds.

He'd told her he loved her. She'd felt it for weeks, but now she knew.

And there was no way she'd let him send her back to the Earth realm.

THIRTY-TWO

Sometime later, something pulled Lex from sleep.

Garrin stirred, possibly sensing her alertness.

And then the sound of a bomb going off rocked the cave, with dirt and debris raining down.

Garrin jumped to his feet.

"What is it? What's going on?" Lex reached for her clothes and looked up to make sure the ceiling wasn't collapsing.

He pulled on his pants and jerked his head through the hole of his shirt, his eyes blazing with intensity. "Stay here. Do not come out."

"What if you need me?" she said, and rapidly put on her pants.

"My father is here. We're moving forward with the contingency plan. Camille will come back and portal you away."

"*Only me?* How do you know it's your father?" Lex wrestled with the rest her clothes as Garrin melted the ice wall and solidified it behind him.

Oh, *hell no*. He was not leaving her behind. "Garrin!"

He wanted to protect her, but she was powerful in her own right. True, practicing with Elena and Reese had shown her how little she knew of her ability. But she was tired of being afraid. Tired of being coddled or left on the sideline.

Lex pulled on her boots and stared at the wall that appeared to be sturdier than before. Had he thickened it?

Darn Ice Prince!

Last night, she'd managed to read Elena and Reese's powers, but Elena's transformative ability was complicated, and Lex couldn't replicate anything the Halven did. Reese's magic was like Lex's in some ways. She'd managed to block Elena from using her powers by calming her to near sleep. For all of two seconds. It wasn't enough, but there was potential. Which was all she could say about any of her attempts at magic.

A massive wave of discordant powers hit Lex's chest, followed by the sound of swords clashing.

She had to get out. Had to help.

Lex kicked the ice barrier separating her from the others, and though she was stronger in Tirnan, it didn't budge.

Overprotective boyfriend!

She threw rocks at it and barely scratched the surface.

A scream rent the air beyond the ice wall, and Lex's heart nearly stopped. *Em? Mom?*

She closed her eyes and focused on the tendrils of Garrin's power. And then she pushed it at the ice wall with all her force.

The wall didn't melt. It didn't mist away. It burst in an explosion as loud as the one minutes before, shards flying in all directions.

She hunched and covered her head, ice cutting through thick fabric on her back and arms.

Lex looked up and saw Garrin skid to a stop on the other side of the alcove, his chest heaving. "Are you hurt?" he said, before turning and throwing his arm out, the tendons in his neck strained.

A male voice down the hall yelped in pain.

"I'm fine," she said.

A liveried soldier made it to the front of the alcove, and Garrin snarled, slashing his sword and sending the Fae stumbling backward.

Lex ran past Garrin and the soldier to the main cavern.

The sun hadn't fully risen, and a faint glow filled the room where the ice wall had stood, its fragments splayed across the dirt floor.

Everywhere she looked, castle soldiers fought her friends. Too many soldiers.

Jas fended off a guard and swung his leg back to kick another in the chest. Then there were two Jases—one a wavery illusion and the other the real version.

Lex could see how his power, weak though it may be, was useful, because the soldiers were distracted long enough for Jas to get the upper hand and push them back with his fists and sword.

But no matter how much Garrin and Jas and the others pushed the soldiers out of the cave, more poured in.

Lex vaguely heard Garrin shout for her to stay back. As soon as she looked up, she understood why.

Dressed in an amethyst robe with gold embroidery down the sleeves stood the Dark King, men flanking him.

His square jaw and refined nose no longer seemed jovial, like the last time she'd seen him. Casone Branimir was all business, and he was terrifying to behold.

Lex sensed no power wafting off him. He wouldn't need it because his men backed Lex's friends deeper into the cavern three to one, with a fresh influx of soldiers behind them.

But her friends weren't giving up.

Elena threw small, lethal lightning bolts at soldiers as they poured in, while Keen fought off four soldiers at once. Reese stood off to the side, her expression focused as she jumped and kicked a soldier square in the chest. He stumbled, turned, and stabbed his comrade in the leg.

Reese's magic had sent anger in the wrong direction and confused the soldier into stabbing his companion— until an alchemist snuck up behind Reese and extended his hand.

Lex called out, but her voice didn't rise above the cacophony inside the cavern.

Reese convulsed and dropped to her knees.

"No!" Lex shouted.

Zirel ran forward and stabbed the alchemist attacking Reese. He reached over and touched her temple.

Reese shook her head and stumbled toward Elena.

Camille dodged the fighting and raced to Lex's side. "We must leave."

Lex's palms sweated, and her heart thundered in her chest. "I can't." These were her family, her friends...her lover.

A handful of Fae not an arm's length away were suddenly frozen in their steps by a sheer film of ice. Two more screeched in pain as the hilts of their swords burned bright blue.

Lex looked back. Garrin was fighting off several soldiers and throwing out magic at the same time.

Not far away, her mother's refined, delicate hands

worked quickly as she jabbed a Fae with a small knife. Though he was twice as big as her, the guy was losing the fight. Because fist-sized stones were pummeling him in the head.

Come to think of it, Lex had never asked her mother what her power was, but she saw it now. Isle could move objects, including people. Just as she'd stopped Lex and Garrin from falling to the bottom of a ravine.

Her powers must have limits, or she'd be throwing the soldiers out of the cave.

She was good, Lex's mom. But they were *outnumbered*. Massively. There was no way they could fend off the king's soldiers for long, with scores more pouring in every second.

And then Lex sensed it.

The Dark King's power coiled in the air above them like a snake ready to strike.

Garrin cut down one soldier after another, giving the king barely a glance. And that was when Lex realized something so obvious: she was the only one who could see everyone's power.

Others could sense power levels, but not even Camille and Amund could *see* power move to its next target. And that was useful. Really useful, considering the size and intensity of magic coming off the king. Something was about to happen.

"Garrin!"

Somehow he heard her above the noise and looked up, while blocking blow after blow.

"Leave! Now!"

The Dark King's eyes narrowed on Lex, and his mouth twisted into a dark smile. He motioned behind him, and Mertha's husband was shoved forward.

The older Fae's back was bowed, and suddenly the

fighting stopped. Because Mertha's husband had sent a surge of calming power that felt like a warm shower, subduing everyone, including Garrin.

"He's like Reese!" she said to Garrin, which didn't have the effect Lex intended.

The king leered at Lex happily as though she'd done something to please him.

Had she given away her ability?

The king glanced at Mertha's husband. "Thank you, Felix. You've done well."

Felix looked pained as he turned to Garrin. "They threatened to keep me alive past my time. I wish to be with Mertha. I told them I didn't know anything."

"Oh, but you knew things, did you not?" the king said. "You knew a great deal, once we convinced you to remember."

Felix dropped his head, looking anguished.

Garrin stepped forward. "Father, why are your warriors fighting us?"

The king looked straight at Lex, making her skin crawl. "Were you attempting to hide your bride, Garrin?" He looked her up and down, his gaze simmering with something Lex didn't want to analyze.

Garrin's jaw tightened. "She is not hidden. She is with me."

"Did you know," the king continued, "that Mertha often shared information with Felix? It turns out she knew of your intended, Lexandra Meinrad. She also knew of her mother. And who Lexandra's father is."

Garrin stiffened. "Lex is innocent."

The king crossed his arms and looked up as though considering. "Innocent? I think not. She has avoided her duty as a noble Dark Fae in my court." He stared straight at Isle. "As has her mother."

"How did you know we were here?" Garrin said, deflecting, from what Lex could tell.

Lex swallowed. They were outnumbered, trapped, and the king knew far more than they hoped. Not to mention, he'd somehow managed to enter the cavern without anyone the wiser, including Camille or Amund, who should have sensed him.

The Dark King grinned. "Don't you know by now, son? My alchemists are very talented. There is nowhere you can hide in my land."

Garrin's eyes darkened. "I never thought I needed to."

"Oh, you don't, son, you don't." Casone stepped several paces forward and gripped Garrin's shoulder awkwardly.

Garrin didn't flinch, but there was something going on. A silent exchange.

Camille grabbed Lex's hand. "We must go," she said under her breath.

"Go?" The Dark King looked straight at Camille. "I heard you'd returned." He clicked his tongue. "You should have taken the gift of escaping Dark Kingdom for what it was. Something never to be repeated. I don't know how you accomplished leaving our land and surviving, but I will find out. And you will never know such freedom again."

Lex's mind raced. The king *wanted* them trapped in Dark Kingdom.

Camille's eyes glowed with fury. "I returned for my son."

"You have no son," the king said, his voice hard.

"You know that I do. He was taken from me during the night not long after his birth."

"And yet you left Dark Kingdom without this precious child?"

Camille vibrated next to Lex, her anger sizzling. "I sensed the soldiers coming and fled. But not before I saw my infant son in your wife's arms."

The king's eyes narrowed. "My heir, you mean."

Camille looked at Garrin. "Not if I bore him. Garrin is my child—conceived after you forced yourself on me."

Garrin's dark head swung to Camille, his lips parted in shock.

It couldn't be… Garrin turned to his father. "What is she talking about?"

Camille was older than Garrin, by more than a hundred years, if he had to guess. Enough for her to have given birth to him. And she had Garrin's exact coloring, with bright blue eyes and black hair. Coloring neither of his parents possessed.

The king shrugged one shoulder. "I hardly know her."

That wasn't an answer.

This was madness, yet it *was* possible. Anything was possible after what Garrin had learned about his father. After what he'd learned of Lex's lineage.

They were outnumbered by his father's legion. "Let us leave here and talk somewhere else, Father."

He had to get the king away from Lex, and he had to get Lex away from Dark Kingdom. And now his backup plan was his real mother?

Casone looked around and raised his arms, palms up. "But this is the place you chose. We will talk here. Besides, this woman is confused about her role in my kingdom." He glared at Camille.

Garrin had seen that look on his father's face before. Camille was in grave danger.

His father made a sharp motion with his hand, and Garrin cried out, "No!"

But it was too late.

Camille was gone. Though not captured by the king. Camille had disappeared, which meant she'd escaped through one of her portals.

Only she'd left without Lex.

"Find her!" Casone shouted.

Several soldiers peeled off, and a man and a woman were shoved forward.

"Mom!" Em shouted, and moved toward her parents.

Amund grabbed Em, blocking her from rushing into danger.

Casone looked at the couple. They'd been beaten, their lips gashed, their clothing torn. "My cousin was kind enough to tell me where you were." He looked around. "Not my preference for a love nest, but to each his own. Some women like dangerous men, and you've certainly shown Lexandra danger by taking her to the graves."

Fae healed quickly. The injuries Em's parents bore weren't healing. Which meant their powers were being controlled and they'd been beaten until their healing slowed.

"Child," Em's father said. "Do not be afraid."

Em whimpered.

And then Casone made the motion he'd made earlier. Only this time, his power hit its mark.

Em's mother and father were sealed in an ice block in suspended animation.

Garrin winced. He'd seen his father mete out the punishment before, but never outside of battle. Fae survived in his father's blocks of ice, but they were unable to move, frozen for eternity.

Em wept and turned her head into Amund's chest. The warrior held her, his eyes on the king and promising vengeance.

Casone caught Amund's look and laughed.

Lex inched closer to Garrin, and he moved to shield her with his body.

"This isn't necessary," Garrin said. "Your cousin helped me protect Lex. There are some who would harm her." His father, for one, but the Dark King was nothing if not desperate for approval and adoration. If Garrin made it look like Casone was the savior, there was a chance he would release them.

His father studied Garrin. "They are no innocents." He glanced at Felix, who finally looked at Garrin.

"My prince, I am sorry. Please—"

Casone froze Felix mid-sentence. He motioned for one of his soldiers, and the Fae threw the ice tombs of Felix and Em's parents out of the cave and over the steep cliff using telekinetic magic.

Em's scream filled the air, and Amund held her close.

Garrin's chest tightened. His father had sentenced Mertha's husband to an icy grave, never to pass into the afterlife and be with this wife. The king wasn't playing by any rules that mattered, except his own.

Casone observed the back of his hand as though there was something interesting there. "Tell me, son, why would you stay in the ice tombs and not the castle? You were hiding, were you not?"

Garrin didn't answer, and his father shot him a knowing look. He peered past Garrin.

"Amund." Casone tsked. "After all this time, you've come to help me fight another battle. Make yourself useful and create a portal for me and my son. His betrothed will also be joining us."

"No." Garrin shot a warning look to Amund.

His father's eyes flared. "You dare disobey me, Garrin?" He glared at Amund. "Amund Ridel, soldier of the Dark Kingdom army. Do your duty and create the portal."

Amund's eyes flashed with hatred. "I refuse."

THIRTY-THREE

Lex clenched her hands together. They were screwed. The king had frozen their friends and tossed them out like rubbish. Camille was gone, and now the king had ordered Amund to return her and Garrin to the castle.

"Do it now or pay for your disobedience," the king said to Amund.

Amund exchanged a glance with Garrin, and said, "I will create a portal, Your Majesty."

The king's eyes narrowed.

Lex squeezed Garrin's arm. "We can't go. It's too dangerous."

He slid his palm to hers, some wild emotion filling his face. "We're outnumbered."

"And going with your father is safer than staying? Let's fight."

"Don't be a fool, Dark Prince," Isle cried out. "Your father will destroy Lexandra just as he destroyed so many others."

The wave of power that followed hit Lex so hard that

she stumbled back. When she regained her bearings, her mother's expression was frozen, entombed in ice.

Shock filled her, and then tears rushed to her eyes. "Mom!"

"Don't do this!" Garrin shouted at his father.

Lex lurched toward her mother and slammed her fist against the ice, whirls of condensation floating up. Isle's pale face was suspended in outrage.

"Remove it! Let her go!" Lex screamed, attempting to re-create Garrin's power, as she'd done inside the alcove, and break her mother free. But her mind was filled with emotion, and nothing stuck.

"Now, now, Lexandra," the king said. "Anger won't help. You wish your mother free?"

Lex swiveled her head toward the king. "Let. Her. Go."

A sickly smile spread across the king's face. "Not until you come with me, child. Then I will set your mother free."

Was "setting her free" some sort of euphemism for death?

Lex looked at Garrin, but he was staring at his father, the color leached from his face.

"It's up to you, son. More of this"—the king gestured to Lex's mom—"or we can return to my castle and discuss what I want from your future bride. If that is what she truly is to you."

A sour taste filled Lex's mouth. The king knew she wasn't here to marry Garrin. Knew what Mertha had told Felix. And considering his reaction to Lex sensing Felix's magic, he knew something of her ability too.

Garrin surged toward his father. "What do you want? Tell me!"

The soldiers surrounding the Dark King unsheathed

their swords, protecting him in a starburst of metal. "The girl first," the king said.

"Never!" Garrin roared. "You'll never have her."

"Have her? Son, I don't wish to possess her. You have my word. Your bride is safe in my castle."

Garrin's chest rose and fell. He looked around the room at the dozens of soldiers standing behind his father. Likely more they couldn't see beyond the cave entrance.

With only ten of them left.

He turned to her and cupped her jaw. "We must go."

Lex shook her head. How had it come to this? They'd escaped the castle, made their way to the grave caves everyone feared, and were so close to escape. Or had they been? Had the king toyed with them all along?

Lex had never believed herself safe in the Land of Ice. But she'd felt invincible in Garrin's arms. And now, even Garrin worried.

She couldn't blame him. The power the Dark King wielded... Her mother hadn't even time to close her eyes before she was enshrined.

Perhaps the king would honor his word and keep Lex safe, but would he give the same courtesy to his son? A son born out of wedlock, who might not be considered an heir?

Em shuffled over, her face red from crying, and handed Lex her coat.

The way the king had treated Em's parents and Isle... Lex looked up at Garrin pleadingly. "We can't agree to this."

He grabbed her hand. "Do you trust me?"

"Yes." But she didn't trust his father. How could Garrin trust the king after what he'd done? And she couldn't even voice her concerns because the king was listening to everything.

Garrin nodded, but this time, he looked over Lex's shoulder as he did.

"The others will remain here, portal creator," the king said as he approached. "Only Garrin, his bride, and I will return."

Four of the king's soldiers moved in to surround Garrin and Lex, but Amund was quicker.

One moment Lex and Garrin were standing side by side, and the next, they were tumbling through a portal Lex hadn't seen coming. Because it had been formed beneath her feet.

AMUND CREATED A PORTAL, just as the king ordered. Only the king wasn't in it.

Lex screamed as she tumbled ass over teakettle. She wouldn't have expected a smooth landing after such a rough start, but she sure hadn't expected their mode of transportation to disappear entirely.

One minute she was careening through colorful lights, and the next, the lights were gone, and land came crashing toward her.

Lex huddled, enacting the tuck-and-roll maneuver Em had taught her during battle practice. It might have worked under normal conditions, but not from twenty feet above ground.

Lex landed hard, rolling through powder and ice until she came to an abrupt stop.

She coughed, the wind knocked out of her, and lifted her head. "Garrin?" All she could see were white mountains, no castle or village.

It was probably too much to ask to be back in the village. She was lucky to not be under the king's control.

Lex eased onto her knees and stood shakily, hopping on one leg and gripping her wrist and the coat she's somehow managed to hold on to. She'd sprained her left ankle and possibly broken her arm. As a human, that would have been crippling. But in Tirnan, healing came as quickly as the pain.

She looked behind her and caught sight of Garrin several feet away with blood on his face.

She jerked on the coat and hobbled over, falling to her knees beside Garrin and desperately touching his face. "Are you okay?"

He blinked and grabbed her hand, then he sat up. "Fine."

"You're bleeding."

He lifted his fingers to his temple, the tips coming away red. "Landed wrong. Where's Amund?"

"Over here," came a voice. Only it wasn't masculine.

They looked up to find the queen dressed in a green velvet gown trimmed in gold embroidery, her long, wavy, light brown hair swept over one shoulder.

"Mother?" The alchemists who'd taken Garrin at the castle stood beside her. "What have you done?" Garrin asked, and climbed to his feet.

The alchemists weren't the only ones protecting the queen. Large four-legged animals flanked her and the alchemists, their downy white fur blending eerily with the land.

Lex didn't have memories of these animals. Their snouts were bearlike, their bodies like a large wolf's. And their eyes were a bright gold. They were terrifying, with fangs and low, menacing growls.

"Djune," Garrin said quietly. "They aren't good for meat or work, but they are strong. And vicious. They must be enthralled by my mother, or she would be in pieces right now."

"You are correct," the queen said. "Though if we are being specific, these djune are in thrall to my friends here. Under my command, of course." The queen tilted her head. "You didn't think it was your father who'd had you questioned?" She laughed. "I had to know what my child was up to. And what my husband wanted with the female." She looked Lex over and turned her nose down.

"Why?" Garrin asked.

The queen's eyes widened. "Don't look so surprised. You and your father aren't the only Fae who desire power. Your father has held on to it for longer than most. He's rather old, you know."

The queen moved closer, and both alchemists and djune kept pace. "It was a great bother trying to find you and your little woman." She glanced in the not-too-far distance, and her nose scrunched. "Why in the world would you go to the graves?"

And that was when Lex realized they weren't far from the caves. A mountain away, at most.

"If I'd been a second later," the queen said, "you would have arrived at your destination. But my men are very good. They stopped the portal creator from taking you too far." The queen's eyes twinkled, and she gestured behind her.

Lex's heart stopped. "Amund!"

Amund stumbled between four robed alchemists, his face ashen and bruised, blood dripping down his mouth. His left leg dragged behind him, contorted gruesomely.

"Let him go!" Lex shouted, her face heating with rage.

The queen frowned. "How disrespectful. Whatever do you see in her, son?"

"Not your son." Camille walked out from behind a snowbank.

What in the hell? Camille had escaped before the king could get to her. Had she been here all along, or had she followed them?

The Dark Queen snarled. "You?" She sighed and looked to the sky as though pained. "You are *nothing*. Merely the vessel that brought me my son. Garrin was always meant to be mine."

Had the queen lost her mind? Camille hadn't given Garrin up. He'd been *stolen* from her.

Garrin's throat bobbed as he looked between his mother and Camille, his hands clenched at his sides. "Let them go, Mother. Camille has done you no harm, and nor has Amund." His stance was tense, but his tone soft.

"Hasn't she?" the queen said, ignoring the question of Amund. "Now that she has joined the party, I recall many grievances against her. That she lay with my husband at the foremost. That she tried to claim you as her own, the most grievous. Everyone knows you are my child. But if the slightest doubt spreads across the land"—her voice quavered, and her eyes hardened—"there can be no question that you are mine."

Without breaking eye contact, Garrin said, "Why would anyone believe a portal creator over the queen?"

Ailith sniffed, and her chest rose. "Why indeed. Still—"

"Why are we here?" Garrin said. He was deflecting again, drawing the queen's attention away from Camille and Amund, the latter collapsed and not moving.

Camille held a calculating expression, and Lex worried. There were half a dozen alchemists and only Garrin, Lex,

Camille, and a severely injured Amund. So basically, Garrin and Camille, since Lex sucked at controlling her power.

The queen walked closer to Lex until they stood toe to toe. "We are here because the alchemists tell me her power level is distinct." She tapped her lip and glanced at Garrin. "I wonder why that is? Perhaps it is the reason you are drawn to her?" She looked back at Lex. "You know, he didn't give in. Not even when my alchemists blocked his magic during several rounds of torture." The queen smiled with pride.

Lex's mouth gaped. What kind of woman tortured her son?

Garrin hadn't gone into detail about what the soldiers and alchemists did to him inside the castle. That he'd suffered made fury rise in her chest.

"Garrin was trained as a mercenary by his father." The queen shook her head. "But now look at him. What has become of you, son? Every soldier wanted to be you. Every woman wanted to sleep with you. And now you bow to this?" She flicked her fingers at Lex.

"Women still want to sleep with him," Lex said. "Me included."

"Lex," Garrin said. "Don't."

Lex threw up her hands. "How can you listen to this? She wants to hurt you."

His mother laughed. "Hurt him? Oh no, it isn't Garrin I wish to punish. It is his father."

THIRTY-FOUR

Lex shook her head. The queen wasn't after Lex or Garrin? She wanted the king?

Garrin shoved her behind him, threw out his arm, and aimed at a mountain off to the side.

The ground rumbled and snow shot up and into the air.

An avalanche sped down the mountain and buried the four alchemists beside Amund within seconds.

But only the alchemists. Amund was still crumpled off to the side.

Lex's heart raced. Her mother had never actually died in an avalanche, but that didn't mean Lex wasn't woefully aware of how deadly this land could be. And how deadly Garrin was.

Camille nearly carried Amund over to them, his large arm draped over her much smaller frame. His eyes were open and he was walking, if unsteadily. His powers must have been subdued by the alchemists.

"Fool," the queen said. "You think downing a few of my men will stop me? I would have made you heir, and here you betray me."

"I am already heir," Garrin said.

"Not if our people discover you are not a child of my body."

The alchemists on either side of the queen didn't move, barely registering their prince's impressive power over the elements. "My queen," one of them said. "Would you like us to dispose of him?"

The queen's eyes narrowed. "He has become a nuisance, has he not? Allow me."

And just like that, the queen shot a lightning bolt at Garrin, throwing him off his feet and tossing him several yards away.

Lex scrambled to him, touching his face, his chest. "Talk to me," she said as he lay with his eyes closed.

Seconds later, Garrin blinked and sat up, shaking his head as he did. Into the muzzles of two djune snarling above them.

The djune were quick and silent. Lex hadn't felt them near until they were practically on top of them.

She clung to Garrin and sensed his magic flow out a second before the djune yapped and backed away, the scent of singed fur filling the air.

Garrin looked at the queen. "Why are you doing this?"

The queen touched her flawless hair as though ensuring no strand lay astray. "The question is, why not? I had hoped to have you at my side, but you are proving less mercenary and more common by the minute. I haven't decided if it's worth it to wait and see if you'll come around."

She walked slowly toward them, her men giving her a wide berth, the djune fanning out, and Lex's heart thrummed in her chest.

"Why would I marry a man several times my age? For that matter, why would he marry me? We had an agreement. I was blessed with dual abilities—one in particular your father wished to utilize—and I would use my magic to make him more powerful. What else is there?"

Garrin rose unsteadily, his hand pressed to his chest where the queen had struck him. "You feel nothing for our people? For the kingdom?"

The queen smiled. "You always were soft in that way. *Caring* about the people. Our royal magic and lineage keeps the food from freezing. It keeps them fed!" She let out a slow breath as though to calm herself. "Without us, there would be no Dark Fae."

Lex sensed tension radiating off Garrin, but his voice was level when he said, "What did you get out of the arrangement?"

The queen's eyes narrowed, and her mouth turned up slightly. "That is the question, is it not? Your father, in his infinite wisdom, thought being queen was all a young woman of his realm could ever desire. That I would be satisfied with the power my new status provided." She chuckled. "He never did understand women." She glanced at Camille, still holding up Amund. "Not your mother, and certainly not his first wife.

"To be fair, his first wife hadn't my ambition. She was more like you and cared for every little whim of the people. And look where that got her? A frozen grave. Ironic, is it not? Your father's first wife wanted nothing more than to continue the legacy of Dark Fae, and in the end, her demise and your father's punishment is what entrapped us. Well, you can see why he needed me."

She strode closer, power emanating off her in waves. "Your father needed someone to help him...navigate. *To persuade.*" She grinned, and a chill ran up Lex's arms.

Lex read the power and realized the queen was using it

to dampen Garrin's anger. Using it to make them believe the queen only wanted what was right, and even Lex felt the pull to side with her.

Garrin squeezed his brow. "Stop it, Mother. You don't need to convince me of your innocence."

Had the queen persuaded Garrin into believing her?

Before Lex could figure out the answer to that question, the air shimmered next to them.

Lex held up her arm to block her eyes against the glare of magic on white snow, and then a portal opened.

The king and two guards stepped onto the mountaintop.

One of the guards immediately threw up and collapsed, his face ashen.

The king looked at the sick soldier and snarled at Garrin. "You will suffer for your disobedience. Look at what you subjected me to. I had to use the only other portal creator in the land. His power is so weak after a couple of leaps, he is barely conscious." The king's gaze slid to the queen. "Wife, what precisely do you think you're doing?"

The queen smiled. "Holding our son for you, dear husband." She waved her hand, and a light sparked from the alchemist beside her before she and the alchemists disappeared in a cloud of smoke.

The queen's retinue was gone, except for the dozen or so djune who'd been tethered to her, and no longer were.

The djune tore across the empty space toward Lex and Garrin, wide paws and claws cutting through the powder.

Garrin sent a burst of power at the animals, and an upwelling of snow and mist formed a menacing wall. His magic was so tangible to Lex now—whether because of their bond or otherwise—it had become more familiar than all the others.

The djune sniffed the air and scampered back.

They must have decided Garrin wasn't worth the risk, because they turned and disappeared down a ridge and into the snowscape.

Though she could easily see Garrin's magic, Lex hadn't seen the alchemists' magic that allowed them to disappear—because they'd moved themselves and the queen without innate ability. And that made Lex nervous.

If alchemists didn't use Fae magic, she couldn't see what they were doing. And if Dark Fae had alchemists to move them from one place to another, what else could they do?

The king and queen seemed capable of getting around Dark Kingdom well enough, but if there was one thing Lex had learned, it was that you could not travel the Land of Ice on limited magical ability. The alchemists might be capable of getting the queen here and there, but they couldn't cross the Land of Ice, or the queen would have done it by now. Wouldn't she?

The king's gaze flickered to the snow-covered mounds where the buried alchemists were making their way out. "I see you've been busy, son."

Garrin stepped back, inching Lex along with him. "I don't want to fight you."

"Don't you?" the king asked. "Why else do you run from me? Cowardly, that." He leveled a look at Camille, who was no longer holding up Amund. "You've returned. How predictable."

"I returned for my son," she replied.

The king ignored Camille and stared at Garrin. "Let's make this easy, shall we? You and the girl come with me, and I'll allow this woman to live."

Garrin stepped toward his father and away from Lex.

Lex glanced between king and prince. "What are you doing?" she whispered.

Garrin's shoulders stiffened, and he slowly turned toward her, his eyes cold. Cold in a way she'd never seen before. "There's no place for you here."

"Now, now," the king said. "I need her. Don't run her off just yet."

"Leave!" Garrin shouted, and he looked over Lex's shoulder at Camille.

Before she knew what was happening, Lex was grabbed from behind and shoved into space. *Again.*

"Nooo!" But it was too late. Lex spun through light, caught off guard. Only this magic she'd come to understand. She pushed out her own, and the pressure changed.

Lex landed, along with Camille, on a different mountain —and nearly rolled over the edge.

The beautiful woman who was Garrin's true mother climbed to her feet. "Are you all right?"

Lex crawled off the edge and dusted snow from her clothes. "We can't leave Garrin. His father will kill him."

Camille closed her eyes as though pained. "I promised Garrin in the cavern that I would take you away should the king find us. If this is the only thing I can give him, I will do it. We must leave and return you to the Earth realm."

Wind whipped Lex's hair, cutting through her heavy coat and chilling her to her bones. The one thing she'd wanted when Garrin first found her was to return to her dorm and her old life. Now, she couldn't even picture that life, let alone the person she used to be. "I won't leave without him."

Lex walked in the direction they'd just come from, then stopped. She was headed the wrong way; the magic was behind her. But when she turned in that direction, none of the mountaintops looked familiar.

She growled in frustration. "Take me back."

"I cannot."

Lex closed her eyes briefly and took a steadying breath. "If Garrin is truly your son, how can you abandon him?"

Fire burned for the first time behind Camille's blue eyes. "I have never abandoned my child. He was stolen from me."

Lex wrapped her arms around her chest and rubbed them. "Neither the king nor the queen can be trusted. They're traitors to their own people."

"That is precisely why I cannot do as you say. I won't do the very thing his father has done his entire life and betray him. We will not go back," Camille said, but Lex sensed doubt in her voice.

Lex looked in the direction of where they'd left Garrin and drew on her power. Her arms lightened and a familiar tingling coursed through her. She focused her energy on the magic Camille used to get them here, studying it—the shape, the weight, the force behind it—and created a portal.

That sputtered and dissipated into thin air.

Lex screamed in frustration.

Camille walked over, looking astonished. "Child, you are getting better. With your magic, we will surely survive the Land of Ice even without provisions. I promise, I will return for my son once you are safe."

Ignoring Camille's words, Lex tried to create a portal again, and the same thing happened. She was no longer cold, but warm from the exertion of molding her magic into Camille's. "It won't work."

"You will practice along the way," Camille said, and placed a gentle hand on Lex's shoulder. "With both of us portaling, we will arrive in New Kingdom and then the Earth realm in no time."

Camille wasn't listening. Lex looked her in the eye. "I will not go to New Kingdom or Old Kingdom or the Earth realm. I will return for Garrin or go nowhere at all."

Garrin's true mother went silent for a moment and looked off. "We are only two against many. If you should die, my son..."

She was right. Garrin would not be happy to see Lex. He'd told her to leave. He even spoke harshly, when he never had before. But he couldn't have been serious. He'd wanted to protect her from the king, that was all. "We can do this, Camille. The others are not powerless. We'll find Garrin, and then we'll find our allies."

Camille let out a shaky breath. "If I agree to this, it is only because I want what is best for my son. But if there is a moment when your life is in imminent risk, I will take you away and not return."

It was enough. Lex nodded in agreement.

She didn't know how much longer Garrin had. They couldn't wait.

As Camille's portal began to form and shimmer, Lex studied the power, truly absorbing it this time. And when they entered, Lex added her own strength to it.

One second they were on one mountain, and the next second they were on another, as though blinking in and out.

Camille stared in surprise as they stood on the mountain where they'd left Garrin and Amund. "I've never experienced a portal like that."

Lex looked around, her hands shaking with adrenaline. "They're not here." Garrin and the king were no longer on the mountain where the queen had intercepted Amund's portal. "Where did they go?"

Camille closed her eyes, and Lex sensed her drawing on her powers again. She observed this too, different, though similar.

Camille pointed across mountaintops. "Over there. They've returned to the grave caves."

THIRTY-FIVE

Lex and Camille didn't head straight to the grave caves. They stopped at an overlook just beyond. And Lex couldn't believe what she saw.

Garrin stood with his back to her, facing his father. But that wasn't what had her growing cold. It was the frozen monoliths of her friends lined up next to the king: Jas, Elena, Derek, Em, and every single one of the others. And not only Lex's friends; the Dark Queen was frozen beside her husband as well, her alchemists now standing among the king's army.

Camille sucked in a breath. "This won't work. We must leave."

Lex swallowed, unable to look away. "Why would the king do this?"

"Power, fear... Who is to say? He will commit terrible acts for what he desires."

The king had raped Camille. She knew better than anyone the lengths he was willing to go in order to gain what he wanted.

Lex should leave. It was over. Everyone she'd counted

on to help her get Garrin out was frozen in ice, including her mother. But her feet wouldn't move, and her chest was tight with adrenaline.

She couldn't stop staring at Garrin's back as he faced off with his father. He was alone. "There has to be another way."

"There is no other way." Camille touched Lex's shoulder. "Child, I am powerful, and I barely escaped Dark Kingdom with my life. There is no match for the Dark King and his army."

Lex couldn't see Garrin's face, but she could see the king's expression. He smirked.

Lex gritted her teeth. There was no one to help her and Camille fight off Casone. And yet... "I can't leave." Garrin had never abandoned her. Regardless of if she was obligated to risk her life for his, she was about to. "We can do this, Camille. You'll create a portal, and I'll boost it. We'll pop in, grab Garrin, and leave just as quickly."

Camille closed her eyes and pressed her thumb and forefinger to her forehead. "That is a terrible idea."

Lex swallowed, her throat tight. Everyone she loved was frozen. And Garrin was trapped. "You're probably right. But will you do it?"

Camille moved closer. "It will take me seconds to create another portal to escape. Seconds that will see us captured."

Lex closed her eyes and extended her senses. "I feel them. The powers of my mother and our friends. They're not dead. They're still there, and so are their abilities."

"And frozen as they are, our friends cannot do anything with their powers."

"No, they can't. But I can."

Camille's eyes narrowed. "What are you saying?"

Lex looked across the clearing. "I see their power...just as easily as I see the wind blowing snow off that mountaintop. Just as easily as I see the condensation of our breath in the frigid air."

Camille's brow furrowed, and then she looked at Garrin. "What do you propose?"

"I'm most familiar with Garrin's power. We'll portal to the cavern entrance where Garrin stands, and I'll cover the soldiers and alchemists in snow. Enough snow to slow them down and create a distraction. In the meantime, you'll create a portal for us to escape." Lex's eyes burned and emotion filled her chest. "We can't take the others. I'm not confident in my abilities to do more than distract. We'll leave, as you said, and return to fight for our friends another day."

"It is all we can do for now," Camille agreed.

Lex's hands shook as Camille formed the portal. She didn't know how much longer Garrin would be in front of the cave, and she didn't want to risk the king returning to the castle to an even greater stronghold. They had to act quickly.

She focused on the energy Camille's magic gave off, stepped inside the portal, and boosted it, as she'd done before. One moment they were on the overlook and the next they were beside Garrin, minus the bumpy landing of a regular portal.

Lex called to the snow.

But not before one of the alchemists caught sight of her and threw out his hand.

The snow dropped midair, some of it scattering on top of the soldiers, but most of it drifting off.

"And here we are," the king said, and clasped his hands as though pleased. "Just as I predicted."

Garrin turned to Lex, angry red welts, blood, and bruises not hiding the resignation on his face.

Lex's chest rose and fell rapidly. He'd been beaten. Worse, a massive gash in the region of his heart left blood puddled in the snow at his feet. A puddle Lex hadn't been able to see from behind.

The king's expression was smug. "We waited so patiently for you, Lexandra. Or should I call you puppet master? I'm told you draw on others' powers. How convenient. My son was convinced you wouldn't show, but I was more optimistic."

Lex tried to call to Garrin's magic. And then to Camille's. Her mother's magic wouldn't rise either. Lex could see everyone's ability, including the soldiers', but she couldn't make any of it work for her.

She looked at the alchemist who'd reached out to her, strain contorting his expression as he kept his arm raised. He was blocking her power, and that hadn't been a part of her plan.

"Yes, my men have you well in hand," the king said. "My alchemists suspect that, with practice, I'll be able to use your powers to access all magic." He smiled and shook his head. "The possibilities are limitless. With an infinite ability such as yours, I'll be able to enlarge crops and create summer houses. But it seems we'll need to wait until you see things my way. I cannot have an unruly magic-wielder in my land."

Casone flicked his fingers, and just like that, Lex was frozen too.

Panic made her mind race. She couldn't move, not even to close her eyes. She felt no cold, no physical pain, though she was aware.

Oh my God. Oh my God. She'd be trapped inside ice for as long as the king wanted.

Muffled voices filtered through the block of ice that entombed her. Her eyes that wouldn't blink provided a hazy view of Garrin fighting soldiers off to reach her.

A moment of sheer panic percolated up her chest. But she couldn't breathe. She couldn't do a damn thing.

Garrin wrenched out of the grip of a soldier and placed a hand to the ice surrounding Lex. She felt him push magic at her. But it was so darn weak. Weaker than she'd ever sensed from him before. And blood continued to trail at his feet. He was dying.

Nooooo!

Garrin's gaze was pure anguish. And then rage. Even as his life's blood poured from his chest.

He backhanded one of the soldiers and stole his sword, then charged the king, clashing metal with the guards surrounding Casone.

The king turned his head from side to side as though disappointed. And then Lex heard his muffled voice. "Had I any notion of your success in finding the prophesied one, I never would have sent you on these quests, son. I needed to appease the people, and I thought the prophecy a good distraction. I too raged at the magical barrier when Kushiel first created it. But now? Now I see its benefits. No one in this land can stand against a Branimir. We are all-powerful."

Casone pinched his chin thoughtfully. "Lexandra is special, I'll give you that. Once she cools off for a hundred years or so, I'll make good use of her." He pulled out his sword. "Until then, you will pay for attempting to remove her from my land."

The Dark King lashed out in a motion so swift that Lex barely caught it.

Blood poured down Garrin's torso, his severed arm sinking into the snow.

Lex mentally screamed.

Casone Branimir would kill Garrin if it made him more powerful.

Garrin collapsed to his knees, his head bowed. And then he tipped to the side, unmoving.

Lex's mind was a haze of anger. And then she sensed it. The heat in her hands. She was no longer being controlled by the alchemist, either because he was distracted or too arrogant to believe she could use her power while frozen.

But she could. It was right there at her fingertips.

She didn't release the power she'd used to heat ice until it shattered. She allowed it to emanate off her slowly, heating the monolith from the inside until her body was as nimble as her mind and she could blink again.

And no one noticed, too preoccupied by the king and Garrin.

"Camille, dear," the king said, "take us back to my castle."

Camille moved to her son, whose face was ghostly white. She touched Garrin's leg, and Lex sucked in a breath. Camille looked up at the king. "I will never do as you say."

Lex felt the burst of power that swept off Camille. She was holding on to Garrin, which meant she could escape with him.

But the king and his men were faster.

Two soldiers lunged forward and stabbed Camille just as she opened her portal. She crumpled to the snow beside her son.

A low growl came from Lex's throat. Garrin was dying.

Camille was dying. Her friends had been buried alive in ice tombs...and Lex was furious.

No longer slow and controlled, Lex sent out a burst of fire energy, and the ice surrounding her shattered. She fell to the ground and looked up at the king with pure rage.

The king's eyebrow rose, and he held up his hand to the alchemist. "Interesting. What else can you do, I wonder?"

A lot, thought Lex, as some of the puzzle pieces of Mertha's memories finally came together.

She slammed her fists to the ground, so hard they went through snow and ice and vibrated off solid stone. She drew on every ounce of energy she possessed, and some she didn't know she had, and pushed heat into the rock and beyond.

There was a fraction of a second between her fists slamming and the snow melting around them. But like a breeze sweeping a cornfield, the magic burst out and melted every droplet of snow and ice as far as the eye could see.

The king's head jerked this way and that, and he stumbled on the fresh stone beneath his feet. "What have you done?" He turned to the alchemists, who were cowering. "Block her magic!"

Even if the alchemists didn't look frightened, Lex wasn't about to let them control her again. She tossed them off the cliff with her mother's power.

In the next moment, her mother and all their friends rose from the side of the cliff in midair. They must have unfrozen along with the land. And they looked *pissed.*

Isle threw out her arms, and she and their friends landed on solid ground, swords drawn.

And they weren't alone.

THIRTY-SIX

The only way to convince Lex to leave was for Garrin to make her believe he'd sided with his father. But his father hadn't been satisfied with only Garrin. He'd wanted Lex and her power too.

Garrin fought off ten soldiers, until his father had stepped in—and nearly cut out his heart.

"Now, now, child," the king had said, re-sheathing his sword. "Stand down while we wait for Lexandra to show."

"Don't," Garrin had begged. "Leave her be."

His father had snarled in response. "You don't actually care for the female? What a deplorable notion. I concede, with Lex's powers, Dark Kingdom will become the strongest land in Tirnan. Particularly now that the queen has found a way around the magical barriers, with help from my alchemists."

The king shook his head. "Never fall for a woman, Garrin. She will only betray you. Your mother was up to something, but I never imagined she'd cook up such magic. Clever, that." He glanced at the queen. "And she still maintains her beauty even frozen in ice. She'll return with us as a reminder for all who think to betray me. Not even the queen is spared punishment."

Drained of power, Garrin had been prepared to bleed out on that mountain, where he'd given his heart and body to Lex. And then she arrived.

Whatever blood he'd had left drained from him. His only hope had been the knowledge that Lex had gotten away. And now he hadn't even that.

The king entombed Lex in ice, just as he had the others.

Unable to move and barely able to breathe, Garrin mentally railed at the universe.

And then, as though in a dream, he heard Lex's voice above him.

"Zirel, can you heal him?" she asked.

Garrin opened his eyes and saw Lex's beautiful face. He didn't know how she'd broken free, but it was the best dying wish he could ask for. He wanted to reach for her, but his body wouldn't cooperate, and his vision blurred.

"He's gone without power for too long," Zirel said, his voice strained. "He will live, but he will not be the same."

"Prince!" Amund shouted from somewhere.

Lex looked behind her, and Garrin did to.

The king was storming toward them.

Lex didn't bother to raise her hand. She simply froze the Ice King where he stood, giving Casone the same punishment he'd carelessly bestowed on others.

Garrin's eyes fluttered. He'd lost too much blood. His power had returned, but he was too weak to use it. "Leave," he said hoarsely. "Quickly, before the king breaks free."

Lex looked at Garrin in disbelief. "Have you lost your mind? I'm not leaving you." She placed her hands on his chest and pumped power into him, a surge of energy so strong it burned down his limbs and made his head pound.

Warmth spread through his chest and to the arm his father had cut off. The arm that would never grow back given the circumstances, and yet it was—first thin and pale pink, then increasing in size and definition, a glow of life coming off it.

Zirel fell back. "I'm not doing this, Your Highness. It is not my power."

Lex lifted her hands off Garrin's chest. "It's your power, Zirel. I borrowed it. And magnified it."

Garrin sat up, his arm formed fully, red but whole, and he opened and closed his palm. He looked up at Lex in astonishment. She radiated, her light bouncing off the walls of the cave. She was magnificent.

Garrin rose to his feet and pulled her to his chest, breathing in her scent. Of course Lex hadn't listened to him when he'd ordered her to leave. It had been a slim chance she would, but he'd been desperate.

Garrin kissed Lex's forehead and finally looked out at the battle going on around them.

The land was unfrozen, and there were soldiers. His father's, yes, but also other soldiers fighting his father's men. And they weren't from this century. He looked down at Lex. "Did you do this?"

She glanced up hesitantly. "I might have unfrozen things a bit."

He shook his head. Isle's prediction had come true. Lex was more powerful than the Dark King. More powerful than all of them combined.

"What's happening?" Lex asked.

Garrin looked around. "You raised the dead."

She peered back at the men and women. "They weren't dead. I've always felt their power, if I think back. I thought it was some creepy energy remnant from dead Fae, but it was them all along."

"No, not dead," he agreed. "Waiting. And furious, from the looks of it. They have great reason to hate my father and his soldiers."

Isle had brought people from the bottom of the ravine Garrin thought to never see again, and some he'd never seen before. Some wore liveried clothes; others were dressed in court attire, and others wore the simple woolen garments Mertha and her husband had worn.

These Fae had been buried in the caves alive. Just as Casone had done with others who'd crossed him. It had never been a graveyard. This place was where the king had stashed his dissenters.

Amund ran over. "The battle will be over soon. Royal soldiers are accepting defeat without their king. Where should we put them?"

Garrin wasn't truly a prince, and his father should have never ruled. "For now, let us take them to the dungeons. We will meet with the men and women of Dark Kingdom and figure out a way forward. I will not rule this land. I'm not a legitimate heir to the throne, and my father has left a stain on the Branimir reign."

"None of this was your fault," Lex said.

He smiled down at her. "No, but I have no wish to rule Dark Kingdom. I find myself inclined to return to the Land of Sun with my fiancée."

THIRTY-SEVEN

Lex tossed a grape into her mouth. Well, not exactly a *grape*. Some kind of Tirnan variation, but it tasted like a grape, except tangier.

She scanned the inside of Em's new digs, previously the king's quarters. "I don't know. The gold accents give it a certain feel. You could be Em the Gold Queen."

Em's mouth puckered. "I'm not queen yet. And Casone Branimir had no taste."

"I'll give you that," Lex agreed. The king had installed a pretty swanky bathroom for a castle this old, with a four-person bathtub that overlooked the now defrosted Dark Kingdom Garden, but the toilet was gold. *Gold.* Who installed a gold toilet?

Velvet drapes in emerald boasted hand-painted images of Casone Branimir. Talk about narcissism. Even the bed Lex lay on was draped in gold silk and could fit an entire soccer team. The Dark King didn't do anything in half measures.

Lex looked around with her nose scrunched. "You really want to stay here?"

Em shrugged as she lifted down a Fae-sized painting of the former king. "Someone needs to protect the land."

Lex was referring to the bedroom, but Em had a point. "Elena and Keen won't attack Dark Kingdom now that your parents are in charge. They only came because Camille detected Garrin when he entered their land. It was more of a reconnaissance mission. And apparently Jas was putting up a stink to get me back."

"It's not them I fear. The queen escaped the king's ice magic when you unfroze the land, and we are missing two alchemists. My father believes they are together in Tirnan or the Earth realm." Em's mouth twisted. "I do not trust the previous queen. She was most unmotherly in how she treated Garrin."

Lex choked on her next grape. "Um, that's putting it mildly. She was power-crazed."

Em batted at the velvet drapes, looking at them sideways.

Lex lifted her finger. "As your stylist, I suggest you burn those."

Em made a sound of agreement, then sat on the bed beside Lex. "My parents were handed the kingdom because we are the closest relatives to the Branimir line, though we don't take the task lightly. I'll make sure my court protects the land from the Dark Queen."

"Former Dark Queen," Lex pointed out. "She's been stripped of her royal post, remember? And I suppose that's an ignoble reason to hang around."

Lex sat up and inspected a piece of cheese, wondering benignly what animal it had come from. "What about the king and prince's harems? What will happen to the women?"

"The prince's harem wishes to become a part of the

royal guard, and my mother and father have agreed. The king's harem wishes to leave this land."

Garrin valued and trained his court females, and the king belittled his. The women's decisions spoke to their treatment by the most powerful men in the land.

"And Amund, what will you do with him?" Lex sent Em a teasing grin.

"He is infuriating."

"Please elaborate." Lex rolled onto her stomach and rested her chin on her hand. "I must know why you hate the Fae beefcake."

Em smacked her lips lightly as though searching for a flavor. "He is like the child that tugs on the girl's ponytail."

"Because he *likes* you."

She made a face. "Or because he wishes to annoy me."

"Same thing, right?"

"No, it is not!"

"So you'll keep him around?"

Em let out a long-suffering sigh. "I suppose I must."

Lex could see the corner of Em's lip twitching. She liked Amund, even if she wouldn't admit it outright. "I suppose if you need a head guard, at least make sure he's attractive. Wait, that's not right, because they're all attractive. At least make it a guard who challenges you and possesses beefcake hotness?"

Em frowned. "Don't you have an appointment with the prince?"

Lex smiled and rose. "Former prince, and indeed I do." She fluttered her fingers. "Ta-ta. Good luck with your remodeling. Call me if you need spray paint for that gold toilet. Oh, and say hello to Amund for me."

Em stuck out her tongue, and Lex felt a sense of pride.

Her human crudeness was rubbing off on the new Fae princess of Dark Kingdom.

LEX ENTERED Garrin's quarters and heard the shower running. She snuck into the dressing room, not wanting to miss the show.

Sprawled on a massive chaise that could fit two football players, she waited impatiently.

A few minutes later, Garrin walked out of the bathroom rubbing his damp hair with a towel, another fitted precariously at his waist.

"Husband, your towel is loose."

He strode over with a cocky grin. "Should I leave and properly cover myself?"

Lex snapped out her arm and plucked the towel from him. "Oh dear, it's fallen."

He tossed the towel he'd been using to dry his hair and covered her with his body. "Devil wife. I left our marriage bed not an hour ago."

"I'll have you know, I was very productive while you were gone. I helped Em redecorate your father's quarters and grilled her for information on Amund."

He rubbed his nose along her neck, seemingly breathing her in. "Did she admit to lusting after the Fae?"

"Not yet, but I'm wearing her down."

He lifted and scanned her body as though considering round two of afternoon delight. "What else have you been doing?"

"*Well*, I stripped my husband and now plan to have my way with him."

His silky hands slid her top up, and she raised her arms,

giving him room to remove it. "I approve of how you spend your time," he said.

"As if you have a say." Her voice came out breathless as he kissed his way down her chest, his large hand covering her breast.

She looked at the top of his dark head. "As much as I'm enjoying our life of married leisure these last two weeks, I'm wondering if we should swing back into the Earth realm now that I've mastered my kick-ass magic."

After she'd melted Dark Kingdom, effectively removing the magic that put their land in permanent winter, she returned their friends to their respective kingdoms in one swift megaportal hop.

Okay, fine, she had to practice a few times, but the third time was the charm.

Her breath caught on something he did with his tongue near her nipple, and she smoothed her fingers along the back of his neck. "We could pass through and check in on Elena and Keen before heading to the Earth realm to make sure your ex-mother isn't wreaking havoc."

He lifted his head, his damp hair disheveled. "We don't know she is in the Earth realm."

"Shouldn't we find out? She was as diabolical as your father, controlling the alchemists and devising a plan to take over Dark Kingdom."

He sent her a disgruntled look. "Must we discuss Ailith?" His gaze skittered down her body. "I had other plans."

She grabbed his chin and kissed his full lips. "You're right. We have business to attend to." And she reached back and grabbed his bare ass.

Garrin growled. "Let's not forget who's in charge here."

"Me?" She grinned.

"Only if you're not putting your life in danger, which you tend to do." He unfastened her pants and slid them down her legs.

Garrin rolled to the side and flipped them so she was on top. He unclasped her bra half a second later.

"I'm not thrilled you know how to do that. I've checked. Fae women don't wear bras."

"Don't they?" he said, and caressed her breasts, making her eyes roll into the back of her head.

"Wh-what?" she murmured, distracted.

He looked at her innocently and positioned her above his hard length.

Lex ran her hands down the undulations of his muscular chest. "I can't remember what we were talking about."

"It's just as well," he said, and lifted her until she sank onto the length of him.

Garrin leaned up and grabbed her ass at the same time his soft mouth enclosed her nipple. It was triple stimulation, and it didn't take long before she was rocking haphazardly, racing toward climax.

Stars burst behind her eyes and pleasure swept over her, incoherent sounds erupting from her throat.

In her lulled state, Garrin kissed her, flipped them, and pressed her back into the chaise. He continued a slow, torturous rhythm that had her thinking about orgasm number two.

Lex touched his strong cheekbone, treasuring the look on his face as he reached his pleasure.

"I love you," she said after he'd caught his breath.

"Not more than I love you," he said, and slid to the side, pulling her close.

She curled into the protection of his chest, and he lazily ran his hand up and down her spine.

He lifted onto his elbow and rested his head in his hand. "I spent hundreds of years believing you were a gift from the angels to save my people. Little did I know you were put here for me."

When Garrin Branimir wanted to woo a woman, he brought out the big guns. "Who knew you were this romantic?" She leaned up and pecked him on the lips. "It's a good thing you're handsome, or I would have run like hell out of that Earth cave."

His brow quirked. "I seem to recall you trying. And handsome, you say?"

She sent him an exasperated look. "I thought you were ridiculously hot the moment I saw you in my dorm. And terrifying. Very terrifying. Which was the reason for my sprint to the cave entrance."

"And now?"

"You're a big puppy dog."

He bristled, but a smile caught on the corners of his lips. "I know to which creature you refer, and I find it mildly insulting. For the record, you nearly barreled over me inside your dormitory. I should have been terrified of the hooded female."

She laughed. "I didn't run into you. I was trying to avoid the big, bad wolf lurking my hallways."

"You called me a puppy dog." A mischievous glint shone in his eyes. "And perhaps the encounter was intentional on my part." His face grew serious. "I sensed it before I measured your abilities—the draw to you. I knew you were mine the moment I saw you, every inch of your face hidden in shadow."

She sighed and encircled his chest with her arms.

"Pushy and possessive. At least I know what my future holds."

Sign up for J. Barnard's newsletter, and **receive a FREE bonus epilogue that takes place after *FATES FULFILLED*,** along with writing updates. By signing up here, you'll also be the first to know when new books go live:

ACKNOWLEDGMENTS

I desperately wanted to wrap up the series in a fun, adventurous, steamy way, and well, it caused stress—a lot of stress. But the final result was worth it. Many thanks to my team of editors: Jessa Slade, Arran McNicol, and Kimberly Dawn. I also want to give Anne H. and Lea T. a huge shout-out for their insightful beta reads.

My biggest thanks go to the readers and listeners of the Halven Rising series. This book took much longer to write than I thought it would, and you continued to send kind messages expressing your eagerness to find out what happens in the final installment. It kept me chugging along, even when I thought I'd never finish.

Finally, many thanks to my husband and children. Maybe it's just this author, but the final weeks leading up to a deadline are filled with very long hours and no days off, and I'm so grateful for your love and support.

ALSO BY J. BARNARD

HALVEN RISING SERIES

Fates Altered (Prequel)

Fates Divided (Book 1)

Fates Entwined (Book 2)

Fates Fulfilled (Book 3)

About the Author

J.Barnard is the fantasy pen name for USA Today Bestselling Author Jules Barnard. Library Journal calls her Halven Rising series "...an exciting new fantasy adventure." To find out more, visit jbarnardauthor.com or follow @jbarnardauthor on Instagram.

Sign up for J. Barnard's newsletter, and **receive a FREE bonus epilogue that takes place after *Fates Fulfilled*,** along with writing updates. By signing up here, you'll also be the first to know when new books go live:

Please spread the love for the Halven Rising series and *Fates Fulfilled* by leaving a review or rating it, and sharing the series on all things social. Don't forget to tag me!